WE HAVE WAYS OF MAKING YOU HAPPY . . .

The science of Hedonics comes to an unhappy world. Now, for the first time, complete happiness is available to all. And the dangling carrot of here-and-now heaven is too good to be rejected. The majority of people in the near–future world plunge headlong into the philosophy and techniques of being joyful. But is it humanity's birthright to be happy, or is it a duty . . . or is it a law?

The climax of this brilliantly conceived and convincing novel is as devastating as it is inevitable . . .

THE JOY MAKERS is one of the most powerful novels of the future of our society since Aldous Huxley's classic BRAVE NEW WORLD.

D1440109

Also by James Gunn

The Immortals

James Gunn

The Joy Makers

Panther

Granada Publishing Limited
Published in 1976 by Panther Books Ltd
Frogmore, St Albans, Herts AL2 2NF

First published in Great Britain by
Victor Gollancz Ltd 1963
THE UNHAPPY MAN, originally published in
Fantastic Universe, Copyright © 1954 by King–Size
Publications Inc. THE NAKED SKY, originally
published in *Startling Stories*. Copyright © 1955 by
Standard Magazines, Inc. NAME YOUR PLEASURE,
originally published in *Thrilling Wonder Stories*.
Copyright © 1954 by Standard Magazines, Inc.
Copyright © 1961 by Bantam Books Inc.
Made and printed in Great Britain by
Hazell Watson & Viney Ltd
Aylesbury, Bucks

To Jane

Part One

I

*Every one of these hundreds of millions of human
beings is in some form seeking happiness.... Not one
is altogether noble nor altogether trustworthy nor altogether consistent; and not one is altogether vile. Not
a single one but has at some time wept.*

HERBERT GEORGE WELLS

He would never have noticed the advertisement if he hadn't
spilled coffee all over the front page of the paper. The coffee
spilled because his hand was shaking. His hand was shaking
because he had drunk too much last night. He had drunk too
much because . . .

But that is following the chain of causation in the wrong
direction.

The drenched front section of the paper was unreadable.
After he had read everything else in the rescued back pages,
he read the ad. It was unthinkable that he should look at
Ethel or speak to her this early in the morning even without
a hangover.

It was one of those little ads, the ones that nobody reads,
about dandruff, itchy skins, headaches, false teeth, and 'a
new way to stop smoking'. They're marked *Advertisements*
for a purpose that has almost nothing to do with regulations.
They're a warning to the reader like a No Trespassing sign:
proceed at your own risk.

Josh had sworn to strangle the first advertising director
who suggested anything remotely resembling it. Both the
oath and the advertising director were safe; electronic components aren't sold that way.

He read the ad, idly, while he was toying halfheartedly

with two revoltingly healthy eggs, and he went on to an ad
for hearing aids, and then his eyes flashed back, and he read
the ad again, carefully :

WHY BE MISERABLE?
Let Us
Solve Your Problems
*"A modern service
for the modern age"*
HAPPINESS GUARANTEED!
Dial P-L-E-A-S-U-R
Hedonics, Inc.

He hadn't been mistaken. The word wasn't 'satisfaction'.
It was 'happiness'.

He started to say something to Ethel about it and re-
considered. Turning masochistically to his breakfast, he forgot the incident entirely. Forgot it, that is, until he reached
the plant.

He stared at the office door. Stuck between the frame and
the frosted glass was a blotter. It was centered, with a nice
regard for balance, exactly below the gold-lettered legend
on the door : HUNT ELECTRONIC MANUFACTURING COMPANY,
Electronic Equipment and Components, '*Hunt for the
Finest*', Joshua P. Hunt, President.

The message on the blotter was a simple, chaste thing –
three short lines of black sans-serif lettering on white, glossy
stock :

**YOUR HAPPINESS
IS OUR BUSINESS**
Hedonics, Inc.

Joshua P. Hunt, president, jerked the card away and
glared at it. Holding it distastefully between two fingers, he
opened the door, stepped into the outer office and walked
purposefully toward the desk of Marie Gamble, secretary,
who was blonde, lovely, and half his age. He dropped the
blotter on her desk.

'Put out an all-department memo,' he growled. ' "The
company regulation prohibiting soliciting or distribution of
advertising material in the plant has not been changed. Disregard of this by any employee will be cause for summary

dismissal." Order me a bicarbonate. Who's waiting to see me?'

'Just Mr. Kidd, the union business agent. He's here about the new contract.'

'That pirate,' Josh grumbled and girded himself for another ulcerating day.

At quitting time Josh pushed his Cadillac through a clotted mass of his employees just outside the plant gate. Their heads were swiveled back to study the sky, and at last they refused to give way at all. Impatiently, Josh shoved open the car door, got out, and joined the skywatchers.

The airplane was almost invisible against the blue of the afternoon sky, but the puffy, white cloud trails were thick and untattered. They spelled out : HEDON. As Josh watched, an 'I' was added, a 'C', and an 'S'. When the plane finished the short slant of the comma and began the long straightness of the 'I', Josh tore himself away and blasted through the crowd with his horn.

II

'I fly from pleasure,' said the prince, 'because pleasure has ceased to please; I am lonely because I am miserable, and am unwilling to cloud with my presence the happiness of ohers.'

SAMUEL JOHNSON

It had been a usual sort of day, hectic, that is; also frustrating, nerve-racking, stomach-cramping, exhausting. . . . The children, luckily, were away at camp. After such a day, Josh couldn't stand them – or, as he had once admitted in a moment of rare honesty, at any other time.

There was only Ethel to contend with.

'Josh—' she began.

'Ummmph!' he grunted and walked past her into the study, shut the door behind him, dropped his brief case on the desk, and mixed himself a tall, cool drink.

'To hell with the ulcer,' he muttered and tossed it down in three thirsty gulps.

After the second highball was well settled, he began to feel vaguely human once more. He settled himself into the cool, rich embrace of the red-leather easy chair – that was, for him, more of a symbol of success than his home, his car, or his mahogany-dark office – and flipped open the evening paper.

This time it was on the front page in the form of a news item. That it was not particularly newsworthy did not matter; such items are the meat and potatoes of the suburban newspaper.

NEW BUSINESS TO MILLVILLE, the headline shouted. Beneath it was a glowing description of the new personal services corporation and the branch office it had opened in the suburb.

The address was familiar. It was in the industrial district, but Josh couldn't quite pinpoint it.

It was a most incomplete and unsatisfying news story. It told everything except the service the new corporation sold. Several times mention of it seemed inevitable, but each time the reporter leaped away from it with admirable agility.

Dinner was silent. Afterward the food lay heavy in Josh's stomach, undigested and indigestible. As he shuffled through the papers he had brought home in his brief case, he tried to dilute the misery with bourbon and soda.

By the time he was able to ignore it, he was unable to concentrate on the papers.

And then he found the card, and the evening was completely ruined. It glistened at him, a picture of a man prey to uncounted, nameless miseries, mouth drawn lower than his chin. Underneath was printed: UNHAPPY?

Josh frowned and leaned forward to toss the thing away, wondering idly how it could possibly have got mixed among his papers. But as he moved, the picture, by some alchemy of printing, shifted.

The man was the same, but his woe had been exchanged

for imbecilic bliss. The legend had changed, too. Now it was : *Hedonics, Inc.*

Josh brushed the card impatiently off the desk. It fluttered to the floor and landed face downward. As he leaned down to pick it up, he read the message on the back : Dial P-L-E-A-S-U-R.

For the first time since he had read the advertisement in the morning paper, Josh let himself think seriously about its meaning. What are they selling? he asked himself. He didn't know. He wanted to know. It had been a very clever campaign.

The second question was : What is hedonics?

That, at least, seemed easy enough to answer. He leafed through Webster's Dictionary. He found the word between *hedonic* and *hedonism* :

> **hedonics** (-iks), *n.* see -ICS. **a** Ethics which treat of the relation of duty to pleasure. **b** Psychology which treats of pleasurable and unpleasant states of consciousness.

He studied it thoughtfully. Ethics? Psychology? It's hard enough to sell psychology, and you can't sell ethics at all. You can scarcely give it away.

Whatever hedonics was, it wasn't an ethics and it wasn't a psychology. But it was logical to assume that it dealt with pleasure. You don't sell pleasure, and you don't sell happiness. You sell products or services and you hope they bring pleasure and happiness, but it isn't the same thing.

Josh couldn't define the service, but he could identify the business. It was a skin game. Josh could smell it a mile away. It was a business for suckers, and there was money in it. They don't give newspaper and blotter advertising away; skywriting is steep; and this reversible image stuff should be even higher – if you could find a printer to do it.

Add them together and it made a tidy sum.

'Josh—' Ethel began as he climbed the stairs to his bedroom.

'Ummmph,' he said and shut the door behind him.

He stared at the night light for a long while before his

mind stopped racing and his taut muscles relaxed. Skin game, he told himself. It had a comforting finality to it.

Let the police take care of it, he thought. It was, after all, none of his business.

On that note of forgetfulness came forgetfulness.

But Hedonics, Inc., refused to be forgotten. The morning paper had a display ad which drew Josh's eye irresistibly. On his way to the office, he saw a billboard with a pure-white background. In the middle was a cage; it held a blue-bird, singing happily. Beneath it were two words : *Hedonics, Inc.*

As Josh walked through the outer office, Marie looked up and said, 'Joy, Mr. Hunt!'

Josh's step faltered. 'Joy?' he repeated.

Marie blushed prettily. 'Good morning, I mean. It was on television last night – "Joy" that is – and it just slipped out.'

'What was on television?'

'A real happy story,' Marie sighed. 'Everybody was happy. It was sponsored by that new business with the funny name—'

'Oh,' Josh said. 'That. Anyone waiting for me?'

'Mr. Kidd and a salesman—'

'No salesmen today.' Josh shuddered. 'I'd rather see Kidd. . . .'

'Good morning, Mr. Hunt,' Kidd said as he came in. 'Are you happy?'

'Am I *what?*' Hunt exclaimed.

'Sorry,' Kidd said sheepishly. 'Don't know what made me say that. Seems to be a new phrase that's going around.'

They worked their way into the usual argument : job specialization versus job enlargement. Josh insisted that specialization had gone too far, that enlargement and rotation meant increased production, improved morale, and decreased complaints, mistakes, monotony, fatigue, and absenteeism. Kidd was convinced that the whole thing was only a sly management scheme to downgrade higher-paying jobs.

It ended, as usual, with both men pounding on the table and throwing their arguments at each other's heads like clubs. Afterward Josh was exhausted, and the taste of old emotion was sour in his mouth.

He sneezed. His head was stuffed with hot cotton. There was no mistaking the symptoms: he was getting a head cold.

The rest of the endless day was still ahead of him.

He felt like putting his head down on his desk and sobbing. He didn't, of course. Men don't do that.

Somehow he struggled through the day. Somehow he resisted the impulse to spring madly at the throats of the five people who greeted him with 'Joy!' and the six who asked 'Are you happy?'

'Marie,' he mumbled, 'I won't be in tomorrow.'

As he dragged himself through the front door of his French colonial home, Ethel greeted him with offensive gaiety. 'Joy, Josh,' she sang. 'Are you happy?'

'I feel lousy,' he shouted.

'Oh, dear,' she said sympathetically. 'What's the matter?'

'Everything,' Josh moaned. 'I'm coming down with a cold, my ulcer is acting up, and—'

'You know what you should do?' Ethel said earnestly. 'You should call Hedonics, Inc.'

Josh staggered back making a strangled, animal sound in his throat. He caught himself, stumbled into the study, and locked the door. Shakily he poured himself a drink, tossed it down, and poured another.

Sometime during the long, blurred evening, the situation became crystalline-clear. What was wrong with him was Hedonics, Inc. It was the breeding pit of all his irritations. If it were gone, he could be happy again.

The only way to get rid of it was to do the job himself.

He had been wrong about leaving it to the police. It was his business; fraud was everyone's business. And the police wouldn't act until after the masses had been mulcted. Mulcted. He liked that word. He said it over to himself several times.

He picked up the telephone. Five minutes later he put it down, frowning awesomely. Millville had a thoroughly unsatisfactory police department.

Yes, Mr. Hunt. No, Mr. Hunt. But we can't do that, Mr. Hunt.

Complaint, indeed! Proof, indeed!

He'd give them a complaint. He'd give them proof.

This time he dialed P-L-E-A-S-U-R.

The voice that answered was delightfully feminine. 'Joy,' it said. 'This is Hedonics, Inc. How can we make you happy?'

'This,' Josh said cautiously, 'is Joshua P. Hunt.'

'Oh, yes, Mr. Hunt,' the girl said. 'We've been expecting to hear from you.'

The implications of that remark didn't register on Josh until long afterward. 'This service you offer,' he said tentatively, 'I'd like to learn more about it.'

'Yes, sir,' the girl said. 'A salesman will call on you tomorrow morning. Ten? At your home?'

When Josh lowered the handset into the cradle, his mouth was twisted up thoughtfully and a tiny muscle was jerking in his left eyelid.

III

Did it ever strike you on such a morning as this that
drowning would be happiness and peace?
                              CHARLES DICKENS

What had seemed like a brilliant idea at midnight was quite another thing at the grim hour of ten. His head ached. His stomach was fiery and rebellious. His cold was straddling his shoulders, jabbing at his sinuses and his raw, dripping nose.

He studied the card unhappily :

WILLIAM A. 'BILL' JOHNSON

Hedonics, Inc.   Graduate, Institute
of Applied Hedonics

He turned it over. On the back was a quotation.

*There is no duty we underrate so much
as the duty of being happy.*

ROBERT LOUIS STEVENSON

He looked back at William A. 'Bill' Johnson. Johnson was a youngish man, not over thirty, with sandy hair, a frank, open face, and an annoyingly cheerful disposition. He was just the type, Josh decided, to mulct widows of their savings.

'Mr. Johnson,' he began, speaking painfully through his nose, 'I—'

'Call me "Bill,"' the salesman interrupted eagerly.

'Bill,' Josh said, surrendering weakly. 'I'm afraid I've changed my mind—'

'Surely you have a few minutes,' Bill said, 'to learn something about the service we offer.'

Josh shrugged and sank back in his chair, blowing his nose sadly.

Webster, it seemed, had been incomplete. Besides '**a** Ethics . . .' and '**b** Psychology . . .' there should have been a third definition labeled '**c** Science . . .'

'Science?' Josh echoed. 'A science of happiness?'

Bill nodded cheerfully. 'That's exactly it. Happiness can

be located more accurately than pitchblende, refined easier than uranium, synthesized more certainly than plutonium, and utilized more efficiently than a nuclear reactor. The entire curriculum of the Institute of Applied Hedonics consists of hedonics.'

'And where is that institute located?' Josh asked sharply.

'Smithfield, Massachusetts,' Bill answered quickly.

Josh silently repeated the name several times.

Hedonics, Bill said, wasn't an overnight miracle. It was a blending of many discoveries, many techniques. Some of them had been available for many years, and some of them had been developed only recently. But until a few years ago, no one had noticed their inter-relationships and combined them into a single master science of happiness.

'And happiness, after all,' Bill said, 'is the aim of living, isn't it?'

'Perhaps,' Josh admitted grudgingly.

'Let me put it this way,' Bill said brightly, 'we shun pain – or, to be more accurate, unpleasure – and we choose between two courses the one that seems less unpleasant.'

Basically hedonics was a discipline. It was a psychological science. As such its greatest value lay in the future, its greatest virtue was in the training of the young.

'That's fine,' Josh said drily, 'but what can it do for me – now – today.'

Hedonics, it seemed, could do many things. Most firms specialized in a single service: cleaning, banking, accounting, plumbing, repairs of all kinds, delivery, employment. . . . Hedonics, Inc., did everything. The client's problems became the problems of Hedonics, Inc. If the client needed a job, a job was found for him; more important, it was not just any job but a job that would make the client happy.

In addition, hedonics relieved pains, cured the sick, reshaped neurotic and psycopathic personalities, toned up the body, straightened out the mind, and removed such sources of unhappiness as salary worries, investment difficulties, budget impossibilities, marital problems, extramarital dilemmas, thwarted desires, and guilty satisfactions. . . .

'In short, Mr. Hunt,' Bill said earnestly, 'we provide the ultimate personal service. We do everything necessary to make you happy. That is our guarantee.'

'How do you make it?'

'In writing, as an integral part of the contract.'

'Fantastic,' Josh muttered, adding, as he looked up, 'that I haven't heard of your firm before. It's a novel and comprehensive service!'

'Yes, it is, Mr. Hunt. The company is new, but we are already on a sound financial footing, and we are bonded against contract failure. We have been doing business privately, on a small scale, for several years, you see, and we are just now opening our service to the public. Actually, this is a test operation in this locality. . . .'

'I see,' Josh said quickly, cutting off the sales talk. 'You can make me well, you said.'

'And happy,' Bill added.

'You can cure this cold?'

'Certainly.'

Josh sat back, momentarily silenced by the beautiful audacity. 'It must be very expensive,' he said finally.

'As some of our advertising material says, it's a service you can't afford,' Bill said, 'to be without. As a matter of fact, it isn't nearly so expensive as you might think, not nearly as much, even, as purchasing those services individually that are available outside the company. During this special trial period, now, you can buy a limited service contract, including full diagnosis and indicated medical and psychological services, for only one hundred dollars.'

'I take it, then, that you have an unlimited service contract?' Josh asked shrewdly.

Bill shrugged. 'Oh, yes. But we aren't pushing it at this time. Now I have a contract with me right here. . . .'

In a few moments Josh was alone. He had a contract, an appointment for that afternoon, and Bill had his check for one hundred dollars.

Josh smiled grimly. If the service was as slick as the salesman, it was a very clever operation indeed.

IV

We have no more right to consume happiness without producing it than to consume wealth without producing it.

GEORGE BERNARD SHAW

Josh recognized the building. When he had leased it, it had been a warehouse. Now it still looked like a warehouse but dirtier, shabbier, more in need of repair. It hardly looked like a chain store for happiness.

Sniffling, Josh sat in the Cadillac for a few minutes watching the procession. A constant stream of men and women entered the warehouse, and a second stream came out. Their appearance and dress placed them in all classes. The desire for happiness wasn't stratified. In those who came out, oddly enough, the distinctions had been largely erased.

But it was the numbers that impressed Josh. In less than two days, Hedonics, Inc., was doing a rushing trade.

The happiness business was booming.

Josh got slowly out of the car and worked himself into the line passing through a propped-open wooden door into the building. As he got inside, he stopped, stunned, and let himself be pushed aside.

The interior of the warehouse was magnificent.

The floor looked and felt like rosy marble. The walls were glowing, a many-colored neutral plastic lighted from within. The whole front of the warehouse had been converted into a broad, towering waiting room, and the décor made it seem even larger.

People streamed across the floor like travelers through a railroad station toward a distant, semicircular information desk and a row of doorways on either side.

The total effect was not immensity but spaciousness, not cold beauty but joyous warmth. Josh took a deep, ragged breath as he turned slowly around.

Carved across the front wall were two fluorescent lines of poetry :

> *All who joy would win*
> *Must share it, – happiness was born a twin.*
>   LORD BYRON

'There's money behind this thing,' Josh muttered.

Only when a deep, pleasant voice answered at his elbow did he realize that he had spoken the thought aloud. 'Obviously, Mr. Hunt. We deal in a valuable service. When happiness is for sale, who would buy anything else?'

Josh spun around, startled. The man facing him was at least as old as Josh himself. But he seemed to be in much better health, and his face was carved with smile lines instead of crow's-feet and wrinkles.

He carried his graying head proudly, but his dark eyes were wise and kind. 'My name is Wright,' he said. 'I'm at your service while you're here. If you have questions, I'll try to answer them. I presume, for instance, that you recognized the symbolism of the building?' He paused questioningly. When Josh was silent, he went on, 'A shabby exterior – but color and warmth inside. Beauty and joy can live inside the ugliest of us.'

Josh let himself be led across the floor, wordless before Wright's easy flow of chatter. They went through a doorway and down a short corridor and into a small room. In the middle of the floor was a single, large easy chair; against the wall was a desk; beside the desk was a straight chair.

'Sit down,' Wright said, indicating the easy chair.

Josh sank into it gratefully and blew his nose.

'Cold?' Wright asked sympathetically, as he sat down at the desk. He glanced at the desk top occasionally as he went on, 'We'll fix that up in a jiffy. Ulcer, too, eh?'

'How did you know?' Josh asked suspiciously.

Wright laughed easily; it was a happy sound. 'I didn't do any research, if that's what you mean : It's the chair. You're sitting in our special, patented diagnostic chair.' His hand moved across the desk.

Something touched lightly against the back of Josh's neck. He jumped to his feet and looked behind him. There was nothing there. His hand, which had gone automatically to his neck, came away faintly damp. 'What's going on?' he demanded indignantly. 'What do you mean "diagnostic chair"?'

'Sit down, Mr. Hunt,' Wright said gently. 'The chair won't hurt you. Hedonics is painless. That's why the chair looks like a chair instead of the steel, chrome, and marble torture instruments in dentists' offices.'

Gingerly Josh eased himself back into the chair, but this time he sat primly on the front edge. 'That's all very well, but what does it do?'

'It gives me an accurate and complete diagnosis of the physical condition of anyone sitting in it.'

'I don't believe it,' Josh snapped. 'Nothing can do that!'

'You mean,' Wright amended gently, 'that you don't know of anything. This chair has been theoretically possible for ten years, technically feasible for five. There's nothing new in it. Given the proper incentive, anyone could have put it together.'

'Nonsense!' Josh exclaimed. 'This is revolutionary – why haven't I heard about it? Why isn't it common knowledge?'

Wright shrugged. 'This is the first public trial, you know. And we shouldn't minimize the natural resistance in the economy that has condemned many inventions to oblivion. You must have heard of the pellet that turns water into fuel, the non-dulling razor blade, the panaceas—'

'Myths! I'm an industrialist, and I know. We make all kinds of tubes and tube-substitutes: vacuum, photo-electric, thermionic, gas-filled, cathode-ray, magnetron, klystron, transistors. And if someone invents one that will obsolete the rest, we'll start making that. No, when something as potentially valuable as any of the things you've mentioned is invented or discovered, a thousand companies would be rushing forward shaking their money in their hands.'

Wright looked interested. 'And you make electronic equipment. We should be able to strike a deal to put the basic design of the chair on the market – as a booth, perhaps. A vending machine for diagnoses: "Get your weight, height, chest X ray, metabolism, blood count, cancer test – only five cents—" '

'Five cents! You'd lose money on it. You'd have to charge at least a dollar or more.'

'That would price health out of the reach of the people who need it most. Contrary to the entire purpose of hedonics. The chair isn't nearly as complicated as you might imagine. But we can discuss it later. The chair here is also a therapeutic tool. Treats diseases and physical malfunctions, adjusts endocrine balances, mends broken bones, that sort of thing.'

'That sort of thing?' Josh repeated weakly. 'How?'

'Oh hypodermics mostly,' Wright said offhand.

Josh laughed with relief. 'The chair diagnoses the case and then cures the ailment, eh?'

'That's right.' Wright smiled. 'How's your cold?'

Josh sniffed. The air smelled wonderful. His nose was clear; his head was unstuffed. 'It's gone,' he said.

'Millions,' Josh muttered. 'A cold cure like that would be worth millions. Why don't you put it on the market?'

'We have,' Wright said simply. 'It's part of the hedonic treatment. From our viewpoint there would be no value in marketing it individually. We aren't interested in alleviating minor ailments – or major ones either for that matter. Our business is happiness, not medicine. Understand?'

Josh shook his head in bewilderment. 'You mean you aren't interested in making money?'

'Of course we are. How else could we support this establishment and build others like it? How else could we make the services of Hedonics, Inc., available to everyone? But money isn't a goal in itself; it's only the best way to get there.'

'Very noble,' Josh growled. 'All right. This chair diagnoses ailments and cures them. What else do I get for my hundred dollars?'

'You've noticed, I presume, that your ulcer is much better?'

An awed, introspective expression spread across Josh's face. He took a deep breath and felt helplessly across his upper abdomen. 'I do believe—' he began, and then his face became suspicious. 'How can I be sure?'

Wright chuckled. 'Go to your own physician. He'll tell you.'

'I will,' Josh said firmly. If it was a bluff, he intended to call it. 'Is this all?'

'You want more?' Wright asked wide-eyed. 'Where else could you buy cures for a cold, an ulcer, and get a complete physical tune-up for one hundred dollars? You're in better shape now than you've been since you were thirty. Is this all? As a matter of fact it isn't. You've had only the first half of the treatment. If it's convenient, the second half will be taken care of tomorrow at the same time.'

'What does that consist of?'

'You've had the preliminaries. Without the rest – without psychological therapy comparable to the physical treatment you've already received – what you've had would be worthless. You'd get more colds. Your ulcer would return worse than ever. I repeat. We're not in the medical business. We're in hedonics!'

'But I don't need psychological therapy,' Josh protested. 'And even if I did need it, I don't think I'd like it. 'I'm not maladjusted.'

'Are you happy?' Wright asked quietly.

Josh realized, with a start, that it wasn't a rhetorical question. 'I think that's an indecent question.'

'Don't you want to be happy?'

'I suppose so,' Josh said slowly. 'But not if it means tampering with my personality—'

Wright sighed sadly. 'Humanity has an infinite capacity for misery. It searches for ways to make itself unhappy, partly, I suppose, out of masochism, partly out of the necessity for self-punishment for subconscious guilt-feelings. Look! Hedonics doesn't tamper with your personality. It only shows it how to express itself in joyful ways; it gives it the techniques of happiness.'

'How?' Josh asked suspiciously.

'We start by relieving the obvious disturbances. The tics, the nervous habits – like the twitch in your left eyelid and the way you stretch your neck.'

Josh felt himself start to stretch his neck, felt his eyelid twitch. He hadn't noticed them for a long time. Now, when he tried to control them, he found it impossible.

'You have headaches in the evening, hangovers in the morning, and shakes before breakfast. You drink too much, smoke too much, depend too much on stimulants. We relieve the first and remove the necessity for the second.'

'A secular chaplain with a club,' Josh sneered.

Wright smiled easily. 'You might call us that. Unhappiness is often no more than a bad habit. We can break that as easily as we can break the others. Then we get at your phobias—'

'I don't have any phobias—'

'I was sure you had most of them. Acrophobia, claustrophobia, homilophobia, even phobophobia – the fear of being afraid—'

Josh shook his head stubbornly. 'You're mistaken.'

'Surely not,' Wright said, his eyes wide. He moved his hand across the desk.

Suddenly the lights were gone. Josh was in dense blackness, so complete it seemed to have texture. It was close around him, stifling. There was a mountain above him, pressing down heavily upon him with its psychic weight, compressing the air. . . .

Panic fluttered in his throat and banded his chest with tight, cold metal. 'Stop it!' he shouted, his voice breaking. 'Turn on the lights!'

The lights came on. Josh blinked angrily.

'That,' Wright said cheerfully, 'was claustrophobia.' His hand moved again.

The ground was a million miles below. People and cars scurried around on it like microbes on a slide. The side of the building faded away beneath him, and Josh felt his insides turn liquid and cold, and his grip on the metal railing over which he was leaning became palsied and weak as if the strength had drained away. He felt himself falling, and it was almost as if he had thrown himself into the hungry void.

A scream started somewhere deep inside him. . . .

Josh was sitting on the edge of the chair, the scream still rising in his throat. He choked it off and glared at Wright.

'That,' Wright said, 'was acrophobia. I could go on, but I think the demonstrations have proved my point.'

By the time Josh had found his voice, he had regained control of himself. 'If the cold cure was worth millions, that device would be worth billions in entertainment alone.'

Wright shrugged as if the matter were supremely unimportant. 'It's a useful therapeutic device. Perhaps you'll have a chance to really see it in action later on. To get on – after we clean up the phobias, we attack your real hedonic problems—'

'All this for one hundred dollars?' Josh asked in amazement. 'This is the special? The limited service contract?'

Wright nodded.

'How do you make money on it?'

'We don't,' Wright admitted, 'although our techniques are so standardized that we break even. This, of course, is an introductory offer and will become considerably more expensive later – for those who can afford it, that is. For those who can't, we do free clinical work. What we make money on, actually, is the unlimited service contract.'

'What is there left for you to do?' Josh asked.

'We take care of everything; we arrange your life so that you never have to worry again. In this age of anxiety, you never have to be anxious. In this age of fear, you need never be afraid. You will always be fed, clothed, housed, and happy. You will love and be loved. Life, for you, will be an unmixed joy. There are additional benefits, such as our researches in longevity – just now bearing fruit, incidentally – which will be used for the benefit of our unlimited service clients first of all.'

'Happiness,' Josh said distantly, 'and a long life to enjoy it in – that would be worth a fortune.' But he could hear warning bells ringing in his head. They said: *Skin game! Skin game!* 'What's the price?' Josh asked.

'As you say,' Wright said thoughtfully, 'it would be worth a fortune. The price is steep, but it's worth it. The price is – everything.'

'Everything?' Josh repeated, his voice squeaking a little.

Wright nodded soberly. 'All assets, including personal and real property and savings, and future earnings are signed over to the corporation. It isn't as exorbitant as it sounds. The client has no more use for money. All his needs are taken care of by the corporation.'

'There's a great inequity,' Josh protested. 'A laborer might have only a few dollars. A wealthy man would have to pay millions—'

'It depends upon your yardstick,' Wright said, shrugging. 'To both it is all they have. For us, it averages out, and it can't matter to the client. Money is worthless to them. They already have, after all, everything that money can buy – happiness. And it couldn't buy that until recently.'

'But what if a man isn't happy?'

'In that unlikely event,' Wright said, 'the contract would be void and the money would be refunded in full.'

It was all very plausible, Josh thought, but there had to be a catch somewhere. 'If I wanted to take out unlimited service, then, I'd have to turn over to you all my property, my business, my savings – everything?'

'That's right,' Wright said cheerily.

'You must not find many customers for that!'

'On the contrary, we have a great many already.'

'This,' Josh said firmly, 'is one you won't get.'

Wright spread out his hands pacifically. 'That, of course, is up to you. Unhappiness isn't a crime. Not yet, anyway.'

Josh picked it up quickly. 'What do you mean, not yet?'

'Eventually hedonics will become nation-wide – even world-wide. And eventually we will need legislation, not for ourselves but to protect the rights of minorities. It must be made a part of the primary school curriculum, and everyone must have the protection of the basic right – the right, Mr. Hunt, to be happy.'

'The right the Declaration of Independence was concerned about,' Josh said slowly, 'was the *pursuit* of happiness.'

'That was when happiness was an art. Now it is a science. We have pursued it long enough. It's time we caught up with it. Well, Mr. Hunt,' Wright said, getting up, 'I've kept you long enough for your first treatment. I'll expect you tomorrow to complete the therapy.'

Josh nodded somberly as he rose from the chair. He would be back. Back he hoped, with a surprise for Wright and Hedonics, Inc.

'By the way,' Wright said as Josh reached the door, 'about the manufacture of the diagnostic equipment—'

'I'm afraid I wouldn't be interested,' Josh said, shaking his head slowly. 'There isn't much profit in nickel business.'

'It depends,' Wright replied, 'on what kind of profit you want.'

And Josh, pondering that remark, walked out of the room, down the corridor, across the vast waiting room, and out into the afternoon.

V.

> *Annual income twenty pounds, annual expenditure nineteen nineteen six, result happiness. Annual income twenty pounds, annual expenditure twenty pounds ought and six, result misery.*
>
> CHARLES DICKENS

J. M. Cooper, M.D., looked up, bewildered. 'Well, yes, as far as I can tell, if your ulcer is not completely cured it is so much improved that it is inactive.'

'What about the cold?' Josh asked.

Dr. Cooper put his hands together thoughtfully. 'Cleared up – that is if you really had a cold.'

'What would be the point of lying about it?' Josh roared. 'I've had thousands of colds, and this one was a dilly.'

The doctor nodded agreeably. 'I suppose you know. But also, I'm sure, you've had colds that cleared up spontaneously in one or two days. That's why cold remedies – and other so-called "miracle drugs" – must be tested, with controls, in a careful, scientific manner before any judgment can be passed on them.'

'But if the ulcer and the cold were cured, how was it done?'

'I haven't got the slightest idea,' Dr. Cooper said frankly. 'But if I had to guess, I'd say that the method was a cousin to faith healing.'

'But I had no faith in the thing at all.'

The doctor shrugged. 'You expected something to happen. You were impressed. The hypodermic injection was a stimulus to autosuggestion – in effect you cured yourself. Your ulcer, after all, was psychosomatic. Your mind inflicted it on your body; your mind cured it. That's all.'

'Sounds very simple.'

'Oh, it isn't simple. If it were, we'd all be doing it. Much easier than diet, drugs, and surgery, eh?'

'Then, actually, it's all hokum?'

'Well, I wouldn't say that. I've got no doubt that they've stumbled onto something in the autosuggestion line which may prove effective in many cases. We must realize that we are living in an age of stress, and the stress diseases are everywhere – the stomach cramps, rheumatoid arthritis, ulcers, hypertension, asthma, some heart diseases, ulcerative colitis. . . .'

'Aren't you worried about your practice?' Josh asked, frowning.

Dr. Cooper laughed. 'Such cases are necessarily limited, and I've found that germs and viruses are virtually immune to autosuggestion. These miracle cures turn out to be only temporary manias. They run their course and are forgotten. No – as fantastic as these chairs seem – there will always be a medical profession.'

'Could this be a case of fraud?'

'Well, yes, I suppose there is that possibility—'

'If it is, would you help me expose it?'

'I – uh – hesitate to become involved—'

'Don't you think it's your duty to the community and to your profession to make certain that anyone treating the sick in this community is fully qualified to do so?'

Dr. Cooper ran his hand through his close-cropped hair. 'Since you put it that way, I suppose it is.'

Josh nodded curtly. 'I'll let you know what you can do.'

When he left the doctor's office, there were still several hours of the afternoon left. He stepped along in the sunshine feeling better than he had felt in years. That, he thought, is what comes of having an outside interest.

The thought of outside interests reminded him of the business, and he felt a flash of guilt. He turned his car towards the plant.

Marie looked up from her desk, surprised. 'I didn't expect you, Mr. Hunt. You looked so sick last night. But today you look much better.'

'Thank you, Marie,' Josh said jauntily. 'I feel fine. Have there been any calls for me?'

'Mr. Steward, your lawyer has been trying to reach you. And Mr. Kidd has been waiting.'

'Get Mr. Steward for me. Meanwhile I'll talk to Kidd.'

'Oh, and Mr. Hunt, while you're here – I want to tell you that I'm resigning. I'm getting married.'

Josh had been turning toward the office. He stopped suddenly and came back. He realized suddenly how much he had come to depend on his daily contact with youth and beauty. It wasn't a question of gamboling with Marie – at least only in distant and fancy hypothesis – but it had been something to look forward to, to cherish secretly, to make his days endurable.

'But I thought you wanted a career!'

Marie blushed prettily. 'I thought so, too. But I just realized – I mean I was made to realize – that what I really wanted all the time was a home and a family. That's what would really make me happy.'

A dark suspicion settled around Josh like a mantle. 'I see. Hedonics, Inc.'

She sighed ecstatically and nodded.

'All right, Miss Gamble,' Josh said distantly, divorcing himself. 'I'm sorry to lose you, but I'm sure you know best.'

That was the first surprise.

The second surprise was Mr. Kidd, the union business agent. He was almost sickening. He didn't argue. He didn't pound the table. He said, 'You're right, Mr. Hunt. Job enlargement is the answer. I agree with you, and the men agree with you.'

'Wh-what?' Josh spluttered.

'Yes, sir, and we'll sign that contract.'

'What's the matter with you?' Josh demanded.

'I've just realized, Mr. Hunt, that all this blustering and argument doesn't do anything but make everybody unhappy. And another thing I've found out is that I wasn't cut out for this business agent stuff. I was happier when I was a worker in the factory. With your permission, that's what I'm going back to.'

His mouth sagging open, Josh looked at Kidd. Consciously he forced his mouth shut and said, 'Hedonics—?'

'That's right,' Kidd said happily.

The telephone saved Josh from blurting out what he thought about Hedonics, Inc. 'Excuse me,' he muttered, picking up the receiver. 'Hello?'

'This is Steward,' his lawyer said in a high-pitched, excited voice. 'You know this new firm in town, the one that calls itself Hedon—'

'I know it,' Josh cut in grimly.

'They just had a representative in my office. They now own half of Hunt Electronics.'

VI

With these celestial Wisdom calms the mind,
And makes the happiness she does not find.
                                    SAMUEL JOHNSON

Josh leaned forward in his chair, staring intently at Steward's mouth, outlined at the top with a thin, pencil-stroke mustache, as if seeing it move made the words easier to understand. 'I still don't understand what you're talking about,' Josh said. 'You mean my wife signed one of their unlimited service contracts?'

'That's what I've been trying to tell you,' Steward sighed. 'And that contract gives them half ownership of your business.'

'How can my wife sign away my business?' Josh demanded for the thirteenth time.

'Only half of it,' Steward said patiently, smoothing his little mustache methodically. 'It stems from the community property law of this state. She owns half of what you own. She's signed it all over. That gives them a half interest in—'

'All right, all right,' Josh said. 'I get that part. Does that mean they own half my house, too?'

Steward nodded. 'And half your savings, shares in other companies, cars – in other words, half of all your assets.'

'But not half of what I'll earn in the future, surely,' Josh pleaded.

'That's a moot point,' Steward said thoughtfully. 'I imagine that would have to be tested in court.'

'What can I do?' Josh asked helplessly.

'Well, they'll probably accept a cash settlement on the house. Otherwise you'd have to sell. As for the rest, that can be arranged—'

'No, no!' Josh exploded. 'We can't do that. I'll fight it. We'll take it to court! We'll prove that the contract is worthless.'

Steward shook his head slowly and determinedly. 'As your lawyer I've got to warn you that you'd be throwing your money away. Whoever drew up this contract made it airtight and waterproof. The greatest contract lawyer in the country couldn't get out of this one.'

'There's undue influence – and temporary insanity,' Josh cried desperately.

Steward shrugged. 'You know your wife better than I do. And you know what you're willing to go through in court. Insanity proceedings are never pretty. Even so, it's doubtful if you could make it stick. Attached to the contract is a psychiatrist's certificate of sanity.'

'That's evidence, isn't it?' Josh exclaimed, tapping the desk with a trembling finger. 'That shows they were afraid we'd attack there. It's their weak point. It's—'

'Hopeless, Mr. Hunt,' Steward said flatly. 'You'd better save your energy to find a way to keep control of the company.'

'Then this is what they're trying to do,' Josh said slowly, pounding out the words to the rhythmic thump of his fist on the desk. 'Why can't anyone see the danger? In a few weeks they'll own Millville – industry, real estate, municipal property right down to the sewers. They'll own everything fixed in place and everything movable including three-fourths of the people—'

'They can't own people,' Steward objected. 'That's slavery.'

'Read that contract again,' Josh told him sternly. 'It's worse than slavery. That, at least, left the mind free.' His voice became quiet, but its intensity was more frightening than if he had shouted. 'I can see it clearly now. Within a few years Hedonics, Inc. will be the greatest single economic force in the country. They will own the United States. It won't be necessary to take over the government. Hedonics, Inc., will permit the government to take out an unlimited service contract—'

Steward had been studying Josh apprehensively. 'That's a lot of extrapolation from a single incident—'

Josh looked through Steward and the wall behind him into infinity. 'There's nothing that can stop Hedonics, Inc. – this lust for power masquerading behind an imbecilic smile. A snowball is an easy thing to halt when it is little, but let it plunge downhill – laden with the eon-long weight of a people's dreams – and it will grow into an avalanche that will sweep nations and continents in front of it.'

Steward was impressed in spite of himself. 'I suppose there is an element of danger—'

'I'm only the first,' Josh continued. 'After me will come millions who will be overwhelmed and forgotten. The time to stop it is *now* – now while it's still small – or the time will be gone forever.'

Steward nodded slowly.

Josh took a deep breath. 'What did their representative want?'

The lawyer started and shook his head. 'Wanted you notified. Tell him, he said, that Hedonics, Inc. won't be a difficult partner. You are to go ahead and run the business just as you have been running it. They won't interfere.'

'Damned decent of them,' Josh growled.

'One more thing,' Steward went on. 'He said that the corporation would like to suggest the manufacture of some kind of – coin-operated booth, I think it was.'

Josh's sigh was a minor explosion. 'So. I'm to dig my own grave. I won't do it. I was right the first time. We have to fight them. And that's what I'm going to do if I have to throw the second half after the first.'

'But I've explained—'

'Look! The contract is no good if the contracting party is engaged in illegal activities. Isn't that right?'

'Well, yes, in general I suppose that's—'

'It's invalid, isn't it, if the contractor can't fulfill the terms of the contract?'

'That's right, but—'

'They guarantee happiness, don't they? Let's make them prove that they can supply it!'

VII

Those who have given themselves the most concern about the happiness of peoples have made their neighbours very miserable.

ANATOLE FRANCE

The sound of the front door slamming shut was hollow and empty. Josh stood in the hall feeling the silence close around him, and he couldn't control a shiver. He knew then that there was no one else in the house.

He called out anyway. 'Ethel!' A moment later, he called again, but his voice was weak and hopeless. 'Ethel?'

The dark bundle of anger he had carried home with him had vanished. He had not spoken more than a dozen words to his wife that week. Now when he had many to say to her she wasn't there. It was like the woman – like all women, perhaps – that she should be there when she was not wanted, and when she was, was never there.

If he had found her then, he would not have spoken all in anger. At the moment he understood her, better perhaps than he had ever understood her before. But slowly that leaked away and was as if it had never been.

He found the note on the desk in the study. It said:

Dear Joshua:

I have gone to get the children. I have spent too much of my life away from them because of this reason or that reason. I realize now that we worry too much about what is good for people. That is wrong. What we should be concerned with is their happiness.

I know I would be happier if the children were with me. I think the children would be happier, too.

ETHEL

Josh looked at the note for a long time after he had finished reading it, but he wasn't seeing the words. He was seeing Ethel as he had seen her many years ago – young, beautiful, and in love. He was remembering the way he had looked at her then and talked to her then, and he was wondering how it had all changed.

There were no ice cubes in the little bar. Josh poured the bourbon carelessly into a glass and drank it that way, warm and neat. He didn't even taste it.

This was what Hedonics, Inc. had done to him. It had taken away control of the business he had built; it had taken half of everything he owned. And it had taken his wife and children. Beside that the rest was meaningless.

The grief was too great for anyone to bear.

The second glass of bourbon seemed to sweep away the mists of emotion. Everything became clear. He had lost everything. He would fight for it. He would win it all back. Hedonics, Inc. was a racket. He would expose it before the world.

A small, unquiet thought crept into his mind: *But was it a racket?*

Could he be sure that Hedonics, Inc. couldn't fulfill their contracts? Could he be certain that they had not found the age-lost secret of happiness, that they had not located the sealed gates of paradise and found a way through them or around them or over them?

If they had discovered techniques and devices for netting happiness like a bluebird then there was only one thing for a sensible man to do. He should take out an unlimited service contract.

When happiness is for sale, only a fool will not buy.

A man couldn't afford to take chances. The smart thing to do was check. That was simple enough. Josh opened his Webster's Dictionary to the back pages where there was a list of colleges and universities in the United States and Canada. He ran his finger down the column: **Indiana Technical C, Indiana U, Iola Junior C. . . .**

There was no Institute of Applied Hedonics. As an additional precaution, Josh checked under 'Applied' and 'Hedonics.' Nothing.

The Institute of Applied Hedonics was a pipe dream.

So was Hedonics, Inc.

So was happiness.

Question : How could he prove it – legally?

As he sloshed his glass full for the third time, he pondered the mystery of the bourbon that refused to make him drunk. His mind was crystal-clear.

He sipped the amber stuff this time, and it went down like water. Something was beating, rhythmically, at the gates of his mind. He swung them open and let it in. It was two lines of poetry :

> *I wonder often what the vintners buy*
> *One half so precious as the stuff they sell.*

That was it, of course. That was the logical proof he had been waiting for. It would be worthless in court, but to Josh it was conviction.

If they were happy, if they had that bluebird fluttering in their cage, why did they want to sell it? If a man has found paradise, why should he sell guided tours? After all desires are satisfied, what is the incentive for further striving? What did they buy?

Answer : there was nothing they could buy. They already had everything.

Hedonics was a fallacy.

Now to expose it.

He dialed the number with a steady finger. 'Lieutenant Marsh?' he said.

VIII

> *To crave for happiness in this world is simply to be*
> *possessed by a spirit of revolt. What right have we to*
> *happiness?*
>
> HENRIK IBSEN

'You don't have to vocalize,' Wright said. 'In fact, I'd rather you didn't. What we're after is your reactions to a standard set of key words, and those are independent of your answers.

The diagnostic chair will give me the readings – chiefly from your psychogalvanic reflex – that will be plotted against the stimuli, and we will have a graphic representation of your hedonic problems. Ready, Mr. Hunt?'

Josh squirmed uneasily in the chair. 'No hypodermics?'

Wright smiled gently. 'No hypodermics.'

'All right,' Josh sighed. 'Shoot.'

'Father,' Wright said in a professionally neutral voice. 'Mother. Girl. Children. Money. Property. Wealth. Poverty. Wife. Hopes. Dreams. Work. . . . Roses. Diamonds. Happiness—' He broke off after fifteen minutes and glanced at the desk top. 'That's enough. Do you want a reading, Mr. Hunt?'

'A what?'

Wright's smile was deprecating. 'You know – the gypsy stirs your tea leaves and tells you your past and your future. We can only guess at your future, but we can give you a very accurate picture of your past and present.'

'No thanks,' Josh said firmly. 'I never go to tea-rooms.'

Wright shrugged. 'That's up to you.'

'Is this all?'

'No,' Wright drawled. 'Now we tell you how to be happy. But perhaps you'd rather pass that up, too.'

'Go ahead. Tell me.'

'You'd be much happier,' Wright said seriously, 'working with your hands. Build something. Make something. Even assemble equipment in your own factory. If you could conquer your need for recognition and acclamation, you'd be happiest as a sculptor. You have a strong tactile sense, you see, and a solid feeling for form. . . . But I wasn't to give you a character analysis, was I?'

Josh chuckled. 'And yet I've built one of the finest businesses of its kind in the country. How do you account for that?'

'I didn't say you'd be more successful,' Wright explained slowly. 'I said you'd be happier. That isn't the same thing, and a recognition of true and false goals is an integral part of the hedonic techniques. The challenge of a job a man really isn't equipped to handle can stimulate him to fantastic efforts – and at the same time ruin his temperament, his digestion, and his home. Is it worth it? The only sensible answer is *no*! But, since you intend to disregard the advice, there's no use continuing this.'

'Have I had my hundred dollars' worth?'

'Substantially, yes.'

Surprisingly, then, it was Wright who was on his feet, who was at the door before Josh could move. The door opened. 'All right, gentlemen,' Wright said calmly. 'You can come in now.'

They came in sheepishly, like small boys caught listening at keyholes: Dr. Cooper, Mr. Steward, and Lieutenant Marsh, the police detective, carrying a wire recorder.

'How did you know we were there?' Marsh demanded suspiciously.

'Mr. Hunt should have known better than to have tried to bribe our receptionist. What possible use could she have for money? I presume you have a search warrant?'

'Yes,' Marsh said.

'What is the complaint?'

'Fraud. And other things.'

'Sworn out by Mr. Hunt, eh?' Wright said easily. 'Against me personally or against the corporation?'

'Both.'

'Well, turn your recorder on. You might as well be recording this, too.'

'*You're* recording it?' Lieutenant Marsh exclaimed, his heavy face wrinkling into a frown. 'I don't know as that's legal—'

'I assure you, Lieutenant, it is. Unless you have a warrant for my arrest and wish to take me downtown. No? Well, let us proceed. You, I presume,' he said, turning to the doctor, 'are Dr. Cooper? And you must be Mr. Steward. What are the charges against me, specifically? I'd rather clear up this misunderstanding now than drag it through the courts.'

'The first one,' Josh said, scowling at the ease with which Wright had taken charge, 'is practicing medicine without a license.'

'Oh, dear,' Wright said, 'where did you get that idea? Simply because I don't have diplomas and licenses scattered around the walls? Here.' He reached into a desk drawer that sprang open as his hand approached it, and he pulled out a folder thick with papers. He handed it to Dr. Cooper. 'I think you'll find all the documents you want.'

The doctor leafed through the odd sizes and grades of heavy paper. Josh watched him intently. If Wright thought he could wriggle free so easily, he was in for a rude shock.

Dr. Cooper looked up. 'It – uh – all appears to be in very good order.' He looked at Wright. 'Excellent record, Doctor.'

'He *is* a doctor, then,' Josh insisted.

'Oh, yes. All his diplomas are here, his certificates of internship, residency, specialization – including internal medicine and neuropsychiatry – state license to practice, advanced study at the Institute of Applied Hedonics. . . .'

'All right, Doctor,' Josh said coldly. 'I'll take your word for it.'

But Dr. Cooper wasn't finished. 'Tell me, Dr. Wright, how did you cure that ulcer?'

Wright smiled. 'I'd be happy to discuss the whole matter with you later – including the fact that hedonic therapists must be drawn from the ranks of the profession that would appear to be most threatened by hedonics.' He turned back toward Josh. 'Next charge?'

'We'll want to study your articles of incorporation,' Josh said, 'but we'll let that go until later.'

'Oh, no,' Wright objected, pulling out another folder and handing it to Steward. 'You'll find them all in order. We've been careful to comply with state law in all particulars.'

'We could press a charge of slavery—' Josh began.

'If you're referring to our unlimited service contract – how? It's a simple contractual relationship which can be broken off at any time with a full return of all fees paid by the simple statement of the client that he isn't happy. That can't be considered slavery by any definition.'

Josh was silent for a moment. Explosively, triumphantly,

then, he said, 'Prove, then, that you are contracting for a performable service.'

Wright looked up quickly. He seemed a little startled. I have him now, Josh gloated grimly to himself.

'Prove that we can make people happy?' Wright said. 'That isn't necessary, you know. It's up to you to prove that we don't.'

'That's right,' Steward said unexpectedly. 'The burden of proof rests on the complainant.'

Josh glared at the lawyer. 'And I'm going to prove it,' he said. His head swiveled back toward Wright. 'I'm going to tie you up in court until you can't wiggle. I'll get an injunction against the corporation until the case is settled. Maybe you can't lose it, but you can't win it, either. You'll never get out of court, *because you can't prove that you've made a single person happy!* How can you measure happiness? You can't even define it!'

Wright shook his head slowly, pityingly. 'How long do you think your case would last against testimony like this?' He passed his hand over the desk.

The door opened. There was a woman standing behind it. She took one step into the room.

Josh's face was red. The veins in his neck grew large and swollen. He took one step toward her. 'Ethel,' he said, and his voice was half strangled.

She held up one hand as if to hold him away. 'Don't come close to me,' she said.

'Tell him,' Josh pleaded brokenly. 'Tell them all. Tell them you aren't happy. Tell them it was all a mistake—'

'Joshua,' she said, and her voice was hollow and distant, 'Joshua, I never knew what happiness was until the day before yesterday.'

Suddenly her face changed. Instead of the placid, resigned features of a middle-aged woman beginning to grow gray and old, her face became radiant, haloed somehow with joy so that she became ageless, eternally youthful, filled like a lamp so full of peace and happiness that it overflowed incandescently, bathing everything around.

'But now I know,' she said. 'Do you think I could give that up?' She shook her head sadly at Josh. 'Don't be stubborn, Joshua.'

And she turned and was gone before anyone could move. Josh sprang to the door, but the corridor was empty. When he swung back, Lieutenant Marsh was shifting his weight uneasily back and forth.

'I – uh – guess there isn't much use for me here,' he ventured.

Josh stepped savagely toward Wright. 'I'll make a complaint,' he shouted. 'Hedonics, Inc. hasn't made me happy.'

'I'm sorry to hear that, Mr. Hunt,' Wright said earnestly. 'In that case, according to the terms of the contract, I must do this.' He took a slip of paper off the desk and handed it to Josh.

Josh looked down at it, but he already knew, with a leaden feeling of defeat, what it was. It was a check made out to Joshua P. Hunt for $100.

He stood there with the slip of paper in his hand, dazed, unable to move. The others left – he felt rather than saw it happen : Lieutenant Marsh, muttering an apology; Steward, handing back the sheaf of legal papers with a shrug; Dr. Cooper, with an appointment for a conference.

'You'll never take over the country,' Josh said, and he heard his own voice as if it came from a long way off. 'The government will move in to regulate you before then. There are laws of monopoly and restraint of trade—'

'But we are a nonprofit organization,' Wright said gently. 'That will protect us for a long time. Moreover, a large percentage of congressmen and government officials are already clients.'

A groan broke from Josh's lips. 'It's a fake. It has to be. There isn't any Institute of Applied Hedonics.'

Wright leaned forward intently. 'How do you know?'

'I looked it up in a list of colleges and universities.'

Wright smiled sympathetically. 'The Institute was founded only six years ago. If your list was older than that, naturally it wouldn't include the Institute.'

Frozenly, Josh recognized the truth. He had owned the dictionary since his college days.

'You refused a character analysis once,' Wright said. 'I'll give it to you now. You're a materialist. You believe only in those things you can hold in your hands. Real abstractions are completely beyond you: love, friendship, happiness . . . There is a demon in some men that refuses to let them recognize happiness or seek it. You would reject paradise if you did not build it yourself.'

Josh's head drooped. 'But what do the vintners buy?' he demanded puzzledly.

Wright shook his head without hope. 'The hedonics techniques aren't something magical. They're a reorientation and a discipline – a control not over external events but over our reactions to them. Happiness is inside. All you have to do is recognize that. Oh, it isn't easy. It's hard work, harder than anything anyone has ever done. But it's worth it.

'What do we buy? I'll tell you. We buy happiness. Not for ourselves – for everyone. Sure, money is no good to us. Not if we're happy. But if we're happy, you understand, we want others to be happy, too. That's a law of human nature, just as we want others to be miserable when we are miserable. Hedonics, Inc. is the answer to the question, How can everyone have a chance at happiness?

'Hedonics, Inc. has unusual requirements for its recruits. They must be altruists. Their happiness must lie in making others happy.'

IX

How bitter a thing it is to look into happiness through another man's eyes!

WILLIAM SHAKESPEARE

Josh sat in the red-leather chair, half of which belonged to him, and studied the amber depths of the liquid in the glass. Here, at least, was a kind of happiness – oblivion.

The only trouble was that oblivion refused to come.

Whisky had ceased to affect him. Had Hedonics, Inc. taken that away, too?

There was still no ice; perhaps there never would be any ice. The house was silent; perhaps it always would be silent. It was good for thinking, but there was no longer any point in thought.

How could he have overlooked all the clues that pointed – inescapably – to the fact that hedonics worked. His cold cured! His ulcer cured! Anyone who could do that could not be a quack.

But the proofs had rolled off his well-oiled mind.

Was he what Wright had called him, a materialist? If so, he could, at least, accept the testimony of his senses.

Hedonics worked. He could accept that. It worked physically: it had cured the incurable. It worked psychologically: it had turned Ethel into a radiantly happy woman.

He could accept, too, the inevitability of hedonics' conquest of the nation and after that the world. It was a juggernaut built out of humanity's eternal hopes; nothing could stop it. All over the United States people would be happy. All over the world people would be happy. Everybody would be happy.

Everybody but Joshua P. Hunt.

He took a sip of bourbon and let it slide down his throat and into his stomach. A twinge of pain made his stomach recoil; then it began to burn. It was a familiar sensation. His ulcer was back.

When happiness is for sale, only a fool will not buy.

Perhaps he was a materialist, but he wasn't a fool. He could swallow his pride.

He dialed P-L-E-A-S-U-R.

'I'm sorry, Mr. Hunt,' the girl said, and she actually sounded sorry. 'The clause is in the contract, and we must abide by it for our own protection. Anyone who has broken a contract is ineligible for further participation. Otherwise, you see, there would be no end of people withdrawing and coming back, and the book-keeping problems would be enormous. We must, of course, keep our incidental expenses to a minimum. You do understand, don't you, Mr. Hunt?'

Josh held the telephone for a long time after he had heard the connection broken before he remembered what its strange finality reminded him of.

The Gates of Paradise might sound like that as they clicked shut in front of the forever barred.

Part Two

I

Justice is the only worship,
Love is the only priest.
Ignorance is the only slavery.
Happiness is the only good.
The time to be happy is now,
The place to be happy is here,
The way to be happy is to make
  others so.

ROBERT GREEN INGERSOLL

hedonics (he.don'iks), *n.;* See -ICS. Psychomedical science
dealing with the nature and pursuit of happiness. . . .

hedonism (he'don.iz'm), *n.* 1. *Ethics.* The doctrine that
pleasure is the only good in life and that moral duty is
fulfilled in the gratification of pleasure-seeking instincts. . . .

hedonist (-ist), *n.* 1. One who lives in accordance with
hedonism; *i.e.,* for pleasure. 2. (Since 2005) A practi-
tioner of hedonics. . . .

The day began as more than eight thousand days had
begun before.

'Wake up,' it murmured sweetly in the Hedonist's ear.
'The sun is shining. It's a beautiful day. Wake up. Be
happy!'

The Hedonist rolled over and punched the pillow into
silence. He pried one eye open and peered out the long, low
window that formed one wall of his cottage. The smog
billowed against it grayly like a fat, long-haired cat rolling
at the Earth's feet, needle claws sheathed for the moment
but ready to flash out and slash if the impulse struck.

So much for realism.

The Hedonist suppressed the thought automatically and sat up. Another day, another pleasure.

He glanced at the pillow beside his and the brown hair flung across it like a silk scarf. He sighed. It was time for that to end, too.

He flipped back the covers and brought his hand down smartly against the youthfully rounded bottom. It smacked satisfactorily. Beth turned over and sat up in one startled movement.

'What's the matter?' she spluttered.

His pajama tops were several sizes too big for her. They drifted down around her like a scarlet tent. She yawned and lifted her arms to rub her eyes. When she dropped them to her sides, the jacket bared one creamy shoulder and threatened to slide even farther.

A smile drifted across the Hedonist's lips. Sleep was so precious when you were young. There was never enough of it. There was never enough of anything. As you grew older you were more easily satisfied. He sighed again. That was a pity, too.

Sleepily, Beth caught the slipping jacket before it left her shoulders completely. 'What's happened?' she said in the middle of a yawn.

'Time to get up,' the Hedonist said gently. And, even gentler, 'Time to go home.'

'Home?' she said. She was suddenly awake.

'I'm certifying you today. You can get married whenever you and your fiancé can agree upon a date.'

'But—' she began and stopped, wordless.

With the skill of long experience, the Hedonist studied her face without revealing his interest. Beth's face, normally calm, was troubled. Even troubled, it was the most beautiful face in his ward. He had taken her under instruction with a joy that was not entirely professional. But so young, so young.

His memory, unbidden, offered him the date: February 23, 2035. A Thursday. He remembered it well. Three months ago she had been nineteen years old. He had presided at her birth; now he had prepared her for marriage. Through the nineteen years between he had guarded her happiness. It didn't sit well beside his fifty-three years.

'You still want to get married, don't you?' he asked.

'Oh, yes,' she said, her dark eyes steady on his face.

'Then you have my blessing. I have done my best.'

'I know,' she said evenly.

'The man you're betrothed to – he's from another ward?'

'You know that,' she said.

Yes, he knew. He knew everything that went on in the ward: the problems, the worries, the troubles, the sorrows. He knew everybody: their emotional quotients and what to expect from them and when, and how to treat them. . . . Sometimes he even knew their thoughts.

In this ward, he was – in a very real sense – divine. In his knowledge and his power over the lives and happiness of a thousand people, he was a god. But a god can know too much. Knowledge is a burden, and responsibility multiplied a thousand times is enough to bow the shoulders of an Atlas.

But the girl beside him was deep; he could sense that much, even if he couldn't touch bottom.

Touch bottom! The smile that flickered across his face was almost wry. He had touched that one for the last time.

'You must be gentle with him,' the Hedonist said. 'He may not have had your advantages.'

She touched her soft lower lip with her teeth. 'I will,' she said softly. 'If – I mean – when we get married, we'll come back here. If he needs treatment, I'll send him to you—'

The Hedonist shook his head. 'That isn't wise. Girls are more adaptable than men. You could adjust to another hedonist, but your husband would have trouble. You must move to his ward.'

She was silent, looking at him through a silken veil that had drifted down across her forehead.

'Remember,' he said with an uneasiness he could not pin down, 'your duty – your only duty – is happiness.'

'Yes, Hedonist,' she said obediently.

'Good-by, Beth,' he said. 'Be happy!'

He swung his legs over the edge of the bed and walked the three steps to the necessary with cautious dignity. It wasn't because he was fat, exactly, but fifty-three years had thickened him a little around the middle, and there is nothing aesthetic about a middle-aged man's naked back.

Besides, the Hedonist could sense that Beth was watching him.

The necessary door slid shut, and he was alone in the three-by-four foot cubicle. Fifteen minutes later he was ready for the new day and its demands upon him. His beard had been depilated; warm, detergent sprays had cleansed him; hot sprays had rinsed him; icy needles had jabbed his body into tingling awareness. Hot air blasts had dried him. And he was reluctant to leave the comfortable little room.

Womb-symbol? the Hedonist wondered.

He pressed the bottom button on the right. The lights shifted. One wall was suddenly a full-length mirror. The Hedonist looked at himself and frowned. He was not so thick after all. There was no fat on him; he was tall and well muscled. His close-cropped hair was still black, unfrosted. His firm, definite face was unlined. He looked no older than an athletic thirty.

The last geriatric treatment had been even more successful than usual.

And yet there was something wrong. He had counted six distinct feelings of unpleasure since waking. And there was no reason for any of them.

Quickly, skillfully, he counted his blessings. In a golden age, he held one of the most responsible and rewarding positions possible. He knew his work; he did it well; he liked it. There wasn't the smallest reason for him to be unhappy. And yet he sighed.

As he accepted new underclothes from the dispenser and stuffed the transparent wrapper into the disposal, he told himself that the difference between Beth's age and his was obvious and irremediable. What did he want? A wife?

Nonsense! There was a logic behind the Inconstancy clause of the Hedonic Oath. *'As a hedonist, I shall not love nor wed nor father, but I shall keep my self intact for the proper performance of my duties. . . .'*

A hedonist could not permit himself to become emotionally involved with one person. To the extent of that involvement, his available empathetic energy was diminished, and his carefully cultivated insight was impaired. The ward would suffer. His dependents would feel slighted. They would stop bringing their problems to him; and, even if they still came, the delicate relationship so vital to his work would be destroyed.

Publilius Syrus said it over two thousand years before: 'A god could hardly love and be wise.'

And yet— The Hedonist sighed. After ten years of the Institute's rigorous, specialized training and twenty-three years of practice, he still didn't understand the roots of his own unpleasures. How could he hope to treat the unpleasures of his dependents?

'Happiness is indivisible,' he told himself sternly and concentrated on the devaluation of the desire.

By the time he had finished the hedonic exercise, his feeling for Beth was no different in kind or intensity than for any other girl in his ward. He felt once more – as he had felt so rapturously long ago – the exquisite beauty of hedonics.

When he came out of the necessary, Beth was gone. He felt a quick, cold sense of loss.

The bed had been lowered into the floor. It would have fresh sheets on it, he knew; Beth was a thoughtful girl. His desk and chair had swung out from one wall; from the wall opposite had come the comfortable diagnostic chair. The room had returned to its spacious daytime dimensions of twelve by twelve.

Devaluation and substitution soon took care of his absurd disappointment, and he realized, as he sublimated the emotion into professional enthusiasm, that he had forgotten to cut the cord cleanly and finally. It was always a delicate operation; he dreaded it. But it was vital to the therapy, and he had never actually forgotten it before.

The relationship between a hedonist and his patient is an unparalleled intimacy; transference is inevitable. And if the hedonist has his problems, the patient's problems are even more serious. And he does not have the hedonist's technical equipment and training for handling them. It was the hedonist's duty to break off the relationship cleanly when the therapy was finished.

He made a mental note to call Beth back.

II

It ought to be the happiness and glory of a representa-
tive to live in the strictest union, the closest correspond-
ence, and the most unreserved communication with his
constituents. Their wishes ought to have great weight
with him; their opinion high respect; their business un-
remitted attention. It is his duty to sacrifice his repose,
his pleasures, his satisfaction, to theirs; and above all,
ever, and in all cases, to prefer their interests to his own.
                                  EDMUND BURKE

Habit is a technique for simplifying existence, for saving time and the energy of decision. It is a pleasure tool.

As a creature of habit, the Hedonist had a standing order for breakfast. He pressed the top button on the wall beside the table. A panel slid up into the wall. His breakfast was in the cubicle behind it. It sat on a tray in covered plastic dishes. He drew the tray out upon the table and broke the plastic tab that held the lid on the juice glass. He drank the juice quickly; it was cold and good and acid, as usual.

It had been a good batch; Monsanto was proud of it, and they had a right to be.

The next dish steamed aromatically. The plankton cakes had a delicate shrimpy flavor the Hedonist always enjoyed.

They were especially good fried in the new high-fat chlorella oil. He ate them slowly, savoring each bite.

When he ate, he flicked on the news. He punched the highly compressed channel; the words came rattling from the wall like the rare, accidental hail on his plastic roof. The film was compressed only a little, but the time-compression on the speech sometimes went as high as seventy per cent without audible distortion. He understood it as easily as ordinary speech, and there was little enough time, anyway, for everything that had to be done.

The Hedonic Index, which had registered only 85% at dawn (the depressing effect of the morning smog, the Hedonist thought), *had already risen to an acceptable 93%* (breakfast), *and was expected to go higher as the 0737 shower cleared the air.*

In the corner of the picture, the time was listed as 0736. The Hedonist stopped eating and lifted his head to listen. Over the announcer's voice came a slow, growing spatter of rain on the roof. The Hedonist nodded with satisfaction. Right on time. Through the window, he could see the smog melting away. That was the kind of efficiency that made government a solid, unobtrusive foundation for a nation's happiness.

The Hedonist remembered when some thought it hedonics' proudest achievement: 'They made the rains done on time.' Now it was a commonplace.

There would be sunshine all day, although the weather bureau had scheduled a brief shower for 1916, just at sunset, to clear the air once more. The temperature would be held steady at 85 degrees until dusk, when it would be allowed to drop to 70.

Interplanetary Authority announced the completion of a new ship in the yards adjoining the Old City port. (It gleamed like a jewel, the Hedonist thought, with the sunlight breaking through the clouds to sparkle in the diamond-drops of water the rain had left.) *The ship would be launched shortly when the emigration complement was filled. At the end of the three months' trip was Venus.*

The Hedonist smiled. *Shortly*. The ship would wait a long time there in the yards. How do you recruit emigrants from the promised land? Where do you find people who will trade peace and plenty and happiness for toil, starvation, and misery? Asylums, maybe, if there were any asylums left. But there weren't. There were few people left who were that crazy – at least in that way.

'The ship,' the announcer rattled off, 'has been named the Asylum.'

The Hedonist started and relaxed, smiling. Someone had a sense of humor. Strangely enough, it was a rarity these days. Well, if that could be attributed to hedonics, it was a small price to pay for the tears that had vanished, too.

The culturing of a new mutation had increased chlorella production by 50%. The protein content of the new crop was high. Chlorelloaf would be on the menu in most wards for several days. Plankton would be more plentiful soon. The scooper fleet reported a layer of zooplankton which promised to be almost inexhaustible. Catch was already within the thousands of tons.

The Hedonist uncapped the Kafi and hoped the boats didn't syphon the sea clear of life. Algae was all right and the synthetics were efficient and often quite delicious, but the subtle flavor of once-living protein could not be cultured or brewed. On the other hand, he reflected, he could be thankful that he liked fish; some people didn't, and they had only the synthetics and the algae or an extensive reeducation therapy.

The latest Teleflush Index, in millions of gallons, placed the sensie LIFE CAN BE ECSTASY 11.7 ahead of ONE MAN'S HAPPINESS. . . .

The Hedonist stopped listening, instantly, completely, and lifted the Kafi cup to his lips. He had no time for the sensies and less inclination. Perhaps they had a certain therapeutic value in some cases, but as a general rule he considered them on the dangerous lower peak of imaginary gratification. They were daydreams made effortless.

He had suggested as much in a memorandum to the

Council, but no doubt they were too busy for such minor matters.

The Hedonist shuddered and almost dropped the cup. For a month now, the Kafi had been bitter and acrid. Something had gone wrong in the last synthesis. He supposed the stock had been too great to dump, but he hoped that Du Pont would do better next time. And that next time would be soon.

He braced himself and drank it down without taking a breath. After all, the caffeine alkaloid was in it. It was the only stimulant he allowed himself, and he had a vague premonition he would need it before the day was over.

'The Hedonic Index,' the announcer said with infectious joy, 'has reached 95 per cent.'

The Hedonist switched him off and shoved the soiled dishes into the cubicle and drew down the cover. The lunch menu flashed on, but he turned it off. He couldn't stand thinking about lunch so soon after eating. He would select something a little later when he wasn't so full, he told himself, but he knew he would be too busy. He would forget and be forced to accept the standard meal. Well, that was good enough, and he would be happy with it.

The wall square started blinking at him. A cheerful voice said, 'Message for you. Message for you. Message—'

The Hedonist hit the ACCEPT button hastily. The square steadied and filled itself with letters, black on white:

TO: Hedonist, Ward 483
FROM: Hedonic Council, Area 1

You will report to Room 2943, Hedonic Council building, Area 1, at 1634 for annual examination. Be prompt! Be happy!

You will report, the Hedonist repeated to himself as he brushed the message away with the automatic acknowledgment. The form was standard, and the message was clear enough. But his last examination had been less than

six months ago. They wouldn't be recalling him so soon –
would they?

There was something ominous about it. A sudden shiver
ran down his spine. His adrenals began discharging their
secretions into his bloodstream; in response, his heart beat
quickened, the blood sugar level rose, the coagulability. . . .

The sensations weren't completely unpleasant. They stimulated him to a condition of awareness and excitation he
hadn't experienced in years. But they were also dangerous.

Happiness is basic. Without that, all else is ashes.

The Hedonist suppressed it. He breathed deeply, sitting
quietly relaxed. He damped his heart beat, soothed his
adrenals. The Council waited to discuss his memorandum
on the sensies, he told himself calmly. They stayed within
the standard form for fear of endangering a whole day's
happiness.

He suppressed the small voice that asked, 'How could
they forget that your last examination was so recent?'

When the adrenalin was satisfactorily dissipated, he
slipped on a short-sleeved shirt and a comfortable pair of
tan shorts and glanced down at the day's schedule. According to the microfilm memorandum projected on the desk, he
had nothing listed after 1630. He picked up the stylus and
scribbled across the desk: *1634 – 2943 HCB – a.e.*

He read it once, hesitated, and went back to underline the
last two letters. He had no reason to be afraid of the examination; he had passed them all easily. There was no reason
to let anxiety ruin his day. And with that underlineation the
worry vanished.

If he allowed himself fifteen minutes for the twenty-five
miles between his cottage and the Council building, he
would have to cancel Mrs. Merton's appointment. Well, it
couldn't be helped. The Merton family quarrels would have
to wait until Monday for the weekly airing.

It was certain the continual exchange of bickerings was a
pleasure activity for both parties. He allowed Mrs. Merton
to milk the last drops of emotion from it in his presence.

He didn't approve of it, but he wasn't responsible for the warp, either. And, as a pleasure value, it didn't deserve the time necessary to straighten it out.

He flicked the MESSAGE button, scribbled a note to Mrs. Merton on the desk, and sent it off. The desk was clean again. He placed an order for a cab at 1615 and turned to the day's business.

Sara Walling. The Hedonist punched her number on the square of buttons under the edge of the desk. Her case history appeared in front of him, projected onto the desk in numbers, letters, and symbols, a meaningful, condensed description of twenty-seven years of a woman's life. The Hedonist nodded and wiped it away. His memory had been correct, but it was just as well not to depend on something fallible when a person's happiness was at stake.

It was 0800. The milky square on the outside of his door read. COME IN AND BE HAPPY. The door opened. Sara Walling stood there, her dark, thin face unhappy.

The Hedonist was up to greet her in one fluid motion that took him effortlessly the three steps to the door. He put his arm around her and caressed her fondly. 'Joy, Sara! Come in, darling,' he said gently. 'Tell me all about it.'

When she was sitting in the diagnostic chair, the Hedonist sat down at the desk and, cocking his head sympathetically, divided his attention between Sara and the desk-top readings.

At twenty-seven, she was a lean, sallow girl, an inch under average height at five feet nine. Her features weren't bad, but it was obvious that she was one of the least attractive girls in the ward. She was unmarried, and she had no lover. That was her problem. Or so she thought. The Hedonist knew, with a flash of guilt, that he had failed her.

From the readings flashed from the chair to his desk, the Hedonist put together another story, just as valid. Muscular contractions, pulse, blood pressure, breathing, volume of limb, but chiefly the electrical resistance of the body — often called the psychogalvanic reflex — gave him a running account of her emotional state. Balanced against her recorded emotional quotient, it was obvious what had happened.

The marriage aspect was only the culmination of several physiological and psychological tendencies which were themselves aggravated by the marriage aspect. . . . It was a vicious, cyclic tangle. He would have believed it impossible except that the constantly increasing demands on his time made periodic review of every dependent an ideal he was unable to realize. But now there was no time to be lost in the long but not hopeless task of untangling this girl's life.

'You have something in mind, of course,' he said.

'Yes,' she admitted.

'Has he gone with you to the premarital cottage?'

'Once,' she snapped.

'I see,' the Hedonist said. It was a misfortune all the way around. He suppressed his empathy; the diagnosis was complete. 'Have you any ideas for increasing your happiness?'

She hesitated. 'Can't you make him love me?' she said quickly, hopefully. 'Then I'd be happy and he'd be happy—'

'Is he unhappy now?' the Hedonist interrupted quietly.

'No-o-o,' she sighed.

'Then I can't make him do anything,' he pointed out. 'You know that. The fact that your desires don't coincide with his is no grounds for compulsion. You're the one who's unhappy. You're the one who needs therapy.'

'But that's the only thing that will make me happy!' she wailed.

The Hedonist shook his head slowly, pityingly. 'We can't force life into the patterns we draw for it, and if we let our happiness depend on circumstance we doom ourselves to sorrow and despair. Happiness begins at home – inside. Didn't we teach you that?'

'I was taught,' she groaned, her teeth clenched, 'but it's so hard to learn, so hard to do.'

'Have you tried the hedonic techniques?' the Hedonist asked. 'Have you practiced suppression? Devaluation? Substitution?'

'I've tried,' she moaned. 'I've tried so hard. But it's no use.

It's too—' She broke suddenly. The Hedonist was ready for
it. He caught her against his shoulder and let her cry until
the sobs had dwindled into sniffles.

'How long has it been,' he asked gently, 'since you've had
a diagnosis?'

'I don't remember,' she said in a muffled voice.

'A year,' he said firmly. 'You can afford a nickel every
week. We're going to bring up your blood pressure, increase
your thyroid, tone up your body generally—'

'Will that help?' she asked weakly.

' "Life is swell when you feel well," ' the Hedonist quoted.
'Even the ancients knew that. Humanity is a tangled thing.
You haven't felt well. You've been depressed, moody. That
has reacted on your relationships with other people. That, in
turn, has increased your depression and created psychosomatic conditions. The free expression denied your emotions
has fed your moods – those resonating echoes of the emotions. The spiral continues downward. Now we're going to
start it back up.'

Her thanks were almost incoherent.

'I'm certifying you for minor plastic surgery,' the Hedonist added. He studied her drab gray skirt and blouse. 'And
we're going to get you out of those clothes and into something bright and revealing. Don't worry now. You're in my
hands. You're going to be happy.'

As he watched her leave, there was a shadow of wistful-
ness in his eyes. She was happy already. She had shed her
burdens. He had picked them up.

The next patient was a man. He had a knife in his hand.
'You filthy kinsey!' he screamed and launched himself
across the floor.

III

The world would be better and brighter if our teachers would dwell on the Duty of Happiness as well as on the Happiness of Duty, for we ought to be as cheerful as we can, if only because to be happy ourselves is a most effectual contribution to the happiness of others.

SIR JOHN LUBBOCK

For a fraction of a second, the Hedonist sat in his chair, frozen, watching the revelatory contortions of the man's face as he came close. For all his seeming speed, he approached with incredible slowness. The Hedonist had time for a dozen observations, a hundred thoughts.

He identified the man – Gomer Berns, sixty-two, recently married, a newcomer to the ward. He identified the flashing knife – an antique table instrument, honed down. He speculated about the expression and its probable motivation—

And he was out of his chair, moving with blurred speed, his hand catching the wrist of the hand that held the knife. As he caught it, he twisted. Something snapped. The knife clattered to the floor. Berns sprawled across the desk, unconscious.

The Hedonist bent to inspect the man. He heard a faint, whirring noise, but as he listened, it stopped. He frowned and continued his examination. The wrist was broken; geriatrics was not so successful with the bones. Outside of that, Berns was in good condition. He had fainted from the pain.

The Hedonist straightened up. His pulse was swift and dynamic. The world seemed sharp and vivid around him. He felt immensely competent, immensely strong, immensely alive. There was no task too great for him.

He caught himself with a sharp thought. The exhilaration was being paid for by Berns. It wasn't worth the physical

pain and the mental agony that had fathered it. His emotion
was antisocial. He suppressed it quickly.

Effortlessly, he scooped up the body and propped it into
the diagnostic chair. The chair straightened into a table.
The Hedonist touched the under side of the edge toward him.
The shadowy X ray of the broken wrist was projected onto
the wall.

A slim, metal arm raised a horizontal half-cylinder over
the edge of the table. It picked up the wrist. Gently, firmly,
it drew the broken bones apart and fitted them back into
position as the Hedonist watched the wall picture. A tiny
hypodermic jet penetrated the skin above the break. On the
wall, the line between the broken bones grew cloudy. A
nozzle spun a short, tight plastic cocoon around the wrist.
As the table tilted itself back into a chair, the arm retreated
back into the chair's base.

The Hedonist glanced at his watch. Berns would have to
wait. The case was serious. It demanded time – a lot of it –
and the Hedonist didn't have the time to spare. In five
minutes he was due at the school.

He touched the desk. Berns's head twitched a little as a
hypodermic forced the anesthetic through the skin into the
spinal column. Berns would have to sleep here until he got
back.

Outside, the Hedonist looked back. The milky square on
the door said:

THE HEDONIST IS OUT
IN REAL EMERGENCY
PUNCH WARD SCHOOL
(RRR 1764)

The Hedonist walked through his ward in the warm, clear
springtime, enjoying the pleasant heat of the sunshine on
his head and back, feeling a brief moment of contentment.
The ward was a field of varicolored mushrooms set in a
green meadow; each of the bubble houses had its small but
precious lawn.

In the thirty-by-thirty vacant lot, the long-nosed house-blower was spraying plastic over a flat-topped balloon. Eliot Digby lolled lazily in the cab, glancing occasionally at the unwavering dials. As the Hedonist passed, Eliot looked up and waved happily.

The Hedonist smiled. By next week the new house would be ready for the Wayne couple. He would marry them the same day.

Basic School was a cluster of mushrooms in a bigger patch of green. When the Hedonist walked through the broad front door, the pretty ward nurse was waiting for him. The Hedonist smiled at her, thinking that the instruction of the boys was in capable hands.

'Joy,' said the Hedonist.

'Joy,' echoed the Nurse, but she looked anything but joyful. 'We've had more trouble about the dispensers in the necessary.'

'The neo-heroin?'

The Nurse nodded.

'How many children have bought it?' A frown slipped down over his face.

'None,' she said quickly. 'I put a recorder on the dispenser, just as you said, and only one syrette has been purchased. That was by the salesman himself. But he was here this morning complaining that someone was sabotaging his sales. He said he was going to take it to the Council.'

The Hedonist shrugged. 'If that's all—'

'But the Council has approved the manufacture and distribution,' she went on anxiously. 'And half the profits have been allocated to the Council. The Council has asked all the wards to co-operate, and we've been doing just the opposite—'

'The Council – the Council,' the Hedonist chided. 'The Council isn't some unfeeling, prehedonic bureau to be afraid of; it's made up of trained men, hedonists, bent only on increasing the available happiness. But it's not infallible. In this turn toward delusion, it has made a mistake. At the next Congress, the mistake will be corrected.' He was about to move on when he turned back and asked, casually, 'Did you recognize the salesman?'

She bent her forehead in despair. 'I couldn't think of his name. But I'll remember it.'

The Hedonist smiled; a poor memory was her greatest sorrow. 'Remember: anxiety is the thief of happiness.' He patted her fondly and turned toward the first class.

The morning's lessons were like a fairy tale turned upside down.

To the little ones, he said, '. . . And so the world lived happily ever after.'

As he left the room, one little girl pressed against his leg and lifted up her shining face. 'I love you, Hedonist,' she whispered.

'I love you,' he said quietly and smoothed her blonde hair.

To the beginners, he said, 'What is the greatest good?'

The class answered in unison: 'Pleasure!'

'What is the basic freedom?'

'The freedom to be happy!'

'Be happy, then,' the Hedonist said.

As he left the room, they were singing the familiar sixth stanza to the old folksong, 'Turkey in the Straw':

> *Sugar in the gourd and honey in the horn,*
> *I never was so happy since the hour I was born.*

To the secondary class, he said, 'Who can tell me what I am?'

One boy held up his hand eagerly. 'You're our Hedonist.'

'And what is a hedonist?'

'He's the man who keeps us happy.'

'Once I would have been called many things,' the Hedonist said softly. 'Doctor, teacher, psychiatrist, priest, philosopher, ward-heeler, God-surrogate, father-image, lover-symbol. . . . But none of these did what I can do. Your definition is the best: I am the guardian of your happiness.'

*　　　*　　　*

To the intermediate class, he threw questions swiftly. 'What are feelings?'

The answers ran around the room consecutively: 'Feelings are unique and unspecific.' 'They can't be analyzed; when we try, they disappear.' 'They can apply to any mental process.' 'There are only two: pleasure and unpleasure.'

The Hedonist began again. 'What are emotions?'

'Emotions are specific; they are connected with a particular tendency to action.'

'They are the result of blocked conations; conations are our strivings to get the things we want.'

'Our feelings are directly conditioned by the success or failure of our conations.'

'And the moral of this,' the Hedonist concluded, 'is that we should want the right things – the things we can get. That is the royal road to happiness.'

To the advanced class, he said, 'Once upon a time does not always begin a happy story. It can describe the real world we left behind us.'

Exacerbated desire, doomed to frustration. A rapidly diminishing area of possible satisfaction. Inevitable, daily tragedy.

Want more! Be more! The pre-hedonic world puffed stale air into the balloon of desire; people were overpaid to increase demand. Buy! Own! Enjoy! And slyly the frustrations waited with their pins in hand: laws, social pressures, economics, physical impossibilities.

Illusions. 'There's plenty of room at the top; only the bottom is crowded.' Fallacy. Dangerous, deadly.

'Teach me to earn so that I may buy so that I may ease this torment of desire.' And no one could be found to say, 'Teach me to live so that I may be happy.'

Poor, tortured world! World of tragedy, doomed to periodic violence, priding itself on being free.

Free. Free to make each other miserable. Free to drive each other to insanity and crime. Free to kill in mass and individual slaughters. Free to develop such stress diseases as stomach cramps, rheumatoid arthritis, asthma, duodenal ulcers, hypertension, heart disease, ulcerative colitis, and diabetes. Free to fret themselves into an early grave.

In 1950, thirty-three men out of every one hundred thousand in the United States committed suicide. That was freedom.

' "The function of government is, and of right ought to be, the preservation and promotion of the temporal happiness of its citizens," ' the Hedonist quoted.

The girl stood up, straight as a young elm. 'The Declaration of Hedonism. December 31, 2003.'

'What was the April Fool Amendment?'

'The Twenty-sixth Amendment to the Constitution came three months later. It made hedonism the law of the land.'

IV

It is not true that suffering ennobles the character; happiness does that sometimes, but suffering, for the most part, makes men petty and vindictive.
WILLIAM SOMERSET MAUGHAM

As the Hedonist followed the winding walk to the Graduate School, the Nurse caught up with him.

'I've thought of the name,' she panted happily. 'It's Berns. Gomer Berns.'

The Hedonist carried the implication with him through the rest of his morning's duties. He stood in front of the Hedonic Mural and turned it over slowly with part of his mind while he went through the discussion.

Hedonics hadn't happened overnight. The philosophical consideration went back more than two thousand years. The Greeks asked themselves the question: What is the greatest good? The answer was 'Pleasure'. The philosophy was hedonism.

The interpretation differed. Aristippus, of the Cyrenaic School, believed in 'pure' hedonism – the sentient pleasure of the moment. But Epicurus, following Socrates and Aristotle, recognized that happiness must be rational; many momentary pleasures led to future pain.

Later came a preoccupation with society. Should a man seek his own happiness or his community's or that of everyone else at the expense of his own? Egoism, Utilitarianism, or Altruism.

Altruism was obviously false. If the agent's happiness was worthless, how could anyone else's happiness be valuable? Without a calculus of pleasures, Utilitarianism was unworkable; there was no way of balancing pleasures. Egoism was the only tenable philosophy; no ethics can be successful which does not begin and end in the individual.

Hedonics was, above all, practical. It worked. But philosophy was only one leg to the stool.

Means had to become available to relieve the great psychological anxieties: death, sickness, hunger, cold, and the social relationships.

Geriatrics had reduced the fear of death. Medical research had largely wiped out sickness. No one needed to go hungry while chlorella surged through the polyethylene tubes and the sea fixed 135,000,000,000 tons of carbon every year. No one needed to go without shelter when houses could be built overnight.

Social relationships had been complicated by antiquated mores and laws; its artificial barriers were guarded by society's policeman, the conscience, which punished the instinctive desires. The barriers were torn down, the laws were rewritten, and the policeman's badge was torn away.

Research into the physiology of the human body brought out the exact relationship between the glands and the emotions and slowly brought them under conscious control: the adrenals, the pituitary, and the hypothalamus. The development of that control into something effective and invaluable was the function of the hedonic exercises; they occupied a large part of the Graduate School curriculum.

But the final development of hedonism as a way of life waited on the discovery of the hedometer, which brought statistical significance into the introspective fields of psychology and philosophy. The simple device, which worked through an application of the psycho-galvanic reflex, became an integral part of every room, and its constant reports made possible a nation-wide application of the axiom 'that action is best which procures the greatest happiness of the greatest numbers.'

The Hedonist stood in front of the Hedonic Mural and explained these things, as he had explained them before and would explain them again. And the wisdom he tried to impart was diagramed upon the wall behind him.

The Hedonic Mural. To the left, a valley; to the right, a mountain with two peaks, one below the other. At the bottom of the valley was a low-pressure mattress; a man was asleep on it, curled into a fetal position. At the top of each of the peaks was a naked woman, her arms held out invitingly, but on the lower peak she was hazy and out of proportion.

They were symbols, of course. The valley was *reduced desire*. The mountain was *increased satisfaction*. There are two ways to be happy : want less or get more. It was simple as that.

There were trails leading to the top of the mountain and paths leading to the bottom of the valley. Sign-posts pointed out the way; they were hedonic techniques.

Two trails led to the higher peak : *modify* and *substitute*. A man can actually get what he wants by modifying the outer world, or he can sublimate his frustrations into other goals which can be achieved.

The lower peak with the hazy, dream woman on it was *imaginary gratification*. There were three trails to her : *anticipate*, *daydream*, and *delude*. Anticipation could lead to real satisfaction, but daydream was conscious wishing, and delusion abolished the wall between wish and fulfillment.

There were four paths into the valley. *Substitute*, which pointed up the mountain, also pointed down; it was the route of wanting what we can get. The other paths were :

devalue, *project*, and *suppress*. Devaluation, sometimes called the 'sour-grapes technique', is seen at its finest in the cat; the moment something is proved unavailable, it becomes worthless. Projection attributed the desire to someone else. Suppression was a means of preventing the desires from reaching the conscious mind.

The valley and the mountain. And the mountain, attractive as it seemed, was relatively worthless. Reality will allow only a very limited amount of modification; population increases, limited as control measures had made them, had rationed the amount to the point of insignificance. If a man allowed his happiness to depend on it, he was dooming himself to frustration.

The lower peak of imaginary gratification was positively dangerous. The mind overcomes obstacles so easily that it seduces the person from all other forms of gratification. For the same reason, narcotics and the sensies were to be avoided. They were not far from madness, and madness – the ultimate retreat for the protection of the organism – was antisocial and non-survival, and, therefore, non-hedonic.

In the valley of hedonic discipline was found the heart of hedonics, untouched and untouchable. Its techniques made man independent of environmental vagaries.

'As long as we have these techniques available,' the Hedonist concluded, 'nothing – no one – can make us unhappy. Like gods, we hold our happiness in our own hands.'

Berns was still unconscious, but the neutralizer quickly made him stir in the chair. His dark, deep-set eyes opened and stared blankly at the Hedonist. Slowly, darkly, they drew memory from a secret place.

His face twisted. His right hand groped, lifted. Pain twitched across his face. He stared down at the cast on his wrist. Tentatively, uncertainly, he wriggled his fingers.

The Hedonist stooped and picked up the knife. He looked down at it for a moment. He handed it to Berns, hilt first. 'Is this what you're looking for?' he asked politely.

Berns licked his lips. 'Yeah,' he said. He took the knife

and then held it awkwardly as if he couldn't decide what to do with it.

'Why do you want to kill me?' the Hedonist asked reasonably.

'Because,' Berns said furtively. 'Because of what you done to me.'

'And what's that? Whatever it is, if I can help—'

'What's done's done,' Berns said sullenly.

'That's a pre-hedonic attitude,' the Hedonist said. 'It isn't what happens that's important; it's how it affects us. But what are you talking about?'

'My wife,' Berns said. 'I'm talking about her.'

The Hedonist remembered. Just before moving to the ward, Berns had married one of his dependents – a young girl, not quite out of her teens. There was nothing basically wrong with that. Geriatrics had kept Berns's body young. Hedonics should have done the same thing for the man who lived inside. And yet, Berns had attacked him with a knife. That wasn't a sane thing.

Dani Farrell. The Hedonist remembered her. A quiet girl, a quick, interested student. With her, hedonics had worked well. She was a happy woman, not deep but sound. He had never expected complaints.

'What's the matter with Dani?' the Hedonist asked.

'You know.' Berns's eyes slid away.

'She's made you unhappy?' the Hedonist asked, puzzled.

'Not her – *she's* all right!'

'Then what *is* the matter?'

'She knows too much,' Berns blurted out.

'You're complaining about that? See here,' the Hedonist said with sudden suspicion. 'Is there something wrong with your sexual adjustment?'

'Nah,' Berns said darkly. 'That's what I'm complaining about. With my first wife, it took years. Dani didn't come to me – well – innocent!'

'Innocent!' the Hedonist exclaimed. 'You mean "ignorant". You're objecting to her education!'

'Some things,' Berns said, glowering, 'a man should attend to personal.'

The Hedonist's face grew stern and then was molded by compassion. The man was sick. He had missed the benefits of a hedonic education, and his previous hedonist had been lax or overworked.

He straightened up. These ante-hedonics cases were tough, but he had cracked them before. 'What you want,' he said slowly, 'is the right to make yourself unhappy and Dani miserable for an outmoded, demonstrably false set of values.'

'Well,' Berns asked defiantly, 'what's wrong with that?'

The Hedonist glanced down at the desk and back up. Given the man's emotional state, he was telling the truth. Or, at least, part of it. 'It's antisocial,' the Hedonist said quietly. 'Society can't permit it.'

'This is a free country, ain't it?' Berns demanded. 'A man can be unhappy if he wants to be, can't he?'

'No!' the Hedonist thundered. 'That myth was exploded fifty years ago. The basic freedom is the freedom to be happy. Society must preserve it above all the others, because without it the others are worthless.'

'The way I look at it,' Berns said sullenly, 'it ain't a freedom unless a man can do something else.'

The Hedonist shook his head slowly, patiently. He would have to start from the beginning. 'If people had the right to be unhappy, they would threaten the happiness of everyone else. Men don't live in a vacuum. Fundamentally, perhaps, everyone has the right to go to hell in his own way, but there are boundaries beyond which a man can't go without injuring his neighbors. That's society's business – establishing those boundaries and setting watchdogs to guard them. When a man crosses them, he becomes a criminal.'

'Maybe,' Berns admitted grudgingly. 'But that don't explain Dani.'

'Be sensible, man,' the Hedonist demanded. 'Would you have us teach a girl all the domestic and marital accomplishments except the one that's most important to the happiness of her marriage? Vital training like that can't be left to anyone. You're no hedonist. What are your qualifications as a teacher?'

'I'm going to file suit,' Berns muttered. 'You've infringed on my happiness.'

The Hedonist exploded. 'You've got no grounds. What's more, you've committed a criminal act. For what you've done today, I could certify you for surgery. In fact, that's my duty.'

Berns looked bewildered. 'You're going to operate on me?'

'You're obviously unhappy,' the Hedonist pointed out. 'According to society's standards, you're insane. You should be treated and converted into a happy, responsible member of society. A transorbital lobotomy is the quickest, surest method. Those who can't learn suppression must have it done for them.'

Berns struggled to his feet, his face twisted with fear. 'No!' he said. 'You can't. They won't let you—'

'They?' the Hedonist asked. 'Who are "they"?'

'People,' Berns muttered.

That was a lie. 'You wouldn't argue with society's right to treat the insane. But I didn't say that was what I was going to do. I owe it to myself, as well as to you, to make your treatment as positive as possible. To do that, though, I need your help.'

Berns mumbled something indistinguishable.

'To do that you need to understand my job,' the Hedonist said. 'Like me, you grew up before hedonics became part of everyday life. Like me, your training for happiness began too late, when you were already past the formative years of your childhood. For the new generation, happiness will come easy; they have been prepared for it. We have to work for it.'

'How do you mean?'

'For me, it meant ten years of specialized training in the Institute of Applied Hedonics. Since then it has meant a job that is never done, the guardianship of the happiness of a thousand people.

'For you, it means study, beginning this afternoon. As a salesman, I presume you can take time off?'

Berns started and then nodded. He's afraid, the Hedonist thought in amazement.

'Then this afternoon,' the Hedonist said, as he installed Berns in the necessary on the one seat available, 'you're going to observe.'

But as the Hedonist left the sliding door a little ajar and returned to his desk, he thought : Why did the man register fear when I mentioned his business?

As he engrossed himself in the file of the next patient, he had not found an answer to the question.

V

Happiness is like time and space – we make and measure it ourselves; it is a fancy – as big, as little as you please; just a thing of contrasts and comparisons.
                                                      GEORGE DU MAURIER

After the unusual beginning, it was a usual sort of day. The stream of patients was unending, and the variety of their needs touched the Hedonist often with pathos. A man who was not a god should not have such power nor be burdened with such responsibilities.

And he wielded the power and shouldered the responsibility.

Medical treatment was easy and fast; the diagnostic chair fixed breaks and scrapes, gave immunization and curative shots, adjusted endocrine balances, prescribed diets, treated or removed cancers and tumors, tinkered with faulty organs. . . .

The complaints and applications were more difficult. Three oldsters complained about their pensions and the high cost of living. Two parents wanted public jobs for their children just come of age; the Hedonist helped them prepare applications and added his own recommendations after they had left. There was one case of technological unemployment; the Hedonist arranged to have the man reeducated and reassigned and vouchered the cost to the industry concerned. There were five applications for pregnancy certificates; the Hedonist put them off as best he could: the year's quota for the ward was already exhausted.

But the ones that took time, patience, and skill were the hedonic cases.

Case No. 1: Unfulfilled Ambition (to write tragedy)

Therapy: Devalue and Substitute ('But, if that is impossible, write if you must – I will read it, and then we will burn it together; you can't be permitted to make others unhappy')

Case No. 2: Accidental Death (of a father)

Therapy: Suppress ('Don't let causal events determine your happiness; that is something for you alone to control')

Case No. 3: Jealousy (of a husband)

Therapy: Suppress ('I can prepare an infringement suit if you like, but I ask you to think: How many times have you been to the post-marital cottage?')

Case No. 4: Envy (of a neighbor's new red house)

Therapy: Devalue ('Old houses are the best houses; they are machines adjusted to your way of life')

Case No. 5: . . . .

They were all simple – in theory. They were all difficult in application. Not one of the cases was classic. Each one was individually complicated. Each one needed individual therapy.

It was a usual sort of day. As usual, it made no difference that he had not ordered lunch; he didn't have time to eat it anyway.

Only one incident was disturbing. During a treatment he felt a sudden moment of dizziness. He concealed it from the patient, but he got a quick diagnosis as soon as she was gone. All the readings were normal. He was in perfect condition. He shook his head uneasily.

As 1600 approached and passed, the unease grew. The Hedonist couldn't locate it. Then, with a start, he remembered his appointment with the Council. He would have to leave in a few minutes. Why, he wondered, had he forgotten?

He remembered, too, the call he had forgotten to make. He punched Beth's number. Her mother's face appeared on the wall. A beautiful face. Only an inner maturity distinguished it from Beth's. She smiled inquiringly at the Hedonist.

'Beth,' the Hedonist said. 'Is she there?'

'Why, no!' She started to frown. 'Beth hasn't been home for days. I thought—'

The Hedonist erased the anxiety hastily. 'Of course. She has been here. But she went out this morning. Perhaps she's with her young man—'

'Young man?' the frown returned. 'Beth hasn't any young man.'

'She hasn't?' the Hedonist said blankly. 'That's strange.' And then, hurriedly, 'Of course. How stupid of me to forget!' His face cleared. Almost magically, the mother's frown was wiped away.

The Hedonist stared at the blank wall for a minute after she said good-by. He could deceive her, but he couldn't deceive himself. Beth had lied to him. There had to be a reason for it. After a little concentration, he began to believe it.

He walked to the necessary in two strides and slid the door back. The cubicle was empty. He stepped into the little room and turned around dazedly. There was, obviously, no one in it except himself. No one could have squeezed into the room when he was there.

And yet Berns was gone. The man was gone, and the Hedonist had not left the room, and Berns could not have brushed past him in getting to the only exit unless he was invisible—

The Hedonist remembered the moment of dizziness.

A time-lapse grenade!

He hunted around on the floor until he found the few shreds of plastic left from the explosion of the gas container. He turned them over slowly in his hand.

Berns was gone. Why? He had obtained a time-lapse grenade. How? He had used it to leave the room without being seen. Why? When? The Hedonist estimated the time he had felt dizzy. It had been almost an hour ago.

For once the hedonic techniques were no good. This was no time for suppression, devaluation, substitution. He had to think and think clearly. Very soon he might have to modify the outer reality, and he needed facts to guide him.

But there were so few facts. The rest was assumption. Berns was only partly what he seemed to be. His story was only partly true. He had some relationship with the Council, and the Council had summoned the Hedonist on the day that Berns had attacked. Berns would have to be reported and certified.

The Hedonist filled out a certification form and back-dated it to the time Berns was installed in the necessary. He hunted through the cabinets behind the wall panels until he found what he wanted. He pressed them against his chest and back under the shirt, slipped a small disk into his pocket and turned toward the door.

The idling cab was waiting two feet above the street. It was 1615, as the Hedonist looked back at his door to check the milky square:

THE HEDONIST IS UNAVAILABLE
FOR EMERGENCY TREATMENT
SEE WARD 482 HEDONIST

He climbed up into the helijet. The rotors sighed overhead. 'Where to?' the cabbie asked softly.

'Hedonic Council Building,' the Hedonist said, staring curiously at the red cap covering the cabbie's head.

The cabbie swung around. 'Great sorrow, man! You aren't going there!'

The Hedonist stared at the cabbie's face, stunned.

It was Beth.

'What are you – I mean – how did you—?' the Hedonist spluttered.

'I rented the heli—'

'But you're underage!'

'I forged an IDisk,' Beth said impatiently, her dark eyes brilliant.

'Forged!' the Hedonist repeated slowly. He rejected the word automatically. He couldn't believe that one of his young people could have committed a criminal act, and it was impossible to forge an identity disk. The plastic locket with its radiation-sensitive heart of phosphate glass could not be duplicated. Or so he had always believed.

'See here,' he said, struggling to get off the defensive, 'you said you were getting married—'

'I am,' she said with quiet determination.

'Your parents don't know about it!'

'Oh, I haven't told *them*.'

'I suppose,' the Hedonist said with quiet sarcasm, 'that you haven't told the man, either.'

'He knows,' she said softly. 'But he doesn't believe it yet.'

'You lied to me.' In spite of himself, the Hedonist's voice sounded hurt.

'You poor, blind fool!' Beth said desperately. 'Look! It doesn't matter. Not now. The only thing that matters is to stay away from the Council. Don't keep that appointment!'

'The appointment!' the Hedonist exclaimed. He looked at his watch. It was 1620. 'I've got to hurry.'

'That's what I'm trying to—'

'Are you going to take me?' the Hedonist asked, 'or shall I call another cab?'

'Oh, I'll take you,' she groaned, swinging around to the front. She punched the buttons expertly. With a muffled roar, the heli rose vertically. When it reached two thousand feet, the jets cut off at the rotor tips and the rear jets cut in. They streaked toward the Old City; it rose like a picket fence on the horizon.

The only sound in the cabin was a gentle vibration. The Hedonist sat silent, turning words over and peering under

them: forgery, deceit, disrespect. Was the younger generation capable of this? His world rocked as he considered the
possibilities implicit in what Beth had done. If these hedonically trained young people were not free from immoral and
criminal tendencies, then hedonics was a failure.

It was impossible. The Hedonist shook his head vigorously. Hedonics worked. He was the failure.

'How did you know,' he asked without a quaver, 'that I
was going to the Council Building?'

'I've been watching all day,' Beth said casually.

'Spying!' the Hedonist said with horror in his voice.

She shrugged. 'If you want to call it that. A good thing,
too.'

He didn't intend to ask, but the words were seduced from
his lips. 'What do you mean?'

'That man. The one who called himself Gomer Berns. He
was an agent of the Council.'

An agent. The Hedonist tasted the word gingerly. It had
extensions and implications. 'How do you know?'

'He's been watching you for days. And I've been watching him. He's talked to the Council secretary three times,
once in person. Then, today, he staged this scene.'

'How do you know what he was talking about?'

'I wired the cottage days ago,' she said disgustedly. 'When
he tossed out the grenade and sneaked away, I was afraid it
might be something more deadly. Then I realized what it
was. I followed him, but I wasn't quite quick enough.'

'For what?'

'He'd already dropped the tape into the mail tube.'

'Tape?'

Beth reached onto the seat beside her and flicked something over the back of the seat into the Hedonist's lap. He
picked it up and frowned at it. It was a flat, opaque, plastic
box about half an inch deep, two inches wide, and three
inches long. The back was sticky. He turned it over. Pro-
jecting a fraction beyond the box was Berns's clear, plastic
IDisk.

He turned it back over, bewildered. Something clicked

and moved under his fingers. The box fell open. Inside was
a tiny, empty reel; there was a spindle for another. Printed
circuits were a maze against the plastic.

The thing was a miniature recorder, equipped to pick up
both sight and sound. The lens – for some reason – had been
disguised as an IDisk. Gomer Berns's IDisk.

'Where did you get this?' he asked suddenly.

'Where do you suppose?'

A sudden flash of apprehension turned the Hedonist's
stomach cold. 'You said he *was* an agent. What did you—'

'He's dead,' Beth said calmly.

Before, the world had rocked. Now it revolved wildly. For
a moment, the Hedonist wondered whether the heli had
plunged out of control, and then his hedonic reflexes caught
him and set him firmly back in place. His pulse slowed, his
adrenals stopped discharging. . . . 'You killed him,' he said.

'Yes.'

'Why?'

'It was an accident, I suppose,' she said thoughtfully,
'although I can't say for certain, I was mad enough to kill
him. I tried to stop him from dropping the tape, you see, and
he pulled out a knife. The cast made him clumsy. When I
twisted his arm, he stabbed himself.'

'Go back! Quick!' the Hedonist shouted. 'He might still
be alive.'

She shook her head. 'He's dead all right.'

The Hedonist groaned and passed his hand over his face.
'I'll have to certify you for surgery,' he heard his voice
saying distantly. 'No!' he told himself, sitting up straight
again. 'I can't do it!'

The weight on his shoulders seemed to shift a little.

Beth sighed. 'I was hoping you would say that. It's all
right. Nobody saw me.'

The Hedonist shuddered. He couldn't believe the immorality he was hearing. 'You'll have to undergo treatment,'
he said nervously.

Beth laughed. 'All you want.'

The Hedonist looked down at his hands. He still held the

recorder. He shuddered again, pressed the button that reeled down the right window, and tossed the plastic thing through. He watched it spin through the air until it disappeared below. He wiped his hands on his shorts as if to cleanse them of an invisible stain. *Forgery, deceit, theft, and murder.* But the stain would not come off. It was his fault. It was his duty to protect the bewildered girl.

'Now,' she said, sounding not at all bewildered, 'you see why you can't keep that appointment with the Council.'

'Because you killed Berns?'

'No, because he was their agent. Can't you see what they're trying to do? They want to certify you—'

'They can't do that,' the Hedonist protested. 'I'm not unhappy.'

'When they get through with you, you will be,' Beth said grimly.

'But why? They've got no reason—'

'When have they needed a reason? They want to get rid of you. Why, I don't know. But there could be a hundred reasons. For some reason you're dangerous to them. If you want to stay alive, you've got to stop judging everyone else by yourself.'

It was a web of nonsense. The Hedonist didn't believe a word of it. Beth had lied to him before without raising her blood pressure a fraction of a point. She was capable of anything. It had to be lies.

But there had been gelatin fragments on his floor. And he had held a miniature recorder in his hands, and it had a lens shaped like an IDisk. Or had he? Was it delusion?

He glanced at his watch: 1629.

The Council Building was a flat-topped spire a thousand feet below. He could see the large *HC* painted across the roof. Around it were the deep, darkening canyons that separated the building from its shorter neighbors.

The Old City was little frequented now. Industry was decentralized into small, automatic factories near their markets, and the population had spread far out into almost autonomous suburbs. The parts of the Old City left standing were used only for the functions and services which could not be decentralized: government, major hospitals, and interplanetary commerce.

'Take me down,' the Hedonist said.

'But—' Beth began, swinging around frantically.

'Down!' he repeated firmly. 'I have an appointment in four minutes. I'm going to keep it.' He had to accept it as reality, not delusion. But he was ready for the Council, if he could get Beth away and out of danger.

She sighed hopelessly. 'All right.' She punched buttons savagely. The rear jets cut out. They dropped in a long, swooping descent that clutched the Hedonist's throat, but at the last minute the rotor's tip jets caught and the heli dropped lightly to the roof.

The little devil! the Hedonist thought. She did that on purpose. 'Go home!' he said, stepping down from the cab and standing on the roof. The rotors twisted slowly above his head. 'Tell your mother to give you an alibi for the time of Berns's death.'

'An alibi?' she asked. 'What's that?'

The diabolical innocent! 'A statement that you were home at that time. She's to lie about it. Tell her I said to. And tell her to make herself believe that it's true. As for you – Don't worry! I'll take care of everything.'

'Yes, Hedonist,' she said obediently.

'Now get out of here!' he said brutally. 'I don't want to see you again.'

He stepped back before he could see the expression on her face, and he watched the heli lift from the roof. The rear jets caught quickly with an organe flame that swiftly turned blue and then became a mere wavering of the air.

Except for him, the paved roof was empty. The Hedonist turned and walked to the elevator housing. As he approached, the doors slid open. He stepped in, turned to face the front, and the doors began to close.

'Twent—' he began, but before he had finished, the car started down.

The Hedonist counted the floors as they flashed by. He counted backward from seventy-five, swiftly, for the drop was faster than the one in the heli. When he reached thirty-two, the car slowed suddenly. 'Thirty-one,' he counted. 'Thirty. Twenty-nine.'

On that number, the elevator stopped. The Hedonist considered the implications. Without instructions from him, the elevator had brought him to the twenty-ninth floor. That was true efficiency. But then the Council was efficient.

The door remained closed. It refused to open. The Hedonist looked at his watch: 1633. When the sweep second hand reached the top of the dial and went a little past, the doors parted.

Real precision, the Hedonist thought, and stepped out into a deserted hallway. The resilient floor felt springy under his feet. It was an old building. There were windows at both ends of the hall.

The Hedonist walked quickly to one of them. It was made of glass, not plastic. Far below, the streets were empty. They had a green tinge where the grass had taken root.

There were doors on both sides of the corridor, but 2943 was opposite the elevator. There was a sign on the door. Like his own, it said COME IN AND BE HAPPY.

On the door at waist-level was a button. The Hedonist shrugged and pushed it. The doors slid open. The room beyond was an ordinary waiting room, well lighted, neat. Chairs lined each wall. Beside an inner door was a desk. The room was deserted.

The place was silent. Completely, absolutely silent. The only sound the Hedonist could hear was his breathing and the internal workings of his body.

He stepped into the room.

VI

The life and liberty and property and happiness of the common man throughout the world are at the absolute mercy of a few persons whom he has never seen, involved in complicated quarrels that he has never heard of.

GILBERT MURRAY

The sound was deafening. That was the first thing he noticed. Or, no, it wasn't the first thing. The sound was even louder because his eyes had squeezed shut automatically at the first flash of brightness. He waited and felt behind him with one hand. The wall was smooth. The door was closed.

The noise, he thought, was a recording of every sound ever made. He could hear drums, hammers, a chorus of machines; he heard raspings, scrapings, gratings, screeches, horns, explosions, voices, screams, shouts. . . .

He concentrated on identifying the sound, not shutting it out. It seemed to cover the whole range of audibility, from 15 cycles per second to more than 20,000 cycles. It was loudest, though, in the middle high tones. That was natural enough. The ear was most sensitive for those frequencies.

Question: Was the sound objective or subjective?

Unless it had been set off by his stepping into the room, it had to be subjective. Not even the finest interrupter could phase out everything. And he hadn't heard a sound.

Ordinarily, the tympanic muscles would have contracted reflexively to protect the inner ear. They hadn't. Presumption: His sensitivity had been increased or the receptors of the inner ear themselves were being stimulated.

He concentrated on the 1000 to 4000 cycle range and reduced the sensitivity of the ear. Slowly the sound diminished. What he had been hearing was actually the molecular motion of the air particles.

He could hear the voice now. He tried to distinguish the words. Slowly he made it out.

'This is a test,' the voice said. 'Find your way to the inner room. When you open that door, the test will be over. The test can be discontinued any time you wish. If you desire to do so, lie down on the floor and cover your eyes and ears.'

The Hedonist did not even consider the possibility. It was not only against his nature to surrender, but he suspected that passing the test was vital. It was something new. He withheld judgment on it until the purpose became clearer.

Slowly he opened his eyes, squinting to keep down the intolerable glare. But the light had dimmed. As he opened his eyes wider, the light flared up, and the eyes snapped shut. He opened them a slit; the light was dim and gray. He opened them a little wider; the light blazed. The light – or his sensitivity to it – was keyed to the width his eyes were opened. After a little experimentation, he discovered the optimum width which admitted the most light without risking blindness.

The room had changed. It was no longer a waiting room. It was his own room, and he was leaning so far backward that he was going to fall over into the necessary. He caught himself and straightened up and almost pitched forward on his face.

Illusion, he told himself. The room's tilted, not me. But it was more difficult to convince his eyes of their mistake.

Which way had the inner door been when he looked into the room from the corridor? If this was the same room, and his senses brought him only illusions, the door was directly in front of him about four paces. He hadn't moved.

He felt behind him again to make sure. His hand dipped to the wrist in semiliquid slime. He smelled a strong odor of decay.

He pulled out his hand, resisting the impulse to shake off the slime, and took one step forward, concentrating on the testimony of his semicircular canals and the sense organs in the muscles, tendons, joints, and skin. The room blinked and changed.

He was on a blue desert. The sand was harsh and gritty under his feet. The scorching wind picked it up and threw it against his face and into his eyes. He could taste it, strong and alkaline, between his teeth. Overhead a huge, orange sun burned down on him.

The Hedonist ignored everything. He didn't blink or rub his face or eyes or try to cover his head. He knew now what he was experiencing. This was the sensies without the cumbersome equipment that they needed. This was sensation transmitted to the nerves themselves. But as long as he refused to believe in the reality of the illusion, he had beaten the tests.

Question: What would be the next scene?

Something stirred behind one of the blue dunes. The Hedonist didn't wait to find out what it was. He took another step, concentrating again on the kinesthetic report of his leg and hip muscles to keep him moving in a straight line.

The floor rocked under him. It quivered like gelatin. It was insecurity. There were tall buildings all around him. They were tumbling. He could smell dust in the air. Great masses of masonry were shaken from the buildings by the earthquake, and they fell toward him, turning, growing larger. . . .

He took another step. Now he was falling. He was turning and twisting through the air, hurtling toward the distant pavement. Air became resistant, buffeted him, tugged at his clothes. The pavement came up to meet him. . . .

He took another step. Everything went black. He stood still, trying to see and there was nothing to see, trying to pierce the meaning of the illusion. Or was it an illusion?

The fears the test had played on had not been the learned fears but the old fears, the instinctive ones: the familiar twisted, the completely alien, things dropping and the firm Earth shaking, falling. Baby fears, never forgotten.

What now? Only the dark?

Close to the floor, something hissed. Something moved over his foot, slowly. Something long and thin. There was a second hiss. A third. Things brushed against his bare legs.

Snakes! the Hedonist thought. Snakes in the dark!

Slowly they became luminescent. They glowed in the

darkness, lifting in front of him, weaving wickedly. They were all colors: green, red, blue, violet, yellow, orange. . . . The Hedonist stopped listing them. One of the snakes was poising itself to strike.

The Hedonist reached out and pressed its diamond-shaped head.

The door opened.

Three men were sitting at the far end of a long table. They looked young, but the youngest of them, the Hedonist knew, was ten years older than he was. They had been the first men elected to the Council; they had held office ever since.

The room was big and windowless, paneled in dark, imitation wood. On the right wall was a door, which should be a necessary. There was a faint glimmering in the air in front of the Council. It could be nothing else but a missile-barrier. It would be airtight, too. The Council was being very careful.

The chairman sat at the very end. He had a pleasant, blond face. He was a simple, not particularly intelligent man, who could never have become a hedonist except by legislation.

To his left was the treasurer, a dark, brooding man of unfathomable moods. The Hedonist would have liked to have him in his diagnostic chair for a few minutes.

To the chairman's right was the secretary, a blank, nondescript, expressionless person, but the Hedonist received a subtle impression of tremendous control. He was the one to watch.

'Joy, hedonists,' the Hedonist said cheerfully. 'I hope I haven't kept you waiting.'

'Not at all,' the chairman said. 'Right on time. Joy to you.'

The Hedonist stood in front of them, waiting, smiling pleasantly.

'What did you think of the test?' the treasurer asked finally.

They had mentioned it first. It was a small victory, but it was important. 'Very interesting,' the Hedonist responded. 'What was it supposed to test?'

'Sit down,' said the treasurer, motioning to the chair that faced them.

The Hedonist had the answer he wanted. It was a test, not of happiness and mental balance, but of intelligence and self-control. What was the purpose? To drive him into insanity?

'A hedonist,' the secretary said tonelessly, 'who cannot control himself, cannot help his patients.'

'A truism,' the Hedonist agreed.

'Look,' the chairman said, and moved his hand.

The Hedonist was looking at himself. He was standing just inside the waiting room, his eyes closed. He opened his eyes, blinked several times, and leaned forward and then upright. A little awkwardly, but not too slowly, he walked across the floor. He reached out and pressed the button on the door. He vanished. The experience had taken less than a minute.

The Hedonist looked at the Council. That was it, then. They had wanted evidence for a sanity trial. There was no indication of outside stimulation. If he had reacted to the illusion or if he had given up, he would have been lost. But they had won nothing.

'Are you happy, Hedonist?' the chairman asked.

'Certainly,' the Hedonist said. 'I presume that this is being recorded.'

The chairman nodded curtly.

'What kind of job have you been doing in your ward?' the treasurer asked. 'In your opinion?'

'A man is his own worst critic,' the Hedonist said modestly. 'But if you must have an answer, I think my work has been adequate. But you have better indicators than that. What has my ward averaged on the Hedonic Index? For the record.'

There was a moment of silence. 'Ninety-seven,' the secretary said.

The Hedonist was surprised. 'So high? I've done a better job than I thought.'

'You haven't certified anyone for surgery in more than a year,' the treasurer pointed out.

'There you're mistaken,' the Hedonist said. 'I certified

someone this morning.' He glanced casually at the three faces at the other end of the table. 'A man named Gomer Berns.' At least he had that on the record.

Two faces were politely interested; the secretary blinked once, impassively. 'So?' he said. 'We haven't received the certification yet.'

'No doubt it's being processed,' the Hedonist said easily.

'No doubt,' the secretary said. 'An interesting statement, in view of this.' His hand slid along the arm of his chair.

This record wasn't as realistic as the other. The film flickered, and the sound wavered. But it was interesting. It was a record of the Hedonist's day as seen through the IDisk of Gomer Berns.

It started with Berns's entrance and ended with his departure under the cover of the time-lapse grenade. The Hedonist watched himself at work with a trace of self-consciousness, but he didn't have to suppress it. It vanished before the realization of the fantastic speed with which the Council had acted. The record had been edited skillfully, almost damningly.

'Interesting, eh?' the secretary asked.

'Very. Especially as evidence of infringement of happiness. Consider this notification of intent to file—'

'Nonsense,' the chairman interrupted. 'The Council is immune to suit—'

'Since when?' the Hedonist asked quickly.

'Since February 18, 2054,' the secretary said flatly. 'You received notification of the legislation, just as every other hedonist did. If you had attended the last Congress, you would have taken part in the voting.'

The Hedonist was silent. There were only so many hours in a day. It had seemed better to let the interminable Hedonic Record tapes go unheard than to leave a patient untreated and unhappy. It had seemed preferable to skip the usually uneventful Congress than to leave his ward untended for several days.

'You have abrogated the basic principles of hedonism,' the Hedonist said slowly, evenly, 'and hedonism cannot long survive. The moment one man or group of men is raised above the laws, the laws become worthless. The basic freedom is the freedom to be happy. Anyone who infringes upon it is a criminal, not above but beyond the laws—'

'You may stop mouthing these phrases,' the secretary said quietly. 'We are the guardians of their meanings. Besides' – he shrugged – 'the recorder had been cut off for several seconds.'

'How then,' the Hedonist asked patiently; 'do you hope to establish the record as authentic?'

The chairman's eyes opened, wide, blue, and innocent. 'We will certify it. How else?'

Above the law, above the law, the Hedonist repeated endlessly to himself. It was an accompaniment to the sound of his world collapsing around him.

'Just,' the treasurer growled, 'as we will certify you.'

'On what grounds?' the Hedonist asked quickly.

The treasurer shrugged. 'The necessary grounds. Unhappiness, Maladjustment. Malfeasance, misfeasance, nonfeasance—'

'I'll fight it,' the Hedonist told them calmly. 'You can never justify the charges. Not with the Hedonic Index of my ward.'

'When a prima facie case of illegal therapy, distortion of legal therapy, or disregard of proper therapy, can be made on the basis of direct evidence,' the secretary said dryly, 'the Index is inadmissible and rebuttal is worthless.'

'The definition of legal and proper therapy is that therapy which is contained in the *Journal of Hedonics*?'

'Obviously,' the chairman said cheerfully.

'You've revoked the principle of autonomy, too,' the Hedonist observed. He shook his head. 'You can't standardize happiness. Every person is an individual case, just as every feeling is unique and unanalysable. The best we can do is approximation, and that is best done by the person qualified to understand the needs of their individuals, the ward hedonist. Publilius Syrus said it a long time ago: You can't put the same shoe on every foot.'

'It seems,' the secretary said, 'that you haven't read the May *Journal*, either. It explicitly analysed, contradicted, and exposed the fallacy of your argument. Please don't waste the Council's time by making us repeat it. The official position of hedonism has been laid down: hedonics is a true science, not an art.'

'You've discovered a calculus of pleasure?'

'It's the corollary of the process you just experienced,' the treasurer said darkly. 'We can reduce pleasure to a common denominator by intrinsically reliable physical means. No longer do we have to be content with ninety-seven per cent happiness. We can achieve one hundred per cent happiness any time we wish for as long as we wish.'

'By machine.'

'That is the beauty of it,' the secretary said. For the first time there was life in his voice. 'The means are one hundred per cent controllable, one hundred per cent reliable. The sensations you experienced were real and horrible; the sensations we can project can be real and wonderful. We don't need to reduce desire any longer. We can increase desire and match it with increased satisfaction. We have reached the millennium.'

'Horrible, perhaps. Wonderful, perhaps. But real, no.' The Hedonist shook his head grimly. 'Systemized delusion. Madness mechanized. Now, I suppose, you will have no use for the lobotomies?'

'You suppose wrong,' the treasurer said harshly. 'It will still be used in criminal cases. The projector is a reward not a punishment. It will be saved for those who deserve the absolute happiness it guarantees—'

'Deserve?' The Hedonist picked it up quickly, his head lifting. 'When did that word creep back into the vocabulary of hedonics? We all deserve happiness; that is the basis of hedonism. "Reward – punishment". Oh, I see what you intend. You are bringing back the two-valued world. On the one side, the hell of the mindless, on the other, the heaven of the mad. I wash my hands of it, gentlemen – I no longer call you "hedonists". I'm through with you.'

'But,' the secretary said evenly, 'we aren't through with you. Because of your services to hedonism, we are going to be kind. You are going to have your choice of happiness: you may have your desires reduced by surgery or your satisfactions increased by the projector.'

'Hobson's choice,' the Hedonist muttered. He looked from the dark, brooding face to the happy, blond one to the blank one. They were determined to get rid of him. 'But why?' he burst out. 'Tell me that!'

The chairman looked inquiringly at the secretary. The secretary nodded. 'It's off,' he said.

'You've infringed on our happiness,' the chairman said simply.

'I?' the Hedonist exclaimed. 'How?'

'One,' the treasurer said, 'you've cut off your ward's trade in neo-heroin. The income is vital to the proper functioning of government—'

'It's dangerous stuff,' the Hedonist interrupted. 'It leads to unpleasure and a reduction of real happiness—'

'Two,' the treasurer continued as if the Hedonist hadn't spoken, 'you have been nominated for a place on this Council. If elected, you would replace one of us – and that would be unpleasure, sir! – and you would upset our plans for the future happiness of Earth—'

'But I had no idea—' the Hedonist began. 'I haven't even been to the Congress – I don't want any such—'.

'Your lack of ambition is unimportant,' the secretary said, shrugging, 'except as it affects your own happiness.' He moved his hand along the chair. 'We have given you an opportunity. Choose!'

'And what if I should tell you,' the Hedonist said suddenly, 'that I have been recording this discussion, that the record is in a safe place, and that it will not be used unless this proceeding continues?'

'It wouldn't matter,' the secretary said, unmoved. 'This

room is shielded.' He cocked his head as if he were listening. 'At any rate, your cottage has just been destroyed.'

'I suspected as much,' the Hedonist sighed. 'And so I didn't try.' His face suddenly grew pale. 'Gentlemen – I find that – this discussion – has suddenly – made me ill. If you will indicate – the necessary—?'

Automatically, in the face of the Hedonist's obvious distress, the chairman nodded toward the door in the right wall. The Hedonist pushed himself up, cupped his hand to his mouth, and staggered toward the door.

The secretary followed him with unreadable eyes. 'Don't forget,' he suggested, 'that this is the twenty-ninth floor.'

VII

Happiness makes up in height for what it lacks in length.

ROBERT FROST

The Hedonist nodded dumbly, miserably, slipped through the doorway as the door slid aside, and turned to close it behind him. The room, almost twice as big as his cubicle at home, was decorated in antiseptically clean white tile. But the door had no lock on it.

The Hedonist's face had returned, miraculously, to its normal, healthy color; his breath came quickly but easily. His hand came out of a pocket. The thin, flat disk was in it. He moved it quickly around the edge of the doorway, stopped, slid it back a few inches, and pressed it to the wall.

When he took his hand away, the disk clung to the wall. He pressed the button beside the door. The door didn't budge.

The Hedonist turned around. As he had suspected, the room had a frosted window. He slipped off one shoe, wrapped his hand in the shirt he had removed, and swung the shoe against the window with all his strength. It shattered explosively.

As soon as the pieces had stopped falling, the Hedonist looked through the jagged hole. The sun was gone; twilight was settling over the Old City; the canyons were dark, shadowed places of mystery. He knocked loose some of the lower pieces and looked down. The street was a narrow ribbon below. He shuddered and drew back.

Someone started hammering on the other side of the door. They were shouting. The Hedonist couldn't make it out. Then one word came clear. The word was: *murder*.

The Hedonist turned back to the window and cleared it and the narrow sill of the sharp fragments. He slipped off his other shoe, tied the two together, and hung them around his neck. There were two large flat circles on his chest and two more on his back. The Hedonist dug a finger under them and pried them loose. They left red circles on his body.

He put the shirt back on and, holding the geckopads in his hand, stepped up onto the sill. He fitted the pads on his hands and feet, making sure that they fit securely and there was no dirt or glass among the fine, rubbery cilia that made a deep-piled velvet on the underside.

He slipped his right hand and foot around the edge of the window and pressed them firmly against the smooth, outside wall of the building. He supported himself by his left foot and reached out with his left hand. When it was stuck, he hung by the three pads and brought out his left foot, feeling in his back the sudden, cold weakness that was recognition of the long emptiness beneath.

He slapped his left foot against the chilly magnesium surface and hung there for a moment like a misshapen lizard. In a moment he had controlled his adrenals. He stopped shivering.

He released his right-hand pad with an upward roll and moved it – up. His left hand followed it and then his feet, one after the other. It was forty-six stories and over five hundred feet to the top; he hunched toward it like an inchworm on the utterly smooth, vertical, building face, broken only by the occasional shallow inserts of window wells.

In spite of the greater distance, in spite of the greater effort, he went up. They would be looking for him below, but they wouldn't find his body there. Before he could reach the pavement, they would be waiting with their men and restraints and surgical knives and wires. His only chance was to climb.

After a climb of five stories, sixty feet, he stopped to rest. He glanced down over his shoulder and saw the lights below. They milled in the remote darkness like fireflies churning in a fantastic dance. Occasionally one slanted up the building face, but it never rose any higher than the broken window on the twenty-ninth floor.

At the thirty-fourth floor, the Hedonist had forty-one stories to climb. Almost five hundred feet. His muscles ached and trembled from the short climb he had made and the continual downward pull of his body as it was supported from the pads at an unnatural angle.

He wished he were thirty years younger. In spite of geriatrics, the years told on a body when a man asked too much of it.

The Hedonist sighed and slowly, painfully inched his way upward again. They would think of helis soon enough. The first one sped by him as he reached the fortieth floor. It rocketed through the dark, narrow canyon on its tail jets. Its exhaust was only a few yards away, and one of the idling rotors almost brushed him. He turned his head to watch.

Perilously, the heli stood on its side at the corner and zoomed out of sight. The Hedonist hung from the side of the building and waited for the thunder of the crash. It never came. He would have to change his plans. The helis had found him.

It would soon be back. Before then he would have to be off his exposed wall where he was like a fly waiting to be swatted. He sidled toward a window.

When he as beside the shallow well, he loosened his right hand from its pad and undraped his shoes from his neck. There was no chance of untying them; he didn't dare let loose with the other hand. One shoe dangled as he beat against the window with the other.

The taps were feeble and ineffectual. The extra shoe bothered him, and from his suspended position, he couldn't get any force behind the blow.

A muffled roar came from behind him. He turned his head and looked back.

Fifteen feet away a heli hung from its rotors. It couldn't get much closer without battering the rotors against the building. They whirred and roared only a couple of feet from his head.

The Hedonist tried to see into the darkened cab, but the strain only made his eyes water. Then the lights came on inside. The pilot stared out at him with wide, lovely, frightened eyes. It was Beth.

Hopelessly, they looked at each other, separated by a gulf fifteen feet wide. It might as well have been fifty. The hedonic techniques were no good here; suppression, projection, devaluation, and substitution were worthless. The only thing that could make him happy was modification, and there was no way to modify the impassable fifteen feet that divided them or the five hundred feet of emptiness that stretched below or the hardness of the street at the bottom.

Beth made impatient motions at him. What did she want him to do?

The Hedonist couldn't figure it out. He looked down toward the distant street. A large searchlight was sweeping the width of the lower stories. Soon it would work its way up here, and they would spot him.

Longingly, he looked back at the heli. Beth was still gesturing, frantically. He understood her now: *Come here!*

Gladly, the Hedonist thought. Give me wings, and I will fly to you.

Beth's lips were moving. She swung open the door and motioned down at the frame. The Hedonist studied her lips, incredulous. Again and again they framed the same word: *Jump!*

Jump? Fifteen feet? Maybe. On the ground. But fifteen

feet over five hundred is another thing entirely. As a fraction, it expressed his chances of reaching the heli and hanging on. Three chances out of a hundred.

On the other hand, his chances of escape were zero if he stayed where he was. Beth was right. Three chances were better than none. The watchdogs wouldn't get him.

He redraped his shoes around his neck and walked sideways across the smooth magnesium until the geckopads were clinging to the clear window glass. He wasted only a moment on a glance down the long, bare, unattainable corridor. Break the window now, and he would fall with the shards.

He slipped his feet out of the straps and onto the ledge. He released his right hand and caught the strap and got his left hand free. Slowly, holding tight to the straps, he turned himself around.

The pavement was a mile below.

The Hedonist shuddered and squeezed his eyes shut. He opened them and looked out toward Beth. *Please!* she said with her lips. And: *Hurry!*

The searchlight finally jumped past the twenty-ninth floor. As it swept by, it caught the Hedonist, silhouetting him against the bright window and the brighter walls, like a dark, clinging beetle.

The Hedonist blinked blindly. Gradually he made out the heli again, the lighted cab and the dark outlines around it. Slowly he bent his knees until his arms were stretched full length below the pads. He let the straps go and crouched lower.

Now he was toppling forward. The action was irreversible. He was committed to jump, and the only thing between him and the distant pavement below was the doorjamb of the heli. He straightened his legs abruptly. He hurtled through the air. He rushed toward the heli, and the heli rushed toward him. He realized that Beth had rocked the ship to bring the cab a little closer to the building. Closer, but not close enough.

His agonized fingers missed the doorjamb by inches. And

he was falling, falling through the darkness, falling toward the distant pavement and death.

Beside this, the Council's illusion was nothing. It was irony that he had time to think of that. This was reality; it was blood-curdling, terrible, and final. A man plunged through the thin, cold air toward the Earth that rushed up toward him to deliver the last, deadly blow. . . .

His arms hit something, slipped down past it. His clawing hands caught it, held it while his body fell and came to a jerking, swinging stop that almost tore the hands loose.

The Hedonist dangled above the emptiness and looked up because he could not look down. The heli was above him. He was clinging to the tubular metal landing skid. Beth's face was framed in the door above. Abstractly, he watched the play of emotions across the face – horror changing to relief and joy and back again to concern and terror.

The Hedonist swung on tiring arms and felt the heli dropping with his added weight. Beth's face disappeared for a moment. The heli lifted, leveled off. Beth leaned out again. She stretched far down from the door, but her reaching hand was two feet short of the skid.

She'll fall! the Hedonist thought, and he had a strange sensation in his chest as if his heart had turned over. He shook his head desperately.

With a sudden burst of adrenalized energy, he pulled himself up until his arms were over the skid. He clung there, gathering strength. In a moment he raised a leg over the skid, sat upright, and caught the edge of the doorjamb.

Beth's hand was surprisingly strong as she caught his wrist and helped him into the cab. He collapsed into the seat beside her and closed his eyes. Rapidly his breathing slowed and became regular.

'Let's get out of here!' he said.

He felt the rear jets kick in and boot the heli forward. He opened his eyes. The dark walls of the artificial canyons reeled past.

'I thought I told you to go home!' he growled.

Beth's hand, which had been reaching toward his hand,

jerked back. 'That's gratitude!' she said indignantly.

'Gratitude?' The Hedonist's eyes widened. 'Where did you pick up a word like that? And when did you learn to expect it? Happiness is a man's right in this world, and if he has that, what's left for him to be grateful for?'

Beth was silent. Fnally, distantly, she said, 'I came back because I thought you might need me. You did, apparently. I couldn't go home because the watchdogs are after me. They found Berns's body.'

'So I gathered,' the Hedonist said thoughtfully. 'Watch out for the jog!'

Beth swung her eyes to the front just in time to swerve the heli around the building that loomed up in front of them. The new canyon turned a thirty-degree angle. Slowly the buildings got lower and shabbier. They were getting farther into the Old City.

'I lost them when we reached the City,' Beth said scornfully. 'They didn't dare follow me down. Which way shall we go?'

'The way you are,' he said absently.

'But we're almost to the ruins,' she objected.

'That's right.'

The heli flew on in near silence. An eerie glow grew bright on the horizon, like a low aurora polaris. The luminescence was mainly green and blue but there were flickerings of violet and purple.

'You weren't as confident as you sounded,' Beth said suddenly. 'You had those geckopads with you.'

'I'd have been a fool not to prepare for the possibility,' the Hedonist said casually. 'If I hadn't I would be mindless or insane by now.'

'Lobotomy I can understand,' Beth said. 'But what do you mean by "insane"?'

'Induced delusions,' the Hedonist said heavily. 'The Council has perfected the sensies. Now, they're realies. The Council is going to make Earth one hundred per cent happy.'

Beth shook her head slowly. 'Poor, happy Earth,' she murmured.

The Hedonist glanced at her silently. What did she mean by that? He knew it was wrong, theoretically, but the wrongness wasn't obvious. The goal of hedonism was to make people happy. Why not the happier the better? Because, as in everything else, a man had to be rational. It was inevitable that a man choose happiness, but he could – and had to – forego some immediate and momentary pleasures in order to insure future happiness.

Anything that decreased a man's capacity for pleasure was wrong. Delusion did that. It ruined a man for reality.

Anything that took a man's happiness out of his own hands was wrong. Happiness wasn't a gift to be bestowed. It was a grail, a purely personal goal, which could only be described in general terms. A man could do that, and he could train someone else for the quest and sometimes help that person over the barriers, but he couldn't do it all. He couldn't find happiness for the other person and he couldn't give it to him.

The mile-wide crater swung under them, glowing phosphorescently. Mostly, as it had been on the horizon, it was blues and greens, but there were flickering patches of purple and violet, and here and there flitting wisps of yellow and orange. The crater was almost two hundred feet deep; after fifty years, it was still deadly. For three miles around the crater, the shattered spears of buildings stretched mutely above rubble, weathered a little now, its sorrow blunted.

'Take it down,' the Hedonist said.

'Here?' Beth exclaimed.

'On the other side. Hurry. There's no time to waste.'

The heli hovered above the rubble, lighted obscenely by the luminescence behind. Beth and the Hedonist stood a few feet away.

'I thought you set it for homing,' the Hedonist said, frowning.

'I did. But I had to give us time to get out.'

In a moment something clicked inside the cab. The rotors speeded up, and the heli lifted itself into the sky. It went up fast. When it was high enough, the rear jets cut in. They watched it streak off toward the rising towers they had left.

Distantly, over the City, it exploded and fell in a shower of sparks.

'They shot it down.' The Hedonist sighed. 'I thought they would. That will give us a few hours.'

Beth had pulled out the IDisk that hung like a locket from a chain around her neck. It had begun to glow in gentle sympathy with the crater behind them. 'Look!' she said.

'Don't worry about it,' the Hedonist said. He fished two large pills out of his pocket. 'See if you can get this down without water.'

'What is it?'

'Cysteine. An amino acid. A radiation protective. It'll last long enough to get us out of here.'

She choked down one of the pills; he swallowed the other easily. 'Let's go,' he said.

They walked away from the crater across the rubble. Soil had blown in, and the rock had weathered down. Seeds had drifted down or been dropped by birds. They had sprouted. Most of the rubble was already covered by a kind of green blanket. In fifty more years, this part of the Old City would be gently rolling meadows.

'How it happened I don't understand,' the Hedonist said, 'but somewhere you've picked up a poor opinion of hedonics.'

'No – no,' she protested. 'You don't understand—'

'This is what it saved the world from,' he said, sweeping his hand from the ruins back toward the glowing crater. 'For the warped conations of a twisted world, it substituted the only real goal, happiness, and it taught man how to find it and how to keep it.'

'What is a man profited,' Beth said quietly, 'if he shall gain the whole world, and lose his own soul?'

The Hedonist stared at her in astonishment. 'Where did you learn that?'

'I read it,' she said. 'In an old book.'

'I know that. But where did you find one. It isn't on the

proscribed list, exactly, but it isn't approved, either. I haven't seen one in twenty-five years.'

Beth shrugged carelessly. 'There are things that even the Council knows nothing about.'

'So it seems,' the Hedonist said thoughtfully.

Side by side, not touching, they walked in silence over the silent mounds of the troubled past.

VIII

A wise woman never yields by appointment. It should always be an unforeseen happiness.
MARIÉ HENRI BEYLE (STENDHAL)

Beth was the first to speak. As the buildings around them slowly changed from broken stumps to dark, hollow shafts, she said, 'What do you intend to do?'

'Get you someplace you won't be picked up immediately,' he said slowly.

'Don't worry about me,' she said impatiently. 'I can take care of myself.'

'Don't be foolish,' he said. 'I'm your hedonist. It's my duty to look after you. Do they know your name?'

'The watchdogs? Not yet, maybe. But they will. They're getting smarter.'

'Getting?' the Hedonist repeated puzzledly. 'Since when?'

Her furrowed face smoothed out magically. 'Since recently. But what I want to know is what you're going to do. You're the one they're hunting. You're the one they want. You're marked and condemned. That trick with the heli won't fool them for long, only until they run a protein-alysis on the wreckage. Then they'll be after you again.'

The Hedonist lowered his head and studied the ground. It was more than he cared to admit, but there was no evading her logic. 'That's true. And there's no place to run. I'll have to get the Council overruled and its policies—'

'Folly!' she burst out. In the silence, the word was loud

and startling. 'How many times have you yourself pointed out the fallacy of altruism?'

'True,' the Hedonist admitted. 'But I am a hedonist. That makes all the difference. My life is making people happy. Would you have me turn my back on all that now? That's my happiness. I could no more stand aside and see others unhappy than I could eat while others are hungry.'

'And how many times,' she said quietly, 'have you pointed out the fallacy of special cases?'

The Hedonist was silent. The streets had become discernible. They trudged along them, and the silent shapes of the past shouldered close. The Hedonist's eyes were watchful.

'Once,' Beth said, 'this was misery's last hiding place. Rebellion haunted the streets by night and hid in rats' nests by day. Here was the final stand of violence, grief, pain, sickness, rape, murder. . . . If we'd been here then, we'd be dead by now. The watchdogs cleaned it up.'

The Hedonist stared at her with curious eyes. 'So much for the Council.'

Beth sighed. 'I suppose so.'

They passed into an area where the buildings were sound. Among the dark, looming warehouses, light, occasional and feeble, was evidence of occupation. Twice they had to dodge the sweeping searchlights of mechanical watchmen. They were approaching the space-port and its complex of warehouses, yards, hotels, and fun houses. They stayed close to the sheltering walls until they emerged, suddenly, into a brightly lighted cross street.

There were people here, walking briskly on business or pleasure, dressed in shorts or slacks or dresses. Some of them reeled and some of them wore masks covering their whole faces and some of them had faces like masks. No one looked at Beth and the Hedonist as they joined the traffic, even though they looked cautiously at everyone who passed.

This was the Strip. Here three worlds met to share their secrets and pool their pleasures, and nothing was taboo. Along this colorful, incandescent street anything could be purchased, anything could be sold.

Beth and the Hedonist stared at the riot of brilliance and color stretching into the distance and forgot, for a moment, that they were fugitives from happiness.

In jumping, sparking letters, the nearest of the signs said:

JOY FOR SALE!
ALL KINDS
YOU NAME IT – WE'VE GOT IT!
THREE WORLDS FUN HOUSE
Licensed, Hedonic Council

Except for individual variations in color and design, the others were much the same. Farther down the street were the more modest signs of hotels, restaurants, and shops. Towering above them was the blood-red sign MARS HOUSE.

'What now?' Beth whispered. With fascination, the Hedonist noticed that she didn't move her lips.

'First, food,' the Hedonist said. 'I haven't eaten since breakfast, and the sensation, suppressable as it is, is distinct unpleasure. Then rest, which is necessary to future pleasure. I prescribe the same for you.'

She frowned and then sighed. 'All right,' she agreed. 'You're the hedonist. But what are you going to do about that?' She pointed to the IDisk on the breast of his shirt. It was glowing brilliantly.

The Hedonist slapped his hand over the telltale IDisk. 'I didn't think we'd get so much.' He took his hand away; the disk was gone.

'You can't walk around without one,' she said.

He put his hand back to his shirt, and the disk was back. It wasn't glowing any more. Beth looked closer. The disk was opaque, and the identification on it was meaningless.

'Turned it over,' the Hedonist muttered. 'Don't attract attention. It will fool anything except a close inspection, and I don't intend to get that close. Drop your locket inside your blouse.'

As she obeyed, he turned her toward the door of a modest Foodomat. It was almost deserted. There was a couple at the back, but they were engrossed in each other. At the side, against the wall, a man teetered idly in a straight chair. The Hedonist inspected him with a casually sweeping glance. The staring pupils told their story. The man was deep in the fantasies of neo-heroin. He was locked up tight in his own, private paradise.

The Hedonist took Beth's arm again. 'Come on.' They entered the necessary together. It was big enough for three or four people at a time. 'Got your false IDisk?' he asked. She nodded. 'Coins?' She nodded again, puzzled. 'Go into the di-booth. Bring me the tape.'

'But won't it be reported to the local hedonist?'

'Don't think so,' he said. 'Not in a transient area like this. But in case it is, your fake disk should confuse the matter long enough to make it unimportant.'

While she went into the booth, the Hedonist took care of his own necessities and was waiting for her when she came out. She handed him the six-inch tape. He scanned it quickly.

Height, weight, temperature, BMR, urinalysis for sugar and the keto-steroid indicators of adrenal activity, refined Papanicolau cancer test – he gave them no more than a glance. He skipped over the section dealing with the external senses and the sensory network, scanned the X-ray report and the electrocardiogram, and barely noted the E.Q. The blood cell count was what interested him, the red, white, differential, and hemoglobin.

His sigh was heavy with relief. He crumpled up the tape and threw it into the disposal. 'Let's eat.'

'Wait a minute.' She put a hand on his arm. 'So the radiation didn't do me any damage. What about you?'

He shook his head. 'Can't take a chance. I haven't got a false IDisk. But if you're unharmed, I can't be in any danger.'

She frowned but didn't say anything.

Inside the Foodomat, they walked quickly down the glass-fronted serving line, slipping coins into the slots. The Hedonist went to a table with a tray of planked plankton steak with a high-vitamin chlorella sauce and a hot milk-substitute. Beth chose a lighter meal, chiefly low-fat chlorella patties and Kafi. They ate quickly and in silence, glancing frequently at the door. The couple at the back finished and left, but no one came in.

Beth and the Hedonist got up, stuffed their dishes into the disposal, and walked through the doorway. The door slid shut behind them.

'Where now?' Beth asked.

'You're going to rent us a room.'

Beth's eyes met his levelly. 'One room?'

'Of course,' the Hedonist said, surprised. 'How many do you think we need?'

When they were within fifty yards of the slideway into the magnificent portal of Mars House, the Hedonist drew Beth suddenly out of the stream of traffic and into a shadowed niche. 'Pretend to be interested in me,' he muttered. 'Put your head on my shoulder.'

She put her slim arms around his neck and buried her face in the base of his throat. Her lips moved against it. 'What's the matter?'

The Hedonist felt his pulse quicken. 'Not so—' he began. 'Not so—'

'What?' she asked in a muffled voice.

'Oh, never mind. The clowns are only a few yards away.'

'Watchdogs?' she whispered.

They passed in motley, vivid and gay, but their faces were young and sharp and intent. In their hands were the subduers modeled after the ancient electronic prodders. They searched the faces on each side of them, lifting masks, inspecting IDisks. There was something horrible in the contrast between their unsmiling purpose and their dress.

So passes power dressed in the clothes of joy, the Hedonist thought suddenly. And, Is this the generation that Hedonics fathered?

And then they were gone; the Hedonist felt his body relax. Once more he became conscious of Beth. 'Stop that!'

Her lips stopped moving against his skin. 'What?' she whispered innocently.

'That! Listen, now. We won't take chances. You'll register for a single, using your false IDisk. I'll sneak into the room later. The clerk will want to know your business.' He paused and thought swiftly. 'Say that you're volunteering for the new Venus colony. Got money for the deposit?'

She shook her head. Her lips slid deliciously across the base of his throat, and her silky hair brushed against his cheek.

'There's a pocket inside the shirt. Money in it. Take it.'

Her hand was cool and slow and sensual as it fumbled the money out of the pocket and withdrew. In spite of the Hedonist's efforts at suppression, his breathing quickened. Then she was gone, and he felt suddenly alone, suddenly cold and deserted.

She walked quickly, youthfully, to the slideway and stepped onto it. She disappeared through the rose portal without a backward glance.

'Old fool!' he said savagely, and he walked slowly toward the hotel.

The lobby was remarkably spacious. It must have been at least twenty feet square. The red resiloid floor was sprinkled with red sand that grated underfoot, and the walls were the realistic depth murals of Martian landscapes. The lobby was lighted by a Mars-sized sun suspended invisibly from the ceiling. Periodically, the Hedonist understood, the sun faded out and Deimos and Phobos raced across the dark blue dome of the ceiling, the swift inner moon twice a day from west to east.

Beth was standing at the desk, talking to the clerk; as the Hedonist passed, she slid her IDisk under its scanner. The Hedonist fed a coin into the newsfax dispenser. A sheet of paper slid into his hand. He took it absently and wandered over to the elevator. It was a crude-seeing openwork model in a rough, tubular frame; behind it the wall curved shinily like the outer hull of a spaceship. The Hedonist sat down on a mocked-up luggage carrier and hid his face behind the news sheet.

Hedonic Index at 2000: 94%. Weather for tomorrow:

same as yesterday, sunny and warm after the early morning shower. News bulletin: the flash noticed over the Old City at 2009 has been identified as a meteor. . . .

Meteor, the Hedonist thought with sudden clarity. Unhappiness has been exiled from Earth. The unexpected, the unpredicted, and unpleasant? Deny it; suppress it. Does it flash in the sky? It comes from space. It is an alien.

The Hedonist looked back at the sheet. The rest of it was hotel advertising. One of the ads said:

Visit the Exotic MARTIAN ROOM
(in the penthouse)
Against the Outré background of the *CRATER*
Taste
Strange *LUXURIES* and Stranger *DELIGHTS*
'A pleasure experience without compare'

At the bottom of the sheet was the notation: *Hedonist on duty at all hours. Press 11 for therapy.*

A breeze touched his face with a familiar fragrance. Something small and light landed on his outstretched hand. Beside him, the elevator climbed quietly. The Hedonist looked up. The cage was disappearing through the blue arch of the sky. In his hand was a crumpled corner of paper. Behind the cover of the news sheet, he smoothed it out. There was a number on it: 3129. He squeezed the paper into a ball and slipped it into his pocket.

When the elevator returned, he threw the news sheet into the disposal beside the chair and entered the cage. 'Mars Room,' he said.

The penthouse turned out to be on the thirty-fifth floor, but it was a quick trip. The only light in the room came through one wide transparent wall; it was the phosphorescence of the crater. Wavering blue and green fingers clutched at the room and the huddled shapes in the dark corners. The Hedonist stood there for a moment listening, in spite of himself, to the oddly stirring atonal music, smelling the pungent alkaloids and incenses. But when a tall, thin shape glided out of the shadows toward him with a whis-

pered question, the Hedonist turned quickly, found the fire
door, and ran quickly down the steps.

The stairs were dark and deserted. The Hedonist wondered if they had ever been used. Within a minute, he was
outside a door marked 3129.

The corridor was empty. He rapped gently and the door
slid open. He stepped inside quickly and shut the door
behind him.

The room was empty.

The Hedonist searched the room frantically, but there
was no possible place for her to hide. There were only
eighty-one square feet to the room, and she was on none of
them.

His stomach suddenly felt cold and empty, as if the meal
he had eaten only a little while before had suddenly been
teleported away.

'Hedonist?' she asked. There was alarm in her voice. 'Is
that you?'

He jumped and then sighed with relief. 'Yes,' he said.
She was in the necessary. Now he could hear the muffled
spatter of the sprays behind the door.

'I'll be out in a minute,' she said.

She was. The door opened. She was dressed in something
black, lacy, and clinging, and she was brushing the damp
ends of her hair. The Hedonist had never seen her look so
desirable. Suddenly he wasn't tired any more. He felt young
and alive again.

'Where did you get the clothes?' he asked quickly.

She brushed past him; it was an upsetting experience. She
pushed the button that folded the chairs and tables into the
wall and raised the bed through the floor. 'Ordered them,'
she said carelessly. 'There was money left. We need clothes
that won't be recognized. There's some for you, too.'

She motioned toward the luggage door. It slid open at his
touch. In the compartment behind were two boxes. The
Hedonist opened the top one. Inside was a dark-blue tunic
and a pair of slacks. He never got to look in the other one.
A thump on the floor drew him around.

On the narrow strip of floor beside the bed was a pillow. He looked at Beth, startled. 'What's the reason for that?'

'That,' she said sweetly, tossing a blanket down beside the pillow, 'is where you're going to sleep.'

'I don't understand,' he said in bewilderment. 'We've been sleeping together for almost a week now—'

'But that's over,' she said, wide-eyed and innocent. 'You said so this morning. And this is scarcely the time for therapy. Unless it's a question of *your* happiness—'

His happiness? Of course not. That was absurd. 'Of course not,' he said, frowning. 'Only—'

'Only what?' she asked when he didn't finish.

'Nothing,' he said and settled himself on the hard floor.

He turned over and over in the darkness, trying to find a comfortable place for his hip and shoulder bones. There weren't any.

Absurd, he said to himself. Beth was acting very strange; not like herself at all. He yawned, and a wave of relaxed weariness swept out toward the extremities of his body. Definitely not hedonic.

The bed was plenty big enough for two. . . . It was soft . . . molded itself to a tired body . . . and Beth was softer . . .

IX

Even in the common affairs of life, in love, friendship, and marriage, how little security have we when we trust our happiness in the hands of others!

                        WILLIAM HAZLITT

The Hedonist woke up. He stared into the darkness above him and tried to figure out what had awakened him. There was no sound, no movement, no odor. And yet something – indefinable – was different about the room.

When he identified it, it was only a little thing. He couldn't hear Beth's soft, even breathing.

He sprang up, grunting a little from the pain of sore,

stiffened muscles, and switched on the lights. The bed was empty. Beth wasn't in the room. The little cubicle of the necessary was empty, too.

Beth was gone.

He slid the door open and glanced up and down the hall. It was dark and deserted. Slowly he let the door go shut, walked to the bed, and sank down on the edge.

Gone. Beth had left him. Silently, in the middle of the night, without a word, without – he glanced with sudden hope around the room, but it turned to disappointment – a note. Gone. It was a dismal word; it seemed to fit the way he felt – a cold, drawn-out emptiness.

Maybe she was better off on her own. Maybe he was dangerous to her. But she might have said something. He wouldn't have tried to keep her. He would have—

He suppressed the anguish, devalued the importance. She was gone. The question : What should he do now?

He glanced at his watch. It was almost midnight. Three hours since he had laid down on the floor. He had slept, he supposed, for a little more than two of those. Now, he was still tired, much stiffer, but there would be no more sleep. He felt sure of that.

He got up impatiently and paced the room. Three paces. Turn. Three paces. Turn. It annoyed him, having to sidle around the bed. He lowered it into the floor and kicked his pillow and blanket after it before the floor closed over it.

It was better, but not much. His pacing was still profitless. He shrugged, stripped off his underclothes, and stepped into the necessary. Steamy jets loosened his muscles; icy jets refreshed him. When he was dry, he inspected the dispensers on the wall.

Ethyloid, one of them was labeled. Three positions were available : Scotch, bourbon, gin. The Hedonist shook his head. He wanted to improve his ratiocinations, not dampen them. That meant, too, no neo-heroin and no mescaline. He located the spigot labeled *Coffee*.

Not Kafi? he thought in surprise. He shrugged. No doubt it was part of the Mars House scheme of décor. He filled a cup with the dark, steaming liquid and sipped it. It was the most delicious stuff he had ever tasted.

That was one consolation, he thought wryly. Du Pont had brewed another batch, and it was the best the laboratories had ever done.

He told himself to forget about Beth. He told himself several times. He had to concern himself with important things. . . . Eventually the Hedonic exercises were almost successful. Although Beth was not forgotten, she was pushed into a corner of his mind and imprisoned there where she could not scatter his thoughts in an unwary moment.

He concentrated on the problem of survival.

Decision: His survival depended on the overthrow of the Council.

Question: Was his survival worth the price?

Answer: No, not alone; but it isn't the life that's important; it is Earth and hedonics.

While he had been occupied with individual therapies, the Council had turned off the main road. They were in full cry down the wrong trail. The rabbit they were chasing was an illusory rabbit. It is not correct to say that the quarry is unimportant, the chase is the thing. Unless the rabbit is real and worthwhile, the chase becomes unreal and worthless. The tricked hound soon loses his eagerness for the hunt.

The Council had turned to pure hedonism. It had gone far back, to Aristippus and the Cyrenaic School: the only good is the sentient pleasure of the moment; the true art of life is to crowd as much enjoyment as possible into every moment.

It was false, just as every extreme must be. Happiness had to prepare for the future, or there was no future for happiness. Every moment is important, not just for the happiness it contains but for the happiness it leads to. Every moment must make a man readier to understand happiness, to recognize it, to seize it, and to hold it.

That was what illusion couldn't do. Imaginary gratification dulled the senses and pushed every other type of satisfaction farther out of reach. It even failed itself; eventually unreasoned gratification becomes meaningless.

The only road was the middle road. The only hedonism was rational, the hedonism of Epicurus, Socrates, Plato and Aristotle.

Eventually Earth would realize that. Pure hedonism could not endure. But it was important to save Earth the long detour which might, eventually, discredit hedonics itself.

But how to discredit the Council!

The Council had maneuvered itself into a position of near invulnerability. 1) It had placed itself above the law – even though that meant the inevitable downfall of law itself. And 2) It had legislated hedonics into a science, which is like legislating a silk purse into a sow's ear. It didn't make it one, but it punished everyone who called it by the wrong name.

But it was only *near* invulnerability. There was always the Congress. The names of fifty hedonists on a petition could call an emergency session, and while the Congress was in session every hedonist was immune from arrest and any proceedings against him.

What the Congress had done, the Congress could undo.

The Hedonist's only problem was to get fifty names on a petition. It was not a small problem: he was a hunted man.

He couldn't do it alone. He needed help. He could, he felt sure, get help from the dependents in his ward, but he couldn't drag them into what could be considered illegal activity. The logical choice were the hedonists themselves; they were responsible for the situation, and they could do the most good.

He considered the hotel hedonist for only a second. He didn't know the man, and couldn't take chances. The first poor chance he took would be his last. He closed his eyes and ran over the list of the hedonists he knew. Suddenly he snapped his fingers and moved to the phone.

He consulted the directory on the panel beneath the screen, punched a two-digit number, waited until the screen flickered and buzzed approvingly, and punched a seven-digit number. There was one man he could trust: Lari.

They had gone through the Institute together. Ten intimate years of living together and mutual analyses and shared confidences had exposed a bedrock of character. Their chance meetings at conventions and Congresses had been infrequent, but the understanding and affection couldn't change.

He knew Lari better, the Hedonist thought, than he knew himself.

The screen got gray and defined itself into patterns of dark and light. Lari looked up wearily from his desk, his face lined, his eyes large and dark. The Hedonist stabbed a button. The screen went dark.

'Yes?' Lari said. 'Something seems to be wrong.'

'It does indeed,' the Hedonist said in a deep voice. 'That is why I have called you. Lari, this is – this is—' For a frantic, impossible moment, he groped wildly for the name. He had not been a name for twenty-three years; he had been a position, a manipulator of people's happiness. Then he said, 'Morgan. This is Morgan.'

'Morgan?' Lari's voice was twisted and strange.

The Hedonist frowned, wished he could see Lari's face, but he couldn't risk his own face on the screen.

'Where are you?' Lari asked.

'Never mind,' the Hedonist said. 'That isn't important. I need your help.'

'Yes,' Lari said heavily. 'I guess you do.'

'You know then?'

'Yes. Go on. What can I do?'

'Meet me. I've got to talk to you.'

'Where?'

The Hedonist thought swiftly. 'Interplanetary Strip. There's a fun house called the Three Worlds.'

'How'll I find you?'

'I'll find you,' the Hedonist said. 'Will you come? Now? I wouldn't ask you if it wasn't—'

'I'll come. It'll be about half an hour.'

'Good. See you then.'

The Hedonist turned off the screen and looked around for his clothes. They were gone.

He found his IDisk on the floor beneath the disposal; it had stopped phosphorescing. He held it in his hand and stared around a room that, except for the discarded underclothes on the floor, was as bare as he was. Then he thought of the luggage compartment.

The door was a little ajar. Inside there was one box. In it were the blue tunic and slacks and sealed packages of disposable underwear, socks, and shoes. He slipped into them quickly. In his preoccupation, he almost didn't hear the noise outside the door.

It was a scuffing sound. The Hedonist stared at the door and silently flicked the button that locked it. He scooped up the box and his discarded underclothes and stuffed them down the disposal. He noticed the cup, and that followed. He noticed the IDisk in his hand and stuck it on the tunic, backward again.

Now to get out. He stopped, stricken. There was no way out. Mars House was newer than the Council Building. The hotel had no windows; even if it had, his geckopads were gone.

Someone tried the door and found it locked. The Hedonist glanced frantically around the room. He could, he supposed, hide in the bed, but the floor recess would be searched.

'Open the door,' someone shouted. 'In the name of the Council. Joy!'

Watchdogs! In two silent steps, the Hedonist was beside the luggage compartment. He slid back the door and wedged himself into the box, his knees doubled up against his chest like a fetus. He let the door slip shut until there was only a hairline crack letting light and air in to him.

There was a moment to think. How had they found him? The only answer that came to him was Beth!

No! He refused to believe it. Not Beth. And yet – Beth had sneaked away while he was asleep. But if she wanted to turn him in, why should she have rescued him from his precarious position clinging to the outside of the Council Building. Unless – she had changed her mind and had decided to turn him in to save herself.

No! Not Beth! And yet – she had deceived him before.

The odor of burned plastic drifted into the box with him. Something slammed nearby. Feet tramped into the room. Bright motley crossed in front of the crack. It turned, searching the room. There was a subduer in its hand, like a two-foot ebony club.

The brief whir of machinery told him that the bed was being raised. The feet clomped impatiently, in and around. The Hedonist watched the crack intently, hardly daring to breathe. Suddenly, very close and huge, appeared fingers, reaching . . .

The Hedonist jerked his hand back. The door clicked shut. The box fell out from under him. He dropped, fast. He clutched his hands tight against his sides. They could be scraped off against the wall of the chute. He fell in utter darkness. He was afraid.

A giant palm pressed him down, forced the breath from his body, flattened him against a hard, smooth board, tried to mash him, squash him, break him. The darkness turned red and then became black again. . . .

The Hedonist opened his eyes. His legs were dangling into emptiness. There was a little light filtering past them, and he twisted himself around so that he could look out of the box without committing himself to leave it.

He was at the bottom of the chute. Radiating out from the box in all directions were endless rubberoid belts, lighted only by the dim radiance of machines looming beyond. He was in the service cellar.

Something pressed against his back, pushing him out of the box. He grabbed the edges and tried to hold back, but it was futile. Unceremoniously, he was dumped onto one of the belts. It complained at his weight, but it started him toward a distant and unknown destination.

The Hedonist slid his legs over the edge and dropped to the floor three feet beneath. He stood still for a moment, studying the pattern of moving belts and chattering machines. One of the machines had lights flashing inside it.

They flashed in sequence, and it clucked to itself as if it were counting.

The Hedonist looked it over quickly. There were thirty-five bulbs, and the one that was lighted for a moment was nineteen from the end. He grabbed the handle of the heavy switch on the front of the machine and pulled it open. The machine went dark and silent. He hoped that it had controlled the elevator.

The service cellar was a maze. Tunnels and narrow passageways led here and there with apparent aimlessness, ending abruptly, twisting, turning. The belts took up so much floor space that the Hedonist spent most of his time crawling under or climbing over. The cellar wasn't meant for men.

At last he found a stairway that wound upward in a tight spiral. He ran up the steps quickly. After two turns he saw a glowing button in the curved wall. He pressed it. The wall swung aside. The Hedonist walked into the hotel lobby.

It was dark and empty. The sun had set. Phobos was moving swiftly across the sky toward the east.

He was beside the elevator framework. Distantly, he heard a ghostly voice. 'Hel-l-l-l-p!' it said. '. . . stuh-uck!'

The red sand gritted under his feet as the Hedonist smiled and walked out into the brilliant night.

Money was a problem. Beth had taken all the money he had. The Hedonist solved that one by picking up a dime on the street. He walked into the glittering entrance arcade to the Three World Fun House and studied the slot machines for a moment. Finally he slipped the coin into a dexterity game.

The machine was an enclosed cylinder separated into ten horizontal compartments by transparent, bright, colored disks. In the center of each disk was a hole diminishing in size from the bottom to the top. At the sloped bottom was a hollow plastic ball. Three jets of compressed air lifted it through the holes in the disks, and the intensity of each jet was controlled by a key on the front. The object of the game was to raise the ball as high as possible before it toppled into one of the compartments.

The first time the Hedonist got back his dime. The second time he worked the ball clear to the top and hit the jackpot. He scooped the dimes into the tunic pocket and walked to the next machine. It was a tone analyser.

Within the range of the machine, the Hedonist could hear a compound tone. It was faithfully duplicated on a screen by a swirl of colors. As the Hedonist analysed the tone into its components of frequency, intensity, wave form, and phase, the colors separated into a prismatic layer arrangement. A multiple of the winning could be obtained by identifying the overtones and their intensity.

By the third trial, the Hedonist had corrected for the machine's inevitable distortion and collected the jackpot. The whole business had taken five minutes.

It was not as difficult as it seemed. The machines were shills for the more expensive pleasures inside; they weren't set for a high return. Being public, too, they would never be approved by the Council if they produced too much unpleasure. Most significant, however, was the Hedonist himself. Sensory analysis and its corollary, dexterity, were his business. He had spent years on more difficult exercises than these.

Weighed down by more than fifty dollars in change, the Hedonist walked into the fun house. The clear doors swung open in front of him. When they swung shut behind, the lights went out.

There was a disturbing moment of disorientation, as if he were floating aimlessly in space. It didn't help to identify the cause: an interrupter automatically canceling the wave lengths of light that should have reached him. Laughter poured in on him from all sides. Suddenly there was an apparition in front of him.

It was a satyr with dainty hoofs and shaggy legs and sharp little horns. Its red, sensual lips were curled into a joyful grin and its eyes were alight with laughter and lust. It hung upside down from the ceiling.

'Joy, sir, joy!' it cried. 'Welcome to the Three Worlds.

Name your pleasure. If it exists anywhere on the three worlds, you will find it here. What will you have?'

Before the Hedonist could speak, the satyr had disappeared. In a wink, it was back, floating horizontally.

'Joy, sir!' it shouted gleefully. 'What will it be? Gambling?' He swept out an arm expansively, and a doorway opened in the darkness. The path led upward. At its end was glitter and movement and brilliance, fantastic machines doing incomprehensible things. 'The very latest devices, sir. Those you saw in the arcade are only a poor sample of what we can provide in color, action, and thrill.' His voice dropped to a confidential whisper. 'Eight out of every ten players leave winner.'

'It's surprising you can afford to remain open,' the Hedonist commented wryly.

'It's a rich man's pleasure, sir,' the satyr said quickly with a contagious laugh. 'What shall it be? Sensies? We have all the latest tapes, sir. And many that won't be released to the public for months. The thrill of winning, sir, the ecstasy of success without the danger of failure. Create, achieve, enjoy, love! There is no limit to what the sensies can give you, effortlessly.' His voice dropped again. 'We can even offer you – real pain! Smuggled. Very rare and expensive. What will it be?'

The satyr and the pathway snapped out of existence. When the satyr reappeared, it was still horizontal, but its head and feet had been reversed.

'Joy, sir! How can we please you? Will it be girls?' As it spoke, doors opened in the darkness; behind each door was a different girl in a different pose. 'We have all kinds: amateurs and professionals, ice maidens and nymphs; short ones, tall ones, thin ones, fat ones; girls of every shape and color, of every talent and desire. Name your delight, and she is yours!'

Helplessly, the Hedonist watched the satyr vanish. When it flashed back into view, it was standing on its feet. It threw out its arm dramatically.

'What shall it be, sir?' it demanded stridently. 'The ethyloids? We have them all. List your flavor: Scotch, bourbon, Irish, rye, Canadian. . . . Describe your mixture; we will prepare it. Guaranteed to be without later unpleasure.'

Its arms dropped and it looked cautiously to both sides and whispered, 'We even have some real, vegetable-based, authentic Kentucky sour-mash. Distilled ourselves according to an ancient recipe – at fantastic risk. A most rare, raw flavor!'

Its voice lifted again. 'Your pleasure, sir! Name it and you shall have it if it is available anywhere on three worlds. Narcotics? Of course! All the alkaloids. Neo-heroin. Whisper your addiction, and we will supply it in any form you desire. Or if you have none, let me recommend the unusual sensations of the latest craze – mescaline! It will slow time to a crawl. It will let you be beside yourself – legally and literally. Enjoy the symptoms of schizophrenia – that long-lost mental thrill—'

'A booth by the door,' the Hedonist said quietly.

The satyr broke off in mid-declamation. It looked a little foolish. 'Er – uh – your pleasure? A booth, sir?'

The Hedonist jingled the coins in his pocket.

The satyr recovered quickly. 'Of course, sir. A booth. But here!' The Hedonist felt something slip over his face. 'In the Three Worlds, identity is lost. Only pleasure is recognized! Only joy is unmasked!'

And it vanished.

X

There is only one way to achieve happiness
  on this terrestrial ball,
And that is to have either a clear conscience,
  or none at all.

OGDEN NASH

The Hedonist blinked as the darkness gave way to light. Half-blindly, he followed a small spot of light through a milling crowd of masked men and women. The spot led him to a dark, transparent door in a line of doors that were lighted and opaque. The booth was more like a good-sized room. There were two comfortable chairs, a table, and a pneumatic couch. Against the wall was a row of coin-operated dispensers. The usual things : drinks and narcotics.

The Hedonist sank wearily into one of the chairs and looked through the door. He could see the fun house entrance. Anyone could see him, too.

'For light and privacy,' the table said, 'deposit one dollar for five minutes.'

Into a slot in the table top, the Hedonist fed five dollars in change. The room brightened. Around the edge of the door, a row of strong lights came on. They beamed against it. He could still see out, but no one could see in.

He bought a cup of Kafi from the dispenser and leaned back to sip it. It was the same bitter brew he had tasted in the morning. He shrugged and drank it and watched the entrance. It had been half an hour since his call to Lari. The hedonist should be coming into the fun house very soon.

Other people came through the door but not Lari. One girl came in already masked. Her mask was passion; below it was a young, curved body in revealing red satin. She didn't wait to have the fun-house wares described. She knew what she wanted and ignored the darkness as she brushed past the satyr's image – both of them invisible from this side – into the room.

A heavy-set man in a blue suit and a mask of thick-veined, red-faced rage grabbed her around the waist and tried to draw her close. She let herself be swung in against him while she deftly flicked back his mask and kept on turning right out of his arms. She disappeared in the surging throng.

After five minutes, Lari had not come in. The Hedonist watched the patrons of the Three Worlds stream past his door toward unknown destinations and unknown pleasures. Some were dressed in rich, glittering clothes, and some were dressed in transparencies, and once a girl in a mask of agony and nothing else broke screaming through the mob and dashed across the floor pursued by a naked satyr.

Joy! the Hedonist thought. Pleasure! Here hedonism has reached its nadir. It can sink no lower.

It could, though. It could sink below saturnalia to madness. It could sink to delusion inanimately received, where nothing was important but the senses – the body useless (let it wither), the mind worthless (let it rot).

But wasn't this implicit in hedonism from the start? No. It wasn't. The pursuit of happiness need not be passive, could not be passive. And the freedom to be happy need not be license, could not be license, for license leads inevitably to unpleasure.

Hedonism was right. Pleasure was the only human good. But it had to be balanced against the total pleasure possible. Choice was necessary, and that demanded wisdom.

Like wisdom, happiness could not be a gift. You can teach a man, but you can't make him wise. You can show him the road to happiness, but he must travel alone.

Happiness was unique. Put it in a man's hands and it was ashes.

Lari stood in the doorway, blinking. His eyes were dark, troubled pools. His face was haggard and drawn. He pushed forward out of the darkness, and there was a mask on his face. The mask was fear.

The Hedonist glanced at his watch. Since he had put in the call, almost an hour had elapsed. He watched Lari work his way through the crowd, looking all around him with fear-widened eyes. Lari stopped the man with the mask of rage, but the man shook him off.

No one followed Lari. No one came through the entrance behind him. As Lari passed, the Hedonist swung the door open and caught his wrists.

'In here,' he said softly, pulling.

Lari started and then let himself be tugged into the booth. As the door swung shut behind him, he stared at the Hedonist with terror-stricken eyes. It took a moment for the Hedonist to realize that the expression was in the mask.

But Lari kept staring. 'Great sorrow, Morgan,' he whispered, 'is that you?'

'Yes,' the Hedonist said. 'What's the matter?'

Lari pointed toward the ceiling. 'Look at yourself!'

The ceiling was a mirror. The Hedonist looked up. Gazing down at him was an idiot, loose-lipped and imbecilically happy. The Hedonist shuddered and jerked his head down. He started to lift the mask from his face.

'Never mind,' Lari said, sinking down into the other chair. 'Leave it on. It's safer that way.'

Fear faced the Idiot across the table. 'All right,' Fear said. 'Tell me what you want.'

The Idiot smirked. Briefly he described what had happened to him that day, the summons, Gomer Berns, the Council. . . . But when he started to describe the Council's new devices and its plans for them, Fear cut him off impatiently. 'I know all that,' he said, fidgeting.

'You know and you haven't done anything?'

'What is there to do? So, you escaped. What do you plan to do now? I don't see how I can help—'

'I don't want you to help me,' the Idiot said. 'I'm not important. The important thing is to get the world back on the right road. We've got to replace the Council—'

Fear laughed nervously, choking. 'How do you plan to do that?'

The Idiot outlined his plan for petition. 'Once we have an emergency session, we can throw out the Council and get the world back to sanity. You and I know the proper hedonic techniques; we know that this way is madness. And once the situation is presented to the Congress in the proper light, it will defend the old standards. Well,' he said as Fear was silent, 'isn't it a good plan?'

'A fine plan, a beautiful plan,' Fear said breathlessly. 'It hasn't got a chance.'

'Why not?'

'You're not a hedonist any more. The Council revoked your license, destroyed your office and files. You're a criminal. You'll be picked up any minute and put to surgery.'

The Idiot brushed it aside. 'That doesn't matter. I can

hide until the Congress has acted.'

'Anyone who helps you is liable to the same penalties,' Fear said suddenly. 'But it doesn't matter. That's right. You'll never get an emergency session. And even if you did, it wouldn't do any good. There isn't a hedonist in the country who would sign your petition. The Congress is behind the Council, whole-heartedly.'

'All?' the Idiot said dazedly.

'All! Every one!' Fear pounded hysterically on the table. Suddenly, frantically, he turned toward the wall and slipped a coin into one of the dispensers. A tiny syrette of neo-heroin dropped into his hand.

The Hedonist's eyes were incredulous as they watched Lari push up a sleeve, apply the syrette to a vein, and press the button. There was a quick, sharp, hissing sound. Lari dropped the empty syrette to the floor and leaned back, his eyes closed.

'Neo-heroin?' the Hedonist said.

'Yes, I'm an addict,' Lari said calmly, his eyes still closed. 'It's nothing to be ashamed of.'

'For anyone but a hedonist, no. But how can you expect to help your dependents when your senses are dulled and your mind is depressed?'

'I'm a person, too,' Lari said violently. 'I have emotions and desires like everyone else. I need happiness too.'

'You haven't been happy?'

'Happy?' Lari said softly. 'I haven't been happy since I was a child. None of us have. We were brave and foolish, just a handful of hedonic therapists shouldering the burden of a world's happiness. It was mad. It was wonderful, but it was mad and impossible.'

'But we did it,' the Hedonist exclaimed. 'We did it.'

Lari sighed. 'Yes, we did it. For a little while. Not perfectly, not completely, but we did it. And we paid for it. We sold ourselves to a thousand people each; we were their slaves. They brought their burdens to us, and we took them on. There are few nights I have had as much as five hours sleep, and most of that was allotted to therapy.'

'You don't know what you're saying!'

'Oh, I know. I know too well. It was more than feeble tissue could endure, the labor and the sorrow. And when the Council offered us a chance at happiness, do you think we could turn it down? By then I'd already been on neo-heroin for two years.'

The Hedonist clenched his fist. How could he convince Lari that he was wrong? It was so difficult because there was truth in what Lari said. A hedonist became a machine for making people happy; after a few years he even forgot that he had a name. 'But it's wrong, Lari!' the Hedonist pleaded. 'What the Council wants to do is wrong!'

'How can it be wrong,' Lari said wearily, 'to make people happy? How can it be wrong for me to be happy?'

'The wrong is the wrong we do ourselves,' the Hedonist said quietly. 'You've got to break the habit, Lari. You know how. And you know the techniques of happiness.'

'Oh, I'll break it,' Lari said distantly. 'I'll break it in a few weeks. And I'll be happy.' His eyes were sad behind the mask. 'But you're lost. You've thrown your chance away.'

Inside the booth, the lights dimmed. 'For light and privacy,' the table said, 'deposit one dollar for five minutes.'

The Hedonist was busy dropping coins into the table slot when the door opened. He moved smoothly to his feet. Standing in the doorway was the girl in the mask of passion and the red gown. She stared at him as she moved close. She lifted his mask, and he let her do these things, not knowing why.

She let the mask fall back and threw her arms around his neck. 'It's you!' she sobbed.

It was Beth's voice. The Hedonist pulled down her mask. It was Beth's face. There was a glad smile on her lips, but there were tears in her eyes. They had a strange effect on the Hedonist. They made his heart pound and his knees weak.

'I've been hunting for you everywhere,' she said.

'Where did you go? Why did you leave me?' the Hedonist asked, his eyes never leaving her face.

'There's no time for explanations,' she said, drawing back and tugging at his arm. 'We've got to get away from here.'

'A little while after you left, the watchdogs came,' he said, pulling back. 'They almost caught me.'

'You can't think I had anything to do with that!' she exclaimed. 'I couldn't. Oh, you've got to trust me!'

'Why?' the Hedonist asked. 'You've been acting very strangely.'

'You're the hedonist,' she reminded him sharply. 'Don't you know?'

He shook his head in bewilderment.

'Oh, fury!' she exclaimed. And then, more softly, 'I'm in love with you. I had no intention of marrying anyone but you. I wanted to look after you, to make you happy. I was no exception. All the women in the ward were in love with you, but I was the only one with the courage to do anything about it.'

The Hedonist was suddenly aware that, under his mask, his jaw had dropped down. He closed it with a snap. 'That's fantastic!' And he added, suddenly, 'You made me sleep on the floor.'

A smile slipped across her face. 'You may be the hedonist,' she said, 'but you don't know anything above love. Some desires should be thwarted; it's like shading a flower that's used to the sun – it grows furiously to reach the light.'

The Hedonist stared at her, wordless. 'It's impossible,' he said at last. 'I'm a hedonist. I can't marry or love—'

'Fool! Fool!' she groaned. 'How long do you think you can hold up the sky all by yourself? Just once, think of yourself. That's all over! Can't you see?'

Out of the corner of his eye, the Hedonist caught a flicker of movement. The walls of the booth fell through the floor. Behind the walls was the motley of clowns. A dozen black subduers were pointed toward them.

At first the Hedonist thought they were wearing masks, all of them the same: impassive blankness. But they were faces. The Hedonist realized, with a shock of recognition, that one of them belonged to the Council secretary.

'The girl's right,' the secretary said. 'It's all over.'

His presence meant that it was a trap, carefully planned, skillfully executed. The Hedonist looked at Beth and the mask of passion dangling from her neck.

Slowly, painfully, she shook her head. 'No, no!' she whispered. 'You can't believe that. You mustn't—'

'I don't,' he said suddenly. He turned to the secretary. 'What are you going to do?'

'We're taking you in for treatment,' the secretary said unemotionally. 'Both of you.'

Both of you. Beth and himself. Not Lari.

The Hedonist looked at Lari. Through the mask of fear, he could see his old friend's eyes. They were the eyes of a man who was lost, forever. He had damned himself, and his own private paradise would be his hell. No amount of pleasure would ever drown the pain.

'I'm sorry, Lari,' the Hedonist said softly.

The eyes winced and closed. The mask turned aside.

'Let's go,' the Hedonist said to the secretary.

For the second time that night, the lights went out.

XI

> It is said an Eastern monarch once charged his wise men to invent him a sentence to be ever in view, and which should be true and appropriate in all times and situations. They presented him the words: 'And this, too, shall pass away.' How much it expresses! How chastening in the hour of pride! How consoling in the depths of affliction! . . . And yet, let us hope, it is not quite true. Let us hope, rather, that by the best cultivation of the physical world beneath and around us, and the best intellectual and moral world within us, we shall secure an individual, social, and political prosperity and happiness, whose course shall be onward and upward, and which, while the earth endures, shall not pass away.
>
> ABRAHAM LINCOLN

The Hedonist threw his fist and felt the paralysing shock

go through it and up his arm. But in his shoulder he felt the solid impact of the fist against something that yielded. The secretary grunted and fell backward in a flurry of falling noises. There were shouts and groans and the clatter of feet.

But the Hedonist was too busy to listen to them, too busy even to enjoy the pleasure of striking back against the forces that had taken his life and his world and pulled them down together. He had swung on around, caught Beth, and pulled her through the door of the booth and into the shouting, milling crowd outside. There was laughter at first, as most of the patrons thought it was a joke, and then moans and screams and growing hysteria.

The darkness was absolute. They hadn't left it when they left the booth. Someone had an interrupter focused on the whole area.

The Hedonist held tightly to Beth's wrist and forced his way through the jostling, clutching, screaming crowd. He brought Beth close and yelled in her ear, 'Are you all right?'

He could feel her head nod and then her lips were moving against his ear. 'I can't fight this mob,' she shouted. 'You go ahead. I'll steer from behind.'

'Where?' the Hedonist asked.

'Never mind! Quick! There's no telling how long the darkness will last.'

The Hedonist hesitated, shrugged, and turned. He lowered his numbed shoulder and plunged into the squirming, clawing sea of humanity. She guided him with strong, sure movements of her hand. Fists bounced off his body and face and nails raked him, but he managed to get his partially paralysed arm up in front of his face and forced his way onward, thankful for the first time that his body was big and strong.

It seemed as if the darkness had thickened, as if the night had arms and hands and feet to hold them back. The pressure increased and grew until, suddenly, it fell away before them and there was nothing.

The Hedonist reached with his foot and there were steps going down. He stumbled down them, dragging Beth behind. When they reached a level stretch again, the noise had faded in the distance, and they seemed to be alone. He brought Beth up beside him.

'What is this?' he demanded. 'Where are we going? Who's using the interrupter? Who—?'

'No time now,' she panted. 'Come on. I'll try to tell you as we escape.'

She led him through the darkness with a sure instinct. 'The answer to most of your questions is, the Underground.'

It was a strange new word. The Hedonist let it tumble around in his mind, and everywhere it touched it summoned up an exotic image: men tampering with hedometers; people meeting in dark, hidden places to share their illicit passions of grief, pain, and sorrow; saboteurs spreading infections of gloom. . . .

How could it have existed without his knowledge? 'And you're a part of it,' he said.

'Ever since I realized that what kept us apart was hedonics. Try to understand us! We aren't troubled about the great mass of the people; they're contented with what they have. We're concerned with the few malcontents who find happiness impossible and get into trouble.'

She stopped. The Hedonist got an impression that there was something solid in front of them. In a moment he felt a sudden breath of cool air against his face. Beth led him down another flight of steps and into a straight, level passage.

'Then you aren't trying to overthrow the Council?' he asked, puzzled.

'Of course not. What would be the point? We don't want the responsibility for a world overpopulated with mediocrities. Let the Council have that. All we try to do is to rescue the few who are worth saving.'

With one step they came out of the darkness into the light. The Hedonist blinked at the brightness; the blindness wore off quickly. They were in a long, narrow passage lighted at infrequent intervals by bulbs in ceiling pits. The Hedonist could not see the end of it.

'Then you think hedonics is a failure?' he said.

The struggle through the mob had torn the red gown.

Beth was trying, with only partial success, to hold it together. 'No,' she said with great seriousness – and the Hedonist would have smiled at her youthful gravity if it hadn't
been so real. 'For the great mass of the people, hedonics was
a howling success. As a physiological and psychological
discipline, it was a great step forward. But as a practical
science, it was impossible. How many hedonites practiced
it in those terms?'

The Hedonist looked blank.

'Very few,' Beth said soberly. 'Those few tried and of
them only you and one or two others really succeeded. That
is why the Council had to get rid of you. The rest bowed
before the impossibility and compromised with the world.
To be a hedonist, a man would have to be a god – and men
aren't divine. Not yet. At least, not many of them.' She
looked at him with warm, dark eyes.

The Hedonist felt them melt a cold spot deep down inside
him; it had been there for a long time, so long that he had
forgotten all about it. 'So you rescue the malcontents. Before they go to the surgeon?'

'All we can, and we get most of them.'

'And then what?' the Hedonist asked, frowning.

Beth led the way up the few short steps. They came out
into the night. The real night with the stars overhead.

'We bring them here,' she said.

The Hedonist looked up from her shadowed face. Across
the broad field was a towering, pointed shape, reaching up
toward space and freedom. 'The planets!' he said suddenly.
'Mars and Venus.'

'And Callisto and Ganymede,' Beth added. 'We send them
out to be colonists. They make good ones. They can work
out their discontent against their environment instead of
themselves. That's the best therapy for them.

'And that's where we're going.'

Before the Hedonist could recover his breath, a broad-
shouldered man, who towered above the Hedonist like the
ship across the field, had stepped out of the shadows behind

them. The Hedonist looked up at the dark, scowling, bearded face. He had never seen more obvious self-torment. He itched to treat the man. *Devalue*, he longed to say, and *substitute*.

'You got him, did you?' the man said in a rumbling voice.

'Yes, Captain.'

Captain. The association with the ship across the field was obvious.

'You helped us?' the Hedonist asked. 'You're the one I should thank?'

The man nodded gloomily. 'Me and some of the boys.'

'I don't understand how you could take over a fun house so easily—'

The captain shrugged his massive shoulders. 'We own it. We own most of the Strip. We still need things out there' – he waved his hand toward the sky – 'that Earth can give us – men and tools – and for that we need money. So we give the rabbits what they really want, and they give us what we need. Used to shanghai a few colonists out of the place, but we stopped that. They were no good; died off too quick.'

'Didn't the Council object?'

'Fat lot of good that would do.' He chuckled at the idea. 'They know what we could do if we took it in our minds to – and there's nothing those fat rabbits could do to stop us. But we'd better be moving toward the ship. This might be the time the Council will decide to take a chance.'

'They don't do anything about your aiding the escaped prisoners?'

'Why should they? Gets them off their hands, don't it? That's all they want. They're happy to leave us alone. Someday, maybe, we'll decide to come back and do something about the Council. Not now. We're too busy.'

'Come on,' Beth urged.

The Hedonist looked back the way they had come. On the horizon were the dark towers of the Old City, and in front of them was the ghostly radiance of the crater. They seemed like mute fingers trying to warm themselves before a cold, deadly fire. Their silence and pathos overwhelmed him.

'I can't,' he groaned. 'I can't go. I can't leave Earth like this and go seek my own happiness.'

'But you can't help Earth,' she pleaded. 'There's nothing you can do. You have to accept reality.'

The Hedonist was silent. Could he help? Could he overthrow the Council, all by himself? What was reality?

Deep down, he knew that he couldn't do anything. The black spires on the horizon were not fingers but gravestones. No one can raise the dead.

'Earth is happy as it is, I suppose,' he said slowly. 'It's overcrowded. There's no space left for modifying reality. Perhaps the self-discipline of hedonics demands too much. Maybe the only way to keep Earth from blowing apart from its own conflicting desires is the Council's way.'

'I'm afraid it is,' Beth said.

'All right,' the Hedonist said. 'Let's go.' They started walking across the starlit field. 'I suppose you need hedonists on Venus.'

The captain stopped short. 'Wait a minute,' he growled. 'You got the wrong idea. We don't want missionaries. We're too busy to be happy. We've got a million things to do up there. We've got no use for any of your immorality.' He turned viciously toward Beth. 'I thought you said—'

'He'll be all right,' she said frantically. 'I tell you he'll be all right.' She tugged at the Hedonist's arm.

Immorality, Captain? No, not immorality. The first truly moral society since man first began to congregate. The first society in which a man's instinct didn't conflict with the demands of society upon him.

Morality wasn't everything, of course. It was a little like death, the end of struggle and conflict. In that sense life was immoral, an eternal fight against the leveling forces, and the immoral, criminal, lawbreaking part of humanity was out there on the planets and the moons of Jupiter, some day to be lifting an illicit hand toward the stars.

That was all very true, but to give it all up! To surrender all he had labored to learn and practice! It was like dying.

What was it the captain had said? *We're too busy to be happy.* The Hedonist could see the truth of that. Happy men don't make good colonists. To tame a planet, to remold a world, takes hungry men, angry men. They had to be discontented, and they had to stay discontented. Otherwise, the world turned on them and broke them.

Devaluation was no good. Suppression was no good. Substitution was no good. You can't devalue the need for food. You can't suppress the desire for breathable air. You can't substitute for the necessities of shelter against the heat and the cold and the insects and the viruses. . . .

'I suppose,' the Hedonist said, looking up, 'that you could use a doctor. You need obstetricians and geriatricians, I guess. You have people who get sick, who break bones, who have babies, who grow old . . . I imagine the children need teachers. . . .'

A slow, brilliant smile spread across the captain's face. It reminded the Hedonist of the sun suddenly, joyfully breaking through the dark clouds. 'Sure, Doc,' he said. 'Come on. We've got a million things to do and only a few hundred years to do them in.'

So the Hedonist thought, his training would not be entirely wasted. His medical skill would be in great demand, and then there would be the children. There would be lots of children as humanity became prolific to populate a world. He would teach the children the hedonic disciplines without removing the angers that kept them alive. Hedonics wasn't finished, after all. It was only a new, finer beginning.

He took Beth's arm possessively, and they started walking toward the tall ship that would take them, without regret, from a world that, after the bitter ages, was going to be one hundred per cent happy.

A bright star hung just above the pointed nose of the ship. It was not Venus, but it was, perhaps, an omen.

There was a great deal to be said for the privilege of being just as unhappy as a man wanted to be.

Part Three

I

And if any is unhappy, remember that he is for himself; for God made all men to enjoy felicity and peace.
EPICTETUS

D'glas M'Gregor met the Duplicate in the corridor connecting the motor pool and the elevator bank. It would have been easy enough to recognize if D'glas's mind had been properly disengaged from his autonomic nervous system, but he was well past it, frowning darkly, before he whirled to the control panel.

The corridor wall opened at his touch. For a fraction of a second, the indicator light behind it was steady. Then the Duplicate began to move at a speed of 200 kilometers an hour.

D'glas's fingers blurred as they flashed to the controls. The far panel dropped, cutting off the Duplicate from the motor pool and the surface of Venus. Instantly, it reversed directions. It was moving back toward D'glas at the same incredible speed when the second panel dropped.

For a moment the indicator stood still, burning brightly. Then it was off.

D'glas sighed. The trap had failed again. . . .

The rain was falling on Venus in great sheets; fierce gusts of wind hurled drops with bullet force. The rain had been falling for fifty years. It would fall for fifty more before it began to slacken.

By then there would be seas and lakes and ponds where free water had never existed. Cleansed by fire of its deadly ingredients of carbon dioxide and formaldehyde, breathable for the first time with free oxygen, the atmosphere would be completely changed.

And one day the clouds would break up, and the sun would shine down upon a Venus unveiled, a world transformed by Man.

Venus had been stillborn. Almost a twin of Earth, it had been embalmed at birth, shrouded in stifling clouds of formaldehyde and its polymers.

Beneath those miles of plastic clouds, Man found a desert where nothing lived, where nothing could live. The vital ingredients were missing: free water, free oxygen.

The colonists dug deep beneath the surface to escape the vicious thermodynamic forces of the atmosphere, and then they set methodically about the task of changing a world.

Sponge platinum supplied the catalytic action. Venus itself supplied the power. Every lightning bolt released water and fertilizing nitrates upon the land. And Man himself was busy in great, lumbering combines which crawled the desert, chewing up sand and stone and leaving behind, to soak up the rain, soil rich with fertilizers, long-chain proteins, genetically designed micro-organisms, earthworms, and seed.

In spots that grew steadily. Venus began to assume a second veil, a veil that lived, a veil of green. And the grasses and plants and trees took carbon dioxide from the air, bound the carbon into their stalks and trunks and leaves, and released free oxygen to the atmosphere.

It took Man four hundred years to conquer the relatively benign North American continent. In less than half that time he would change Venus's alien, poisonous nature. Already he had tamed her, sweetened her breath, softened her hard bosom. Now he was making her fertile.

In another fifty years she would be as fair as Earth.

Driven raindrops swirled suddenly against the lens above. In the room below, the scene blurred; rain seemed to stream down the repeater window. As it cleared, a long, blinding chain of lightning danced along the horizon.

Perry closed his eyes. 'So near,' he murmured. 'And yet so

far. All right, D'glas, wake up.'

'I'm awake,' D'glas said. 'You've got the story?' He straightened up in the diagnostic chair, rubbing his arm where the hypodermic jet had irritated the skin.

Perry was seventy years old, and his middle-aged face had settled into wise, tolerant lines and creases. But now it was troubled. 'There's no doubt. It was a Duplicate. Guy Reeder, the lay hedonist, was on a combine at the time.'

'That's how I recognized it. I had just left him—'

'We know,' Brian broke in, motioning at the chair with the mouthpiece of his pacifier in a gesture that summed up the whole, subconscious interrogatory. He was a few years younger than Perry and perhaps a few years less patient. He pointed the pacifier at D'glas. 'And in a foul temper you left him. Which is why you were almost too late in recognizing the Duplicate. Boy, you need treatment.'

Besides D'glas, there were three of them in the room. Perry, Brian, and Floyd – as dissimilar as three men can be, but hedonists all. What government there was on Venus existed here. Whatever these men decided in their wisdom, would be the concurrent decision of three million colonists.

Three hedonists, and D'glas. He felt outnumbered and alone.

'I was angry, I admit,' he said grudgingly. 'To me the combine work is boring and unrewarding. And when Guy tried to convince me that this was modification of reality in the hedonic sense, I quit and came back.'

'What could be greater modification?' Floyd asked quietly from the corner, his dark face shadowed and anonymous.

'To apply it here is casuistry,' D'glas flashed back. 'Our work is drudgery, not pleasure.'

'Happiness comes from inside,' Brian said soberly. 'What hedonics gives us is the techniques with which to make necessity a virtue, with which to make the unavoidable a pleasure. "What cannot be cured must be endured, and what must be endured should be enjoyed." '

' "When rape becomes inevitable—" ' D'glas growled. 'I'll quote Morgan to you verse by verse. I know what he brought us from Earth a century ago. But your hedonism is little different from my stoicism. There should be more for Man than grubbing in the dirt.'

'I would like to point out,' Perry said quietly, 'that the decision is not whether we should or should not grub in the dirt, but whether we will be permitted to do so if we wish.'

As quickly as it had come, D'glas's anger ebbed. This was a good society. There had never been a better. A man had a right to do anything he wished, to be anything he wished except unhappy. And society must be conceded the ultimate right to outlaw those emotions which are destructive of the society itself. An unhappy man is a deadly focus of social disintegration.

It was, D'glas thought, a significant comment on this society that in the middle of the most desperate struggle of its existence it could concern itself with the hedonic condition of a single citizen.

'We have assumed,' Perry continued, 'that the Duplicates were a threat. The threat has become imminent. If we learn anything from this incident, it is this: the Duplicates are telepathic. Let's re-examine the film.'

Perry pressed the side of the window frame. Within it, the surface of Venus vanished, replaced by a dim corridor. A man was walking away from them. As they watched him, the man, without a backward glance, began to run.

'You had just opened the control panel,' Perry said.

The Duplicate did not begin clumsily, as men do, building up momentum. It started at high speed, its legs churning like pistons, blurring even on the high-speed film. Ahead, a panel fell, closing the end of the corridor.

Without hesitation the Duplicate jumped, landing with both feet against the panel, absorbing momentum with bending knees. When they snapped back, they propelled the Duplicate back the way it had come, its legs flashing before they touched the floor. Now they could see its face.

It was the Duplicate of Guy Reeder.

The second panel dropped, completing the fourth wall of the cell. The camera shifted. They were inside the cell with the Duplicate. For an instant it stood frozen. The next moment the only trace of it was a cloud of disintegrating particles.

'That,' Perry sighed, 'was taken at a speed of one million frames a second.'

'Same spectroscopic analysis?'

'Exactly,' Floyd said quietly. 'It is not human. There is, generally, a higher percentage of metal in the Duplicate.'

Perry returned the window to its view of the rain-swept plains of Venus. 'The first one was reported two days ago – almost five hundred hours. This is the fifth one. We have trapped two. Both instantly blew themselves into their constituent atoms. There must be others among us which have not been detected.'

Brian removed the pacifier from his mouth. 'Too soon. We are not ready for contact with aliens.'

'Aliens? You're sure?' D'glas asked quickly.

Brian shrugged. 'Their abilities aren't human.'

'The percentage of metal suggests that they are mechs,' Floyd added. 'And the self-destruction, too. There may be alien races which can blow themselves to pieces at will, but I doubt it.'

'A humanoid mech?' D'glas said, puzzled. 'Why?'

'To pass among us unsuspected,' Perry said.

'What for? They haven't done anything.'

'So far. Perhaps. In our society it is difficult to know when changes occur. At this moment we are under observation.'

Brian and Floyd nodded.

'What the next stage will be,' Perry went on calmly, 'is impossible to guess, but it will not be favorable to a continuation of our society and of our way of life.'

Again the hedonists nodded.

'What are we going to do, then?' D'glas demanded, his dark, young face scowling.

'The first thing,' Perry said, without changing inflection, 'is to make certain we all are human.'

While he was speaking, the partitions were falling. Hedonic reflexes brought D'glas out of the diagnostic chair without hesitation, but it was too late. Already he was locked into a small metal room. It vibrated briefly.

Before he could sit down again, the partitions rose silently. Perry and Brian were looking at the corner where Floyd had been sitting. It was empty. The chair had disappeared. So had the rubberized flooring down to the steel beneath. The wall was scorched and black.

'They are determined,' Perry said grimly, 'that we shall not examine one. . . .'

Brian sucked on the pacifier reflectively before he removed it. 'Did you expect this?'

'No,' Perry admitted. 'It was a precaution. To be truthful, I suspected you, Brian, if anyone. Your dependence on that pacifier seemed a little excessive.'

'It's a small crutch which seems to be emotionally helpful in these troubled times,' Brian said calmly. 'In more plentiful times, I think I would have smoked tobacco in a pipe.'

'And are the rest of us human?' D'glas asked.

'That's what the X rays indicate.'

Brian got up lazily. 'You don't mind if I check on you, do you, Perry?'

Perry smiled ruefully. 'Not at all.' He made room for Brian behind the desk. 'It is unfortunate that Floyd's Duplicate didn't give us time to get a picture of its insides. But how can you trap a telepath?'

Brian studied the desk top, nodded, and moved back to his chair. 'What about Floyd?'

'He's on his way here now – not that there's much we can do.'

'Are we going to let them roam among us at will?' D'glas demanded. 'Who knows what they may be planning?'

'Exactly,' Brian said. 'And so we cannot weigh the risk of preparing for it. Perhaps we could set up X-ray equipment in deserted corridors – deserted, of course, because the threat implicit is not yet dangerous enough to risk the death or injury of the general citizen.'

'Beyond that,' Perry said soberly, 'we cannot go without losing that freedom of action and choice which is an integral part of our society. When the measures for the preservation of our society must, in themselves, destroy it, we must choose inaction.'

Brian agreed gravely. 'Wait and see. I am confident that hedonics can meet the test without additional preparation.'

'Then we are going to do nothing?' D'glas exclaimed impatiently.

'As a group, yes,' Perry said, unmoved. 'As individuals, no. Each of us must act as his intellect and desires direct. That is the basis for our society, and it must so remain. But it would be desirable to warn the other colonies of our danger and ask their advice and help.'

'We haven't heard from Ganymede and Callisto for a hundred years, from Mars for seventy-five,' D'glas pointed out. 'If they were going concerns, they would have contacted us by now.'

'Have we contacted them?' Brian asked quietly. 'Their job was more difficult than ours. We had only to change our atmosphere; they had to manufacture theirs. And yet even our society has been lean; we've had no fat for interplanetary jaunts.'

'It was hedonics that brought us through,' Perry added. 'And we got hedonics only by accident. The original colonies had little use for such frivolities; it was equated with the over-sensualism and overstimulation the colonists fled from. Morgan himself, who did so much to make applied hedonics a true science and then saw it perverted beyond control, came to Venus as a physician and teacher, not a hedonist. There are not many men like Morgan. Perhaps the other colonies were not so lucky.'

'And perhaps the aliens conquered them first,' D'glas said gloomily. 'What about Earth?'

'Earth, too,' Brian said, 'although the case is not quite the same. Earth was never lean, and yet we lost touch with Earth fifty years ago. She may be conquered. She may need help. It may even be possible that she can help us. I think some of us must make the effort.'

'We have scavenged parts enough for four complete ships,'

Perry said, 'One for each colony and one for Earth. After that there is no more, and it is questionable whether any of these will reach their destinations safely. But I think there will be volunteers.'

'The Earth flight,' D'glas heard himself saying. 'I'll take it.'

'Very well,' Perry accepted gravely. 'I wish you luck and happiness – for yourself and us.'

D'glas didn't answer. He was stunned by what he had done. This is what the hedonist had wanted. Skillfully, they had worked him into risking himself on a wild and unpromising errand. Now it was too late to back out.

And yet, he felt a warm backlash of emotional release. For the first time he really understood the meaning of the word 'voluntary'. The job was there to be done. It should be done. Someone had to do it. He, D'glas M'Gregor, who was not happy to grub in the dirt, was the logical choice.

The result was pleasure. It was the hedonic reflex.

'Can you fly the ship?' Brian asked softly.

'I think so,' D'glas said confidently. 'I've done more complicated things in the exercises.'

That was true. The hedonic training program developed muscular, sensory, and nervous discrimination and coordination side by side with mental agility and the all-important psychological control. It was complete.

'Good,' Perry said. 'You can start tomorrow. We have absolutely no time.'

'Less than that,' Floyd said from the doorway.

It was the real Floyd this time. Perry confirmed it by a glance at his desk.

'We're beginning to lose people,' Floyd said quietly. 'An accurate count is impossible in our society, but by my estimate more than one thousand persons have disappeared in the last two days.'

'Where have they gone?' exclaimed D'glas.

Floyd shrugged. 'Venus is a big world, and three million people don't make much impression on it. My guess is that the missing people are in the ships that brought the aliens – hidden underground, perhaps, in the boiling tropics. What worries me: have their places been taken by things that aren't human?'

II

O happiness! our being's end and aim!
Good pleasure, ease, content! whate'er thy name.
That something still which prompts the eternal sigh,
For which we bear to live, or dare to die.

ALEXANDER POPE

It was a rocky landing, but a good one. Any landing a man can walk away from is a good one. D'glas walked away from this one.

The ship was not irreparably damaged. New first and second stages, another load of fuel, and he might even be able to nurse it back to Venus.

He didn't worry about it. Ships stood tall all over the vast landing field, rusty missiles reaching high, aimed at the cloudless sky above. They hadn't flown for many years, but among them all there must be parts and equipment good for one more ship.

More important, he didn't want to consider the return trip. Not yet. The memory of the long, lonely voyage from Venus was still too fresh. Only his hedonic training had saved him from madness.

Now he stood with his two feet on the Earth and shivered. Earth was a mother no more.

Weight was on him again, feeling heavy and strange after the long weightlessness of the trip, and the air smelled flat and tasteless without the omnipresent odor of formaldehyde, and he was trapped between the concrete-covered soil and the naked sky, blue-clear and blazing.

It was horrible. It triggered subconscious and unsuspected reactions. He was afraid.

Ancient names that had almost passed out of the language of the Venusian colonists returned to him: agoraphobia, photophobia— He was exposed pitilessly upon a great plain; a giant eye stared down at him accusingly, watching, condemning. If he moved incautiously he might fall into the transparent blueness above, fall off the surface of the world into the terrible sky—

It was five minutes before he stopped shivering and the perspiration dried on his body. It took the hedonic exercises that long to re-emphasize the unity of mind and body, to damp the feedback of mind to senses. It took that long for the mind to accept the testimony of the senses and construct logical patterns out of it.

No clouds. That explained the blue emptiness above. That burning eye was the sun. The only direction he could fall was down.

D'glas turned to an inspection of the field. It was deserted. More than that, abandoned. The concrete was cracked and uneven. Grass grew in long, green traceries. A nearby sapling was taller than D'glas. It had already begun the mighty destruction it would complete in maturity.

The warehouses and control towers that lined the city-side of the field had been built to endure, no doubt, but they were showing signs of long neglect. Their sides were stained, their windows broken. One had lost a wall; its roof leaned precariously over the void.

Over everything was a sensation of solitude, like an almost intangible brush of cobwebs across the face. There was no movement, anywhere. There was no one to move.

D'glas studied the field through narrowed eyes, but he could decipher no meaning from it. Not yet, The mystery was still as great as why the ships had suddenly stopped coming fifty years ago.

The landing field had belonged to the colonies. The whole interplanetary enterprise had been theirs. The Hedonic Council, Earth's ruling body, had been content to leave it so, seeing no useful purpose in risking its concept of hedonism in a risky attempt to bring the colonists under control.

And to the Council's mind, no doubt, the colonies had served a useful purpose as places to which those few criminal masochists who rejected the ultimate sensual pleasure might exile themselves.

That was what Morgan had written in his book *The Rise and Fall of Applied Hedonics*.

What had happened, then, to the colonists who had worked the ships and run the field and operated the strip beyond?

D'glas frowned and went through the rusting ships nearby. When he emerged from the last of them, his frown was deeper.

Three of them had been unidentifiable. Of the remaining four, one was from Callisto, one from Ganymede, and two from Mars. Why they had come, why they had not left again, and what had happened to the crews were questions the ships did not answer.

D'glas turned toward the distant spires of the City. They rose like supplicating hands against the horizon, and he wished he were a complete hedonist. Perhaps then he could banish the tight, cold feeling of uneasiness that straightened his shoulders and stiffened his spine.

But he wasn't. He couldn't. He would have to live with it until he could answer the questions the silent City proposed.

It waited for him, motionless, deadly. . . .

Cautiously, he moved through the semidarkness of the building called Fun House, his senses alert. But there was nothing to set them off. No movement, no change, no sound.

Glass-doored booths lined both sides of the big room. They were empty. They were clean, too, dusted and scrubbed, the floors, the tables, the long, soft benches that were as wide as beds.

Idly he touched one of the dispensers that lined the wall above the table. White powder dusted from it and powdered the table top. He picked up a few grains on the tip of his finger and tasted them gingerly. They were sweet with an edge of bitterness. He studied the labels on the dispensers:

NEO-HEROIN POWDER
NEO-HEROIN SYRETTE
SCOTCH BOURBON GIN KAFI

He touched the last one: a hot drop of liquid fell onto his palm. He tasted it. It was bitter. Coffee, all right. Not good coffee, but coffee.

It was a puzzle. As far as his investigation had taken him, the strip was deserted. He had seen no signs of habitation, no activity, since he had entered the building through the underpass.

There was no one in this place. And yet it was ready for customers who might find here their definition of fun. It was clean. Dispensers were full. If he had coins to slip into the indicated slots, he could have had coffee or one of the other drinks listed.

It was all ready. Where was everybody?

He turned toward the rear of the room. From the outside this had looked like a multi-storied building. Even if all the levels were as tall as this one, there should be five more above. But he had found no way to reach them.

Then he found it. Where, logically, stairs should have started, where banks of elevators should have waited, there was a wall. Bolted in the middle of it was a metal plaque in archaic but decipherable printing:

> DO NOT DISTURB
> All Rooms Occupied
> Sealed this day: 3-7-05
> by order of the Council

D'glas puzzled over it. Occupied by what? Goods? People? Bodies?

All choices seemed improbable. He rapped on the plastic with his knuckles. It was solid and thick. Too solid and too thick to struggle with now. That mystery would have to wait.

As he approached the front of the building, doors swung open eerily. So all-pervasive had been the atmosphere of desertion, he almost jumped. Photosensitive relays and automatic motors, he told himself.

Beyond the entrance was a kind of arcade lined with

machines. He studied them a moment. There were slots in them, obviously meant for coins. There were chutes from which something – possibly coins again – were returned. There they ceased to resemble each other. Some of the machines had handles, some levers, some no apparent means of control.

They were means, he decided, by which a person could wager coins against odds implicit in the machines or in the difficulties of controlling the gambler's own sensory or muscular system.

Coins, their use almost forgotten on Venus, seemed like very handy things to have on Earth. If he had a few, he might even return to that tap inside marked Kafi, whose dispensation, foul as it was, was still loaded with caffein.

But wistful glances were a waste of time. He turned one of the machines around. Within five minutes he had solved the mystery of the rudimentary lock and picked it with the slender piece of wire which had kept half of his shirt-front neat and straight. Inside the machine, in a little box, were two lonely coins.

He juggled them thoughtfully in his hand, weighing the convenience of the coins against the effort necessary to obtain them, and turned to a second machine. Two coins were little better than none, but it wasn't necessary to spend time extracting them from the coin boxes. He had a stake.

In the second machine, steel balls, released simultaneously from right- and left-hand chutes, spiraled downward through mazes fraught with perils – holes through which they could drop and be lost. Electro-magnets controlled by the player could guide the balls to safety and the jackpot at the bottom.

D'glas hit the jackpot with the first coin. Within ten minutes, he had milked every machine on that side of the arcade. None had many coins, but most had a few. As he turned away, he had a jacket pocket full of coins.

The games had been easy. Too easy. A ten-year-old child on Venus was expected to perform more difficult feats in his hedonic exercises.

Perhaps, he thought, they served as a come-on for the Fun House.

Thinking of the fun house made him thirsty. He could suppress it, but there was no need now that he had coins.

The transparent doors opened to welcome him back. As they closed behind him, the lights went out.

The darkness was total. Suddenly, frighteningly, he was back in the coasting spaceship, feeling again that terrible, weightless disorientation—

Then his hedonic reflexes acted, damped the false sensory impressions, calmed his baseless fears. He knew, theoretically, what caused the darkness. An interrupter was canceling the light that should have reached him with waves 180° out of phase.

The darkness chuckled, snickered, giggled, tittered, guffawed, roared—

Suddenly, where only darkness had been, there was a fantastic figure standing in front of him – a creature who was goat from his wicked little hooves up to the waist, and man from the waist up to his curly hair. Out of the dark hair, like twin reminders, peeked sharp little horns.

'Be happy, be joyful, be gay!' bubbled the satyr. 'Life begins at the Fun House of the Three Worlds, where every pleasure known to man has been brought to ecstatic perfection. What stimulation do your senses lack? Name it – and it's yours.'

Stunned, his senses shocked, his body temporarily out of control, D'glas staggered back. Abruptly, the satyr disappeared, the laughter cut off in mid peal. Light returned, and D'glas realized that the darkness, the satyr, and the laughter had been only a recording, a welcome to the entering customer.

Where were the customers?

D'glas turned and walked quickly out of the arcade into the street beyond. He could explain the darkness inside the fun-house entrance; he could explain the laughter and the satyr. But he had an unreasonable reluctance to press through the darkness and the laughter, to brush past the satyr, to reach a fun house from which the fun had disappeared.

The naked sky had shaken him not long ago, but now it seemed preferable to the unnatural silence of a place that once had rocked with merriment. It was a place of strange echoes and unpleasant stillnesses.

He put it out of his mind. In front of him was a shop whose front wall was a single, broad sheet of glass. Across it was printed the word : FOODOMAT.

He walked along the front, looking for an entrance, and for a few steps he had a companion in the glass – a tall, lean, lonely young man gliding through a silent city.

A thin vertical line appeared in the glass, widened, became a door. D'glas hesitated in front of it, realized his hunger, and went in.

The floor was immaculate; the tables and benches were spotless. Glowing, plastic railings guided him to the right. As he approached the side wall, delicate food odors stimulated involuntary flows of saliva into his mouth.

Set into the wall were plastic, full-color solidographs of prepared foods, some familiar, others strange. Below were names and coin slots. D'glas studied them :

CHLORELLA
Bread Loaf (hi-fat) Patty (lo-fat)
(Choose sauce below)

D'glas knew what chlorella was – a multipurpose omnifood on Venus. An alga whose fat and protein content could be adjusted to fit almost any requirement, it could be grown in vast quantities wherever sunlight (or its equivalent), carbon dioxide, water, and mineral salts were available. On Venus, it was grown in polyethelene tubing, nourished partially on recirculated human wastes; it not only fed the colonists, it renewed the oxygen supply.

Another food was strange.

PLANKTON
Cakes　　　Steak
Rare　　Medium　　Well done
(Choose sauce below)

Beyond were the synthetics: food fats from glycerin and petroleum, starches from the action of sunlight upon carbon monoxide, the amino acid proteins. D'glas knew these well.

He picked chlorella loaf, without sauce, and water. Chlorella was chlorella – there wasn't much anybody could do to it. Synthetics and sauces, on the other hand, were good things to steer clear of in a strange cuisine.

They always depended on the acquired tastes of the chemist and the cook.

The counter that ran along the wall opened up. The foods came through – the chlorella hot, the water cold. The dish and glass slid along the counter and waited for D'glas at the far end.

He carried them to the nearest table and tasted them gingerly. The water was pure within a fraction of one percent. The loaf was a good strain of chlorella ruined by poor seasoning; almost a teaspoon of salt and a dash of a sharp, unfamiliar condiment.

He ate quickly.

Satisfied but not sated, he stood up and walked toward the front of the large room. The glass opened for him, but he stopped, turned, and looked back. The empty dish and glass marred the neatness of the place. He restrained an irrational impulse to go back and remove them.

Who would care?

And who, he wondered, would come out when he was gone, to clear off the table and polish its top, to ready the restaurant for its next patron?

He suppressed a desire to call out, in the fashion of the childhood games played in the corridors and storerooms of the underground city called Morgantown. 'Come out, come out, wherever you are!'

He shivered and went out into the warm, clear air, thinking that this life lived out-of-doors, without mask or clouds or the endless rain, would take a long time to get used to.

The utter silence was oppressive. He stopped in the middle of the street, uncertain where to go next. The tallest building in sight had a sign that was even taller. MARS HOUSE.

D'glas walked quickly toward the red canopy. As he came under it, the walk moved beneath his feet. It was a slideway; it carried him to the portal and into the lobby.

As he stepped off, his feet gritted in red sand.

Overhead, invisibly suspended, was a sun looking oddly small.

The sun might look like that when viewed from Mars.

The back wall was curved and shiny like the outer hull of a spaceship. The elevator installed against it was in an openwork frame, a replica of the portable models he had seen on the landing field.

'Joy!' said a voice at his elbow. 'There are rooms available. May I help you?'

D'glas controlled an involuntary start and turned. He was standing beside a short desk. Above it was a mech consisting of two scanners and a speaker. One scanner studied the desk; the other, and the speaker, were pointed at D'glas. 'I am the desk clerk,' said the speaker. 'How may I be of service?'

'What rooms are available?' D'glas asked slowly and distinctly.

'Only the second and third floors, sir. The other thirty floors are filled. The rooms we have left, however, are fully equipped for temporary or permanent residence. Just slip your IDisk beneath my scanner—'

'What do you mean – permanent residence?' D'glas interrupted, at the risk of jamming the mech beyond usefulness.

'Ah, there you are, M'Gregor!' a strange voice broke in. 'We've been looking for you.'

D'glas spun around.

Close behind him, a smile on his craggy face, was a man D'glas had never seen before.

III

> *That action is best which procures the greatest*
> *happiness for the greatest numbers.*
>
> FRANCIS HUTCHESON

'Sorry to startle you,' said the stranger with an engaging grin. 'To tell the truth, we couldn't resist seeing your reaction to someone's voice when you thought you were in a deserted city.'

It was a likable demonstration of humanity, but it brought up more questions than it answered. 'Who is "we"?' D'glas asked evenly.

The stranger grimaced. 'Sorry again. That's the royal "we", I'm afraid. The name is Hansen.' He stuck out a strong, square hand, its back furry with curly, blond hair.

D'glas took it. It felt hard, warm, and dry. 'How did you know what I thought?' he asked, studying Hansen. He was as tall as D'glas and broader across the shoulders. He seemed about ten years older.

Hansen's eyebrows, almost white against his tanned face, moved expressively. 'Rather obvious,' he said easily. 'Not much else a man can think about the City. Because it's almost true.'

D'glas hesitated. There were so many questions to ask that he had difficulty choosing the next. And Hansen's answers were peculiarly unsatisfactory.

'Look!' Hansen said apologetically. 'You want to know a mess of things – what's happened to the City, how I happen to know your name, where everybody is, and so on. Let's mosey over to the Council building, where we can be comfortable, and the Council will tell you everything you want to know. Okay?'

'It's not okay,' D'glas said dryly, 'but I guess it will have to do.'

'Cigarette?' Hansen extended a metal case filled with

stuffed paper cylinders. 'But no – you wouldn't have picked up the habit on Venus, would you? No oxygen to spare, right? These, though, are rather special – a blend of synthetic alkaloids that supply a wonderful lift without danger of lung irritation. Don't want to short the lifespan with carcinogens, eh? Habit-forming as neo-heroin, though.' He put one between his lips and sucked on it. The tip glowed and began to burn; smoke curled from his nose. 'Shall we go?'

'Just a moment. I was about to get a straightforward answer to a straightforward question from this mech.'

'Touché!' Hansen laughed. 'But that's a simple mech. I'm afraid the answer you get will be just as unsatisfying.'

'What do you mean by permanent residence?' D'glas repeated.

'Permanent residence,' said the clerk mechanically, 'is permanent residence.'

Hansen slapped D'glas on the shoulders. 'See? This mech was built to accept registrations, not to explain itself. That's something even we would have difficulty with, eh?'

'Perhaps,' D'glas admitted.

As Hansen stepped onto the slideway, it reversed itself and carried him toward the street.

Watchfully, D'glas followed.

'This way,' Hansen said cheerfully. He walked to the nearest corner, turned, and started down broad, worn marble steps under glowing letters that said: J.R.T. DOWN-TOWN.

Hansen dropped coins into a turnstile and pushed through.

'You still pay?' D'glas asked when he had rejoined him.

'Absolutely. Be immoral not to, eh? Can't let standards slip when society is depending on you.' He hopped onto an escalator that took them down to a broad platform bordered by slideways. 'This way,' he said gayly, hopping nimbly to the left.

D'glas followed, feeling more at home underground, fighting a delusion of safety.

The slideway paralleled an endless parade of small, two-passenger, moving cars with one seat facing the front. Hansen stepped into one. D'glas sat down beside him.

'Everything still works,' D'glas said. 'Food ready, drinks on tap, transportation system running. Everything ready. And nobody to—'

'Yeah,' Hansen agreed, cocking a pale eyebrow. 'Pitiful, isn't it? Faithful old automaton keeping things all ready for the masters who have gone away. Old Mech Tray; that sort of thing.'

'Or as if someone had gone off and left the water running,' D'glas suggested.

'That, too. Better fasten your safety belt.'

Hansen was already strapping himself down. Glancing once at the smooth, glowing tunnel walls, D'glas shrugged and tightened the belt across his legs. The cars were moving at the less-than-dangerous speed of 100 kilometers an hour. Being linked together, they could move no faster unless the whole, endless chain speeded up.

'Drink?' Hansen asked, indicating the dispensers lining the front of the car. 'All the ethyloids. Synthetic, of course, but then, what isn't? Or maybe you'd like a shot of neoheroin. That would bring the world into focus.'

'Thanks,' D'glas said dryly. 'I prefer my own focus. Your comments seem to agree with my assumption that there are no more people around.'

'That's right,' Hansen agreed. 'They do, don't they? But that isn't quite accurate. They're around – just not *around*. If you know what I mean.'

D'glas resisted an urge to smash Hansen's amused smile down his irritating throat. 'And everything continues automatically, is that it?'

'Right. It follows, doesn't it? Labor is unpleasant. Unpleasure is illegal. Labor is illegal. *Q.E.D.* Therefore, everything is automatic.'

D'glas nodded slowly. The advantages were obvious, the disadvantages not so readily apparent. At the sacrifice of immediate progress, the colonists could mechanize Morgantown and the other settlements, could equip the combines with automatic pilots. And then— He considered the prospect. What then?

'And then,' Hansen continued with inexorable logic, 'everyone can devote himself to pleasure – which is, after all, the only good, eh? And the millennium is at hand – pure hedonism. Let joy reign unconfined! And speaking of joy, boy, hold your hat. Here we go again!'

From the brilliance of the glowing tunnel walls, the car dived unexpectedly into the darkness of an interrupter. *Dived* was the proper word. D'glas felt himself rise from his seat as the car plunged downward; then he was slammed down hard as the car hit bottom and straightened out. Or perhaps it started upward again. Everything was happening so fast that D'glas's perceptions became confused.

Perched on the front of the car, talons disappearing into the hard metal, was an alien horror fluorescing greenly. From the waist up, it was woman – except for the wings, and they belonged with the feathered half, below.

It opened green lips. 'Welcome, mortal,' it drawled. 'You've kept me waiting long enough!'

'Don't mind her,' whispered a voice in D'glas's right ear, the one away from Hansen. 'She's always impatient. She's a harpy, you know.'

Before D'glas could turn his head to see who was whispering, a second winged thing appeared beside the harpy. This one was purple, also female, with snaky hair that weaved as if it had a life of its own. If possible, her face was more horrid than the harpy's.

'Move on, sister,' it snarled to the harpy in a deep voice. 'He's mine. After all, he has sinned.'

'Haven't we all?' snapped the harpy. 'You can have him when I get through, dearie. You've been satisfied with my leavings before.'

'The purple one's a Fury,' the voice whispered in his ear. 'Don't pay any attention to them. They're mad. They're women, you know.'

Out of the darkness in front, the blue, three-headed dog

sprang between the woman-things, its serpent tail lashing, its three jaws agape and dripping. It sprang straight for D'glas's throat.

'Don't flinch,' the voice whispered hurriedly. 'They can't hurt you. They aren't in your cultural heritage at all.'

Cerberus, the dog, hurtled through D'glas's body and disappeared. He was braced for the impact and felt foolish when there was none.

It was illusion, D'glas knew – but real enough. Too real. He did not like the implications at all.

This time he would look at the thing that whispered on his shoulder, he decided, but something stopped him again. The harpy and the Fury had disappeared. In their place was a horned, tailed creature attired in livid, red scales; in one hand he carried a pitchfork, in the other, casually, his spiked tail.

'Well, M'Gregor,' he rolled out with great sophistication and an urbane, man-to-man smile, 'we meet at last. I'll bet you thought you'd ditched me for good back there in the Middle Ages. But there's no escaping the consciousness of sin, is there? Of course not. I've always considered myself the kind of creature who, if he had not existed, would have had to have been invented.

'Where there is sin, there is hell, whether we put it off to the Hereafter or make it now ourselves. To know sin is to feel guilt, or to feel guilt is to be punished. The only limiting factor on the punishment is the limits of our own imaginations. I'm sure we can agree on these things, eh? Come, little ones, let us show our friend what we are talking about.'

They swarmed over the front of the car, the little demons, wielding spears, pitchforks, swords, knives, needles, stabbers of all kinds. Pain started in D'glas's foot, traveled up his calf, tormented his thigh, reached his hips, climbed to his abdomen, reached for his heart—

The car plunged into a red inferno, a pit of molten lava. Heat poured over the car, over D'glas, fantastically intolerably. D'glas lifted from his seat as the car dived straight into the middle of it.

'Mephistopheles, eh?' the voice chuckled in his ear. 'Anachronous psychiatry is what I call it. Freud with hell-fire.'

The scaly thing and its spawn were gone. In the car ahead was an impossibly ugly crone, almost toothless, dressed in filthy rags. She was stirring a pot and dropping indescribable substances into it; nameless things swooped around her head. She looked up, saw D'glas, and cackled.

'A handsome lad. I knew you'd come. He promised me. A young man, strong in the loins, He said, just for me. Oh, we'll be happy together, we two, like a pair of doves. We'll do our devotions together – the kind He likes. When the Coven meets, why we'll be there to share the fun, and you'll be my partner in the orgy. Oh, we'll worship the Goat, we will.' She cackled again. 'All will be afeard of us and pay us tribute, night or day, for the things that we might do: the curse, the evil, the witch's brew. Oh, we'll have fun, lovely, you and I.'

The dark, nameless things circled closer to D'glas's head. He could not control a shudder.

The crone squinted one eye knowingly. 'I don't look too pretty now, but wait till you've sampled what's in my kettle. Then you'll see me with different eyes. To you I'll be young again, straight-bodied, firm-fleshed, and curved like a girl should be. You'll love me then, my boy. You'll never leave my side; you'll never get enough of touching me.'

She lifted a spoon out of the pot and tasted the brew gingerly, one eye squinting judiciously. Lips smacking, she nodded her approval and dipped in the spoon again. This time she held it high with a bony hand and put one leg over the car which held Hansen and D'glas.

'Now it's your turn, lad,' she crooned. 'Open your ruby lips, lovey, and soon the world will be a different place for you and me – a place of light in the darkness and darkness in the light. Come now, lad!' She had both legs over. She was close, the spoon dripping. 'Open up!'

D'glas didn't move.

'That's right,' the voice whispered approvingly in his ear. 'Not your dish at all.'

The spoon passed through D'glas's face, and the crone disappeared, her face twisted with disappointment.

'I'm your dish,' the thing on his shoulder whispered. 'Or maybe you're my dish. It doesn't matter really. We were meant for each other.'

This time D'glas got his head turned. Sitting on his right shoulder was an inky blob. It was nothingness personified. It was unconsciousness. It was surrender. It was the merging of the individual will into the collective will, the betrayal of all personal standards, the collectivization of the psyche.

It was everything D'glas hated. It was the reverse side of the hedonic coin, the sin to match hedonism's virtue, the hell to balance its heaven.

Only these were words, and words are meaningless in anything except a personal sense. In all heavens there is the germ of hell; in all hells, of heaven.

The blob opened bright, blue eyes and a pink mouth. 'There, now,' it whispered. 'Aren't you glad you waited?'

It melted toward him, blurring, filtering through the skin and bones into his skull in an unholy symbiosis. Mutely, D'glas struggled against the intolerable invasion.

Light burst into the darkness, shattered it, sent it fleeing. For a moment D'glas was blind. Then sight returned.

The car was poised on an incredible summit. The sun blazed down on them. The spires of tall buildings were so far below they looked like spikes waiting to impale them. Thousands of meters in the air, they hung between sky and earth, exposed to the perils of each.

In spite of his training, D'glas's heart thundered in his chest.

The car just ahead toppled over the peak, pulling D'glas's car to the edge. It hesitated on the brink of a precipice.

The car dropped, fell, dived, plunged, plummeted. It was worse than the weightlessness that followed the cut-out of the rocket drive on the trip from Venus. They screamed down the side of the cliff into the endless depths below, waiting for them, dark and shadowed.

D'glas gripped the side of the car with desperate hands, feeling himself lifted from his seat, flung outward. It went on and on, the spires of the buildings rising to meet them, flashing past, the windows blurred on either side. And finally came the sickening onset of weight again as the car hit bottom and leveled off in the glowing tunnel once more and rolled peacefully forward as if there had been nothing really to be frightened of.

Hansen was standing. 'Here we are,' he said cheerily. 'Coming?'

He hopped onto the slideway that ran beside the car. For a moment D'glas hesitated. Taking a deep breath, he unsnapped his safety belt and joined Hansen as he moved from highspeed to lowspeed and then to a platform that was motionless.

Ahead was an escalator that took them to the foot of stairs that mounted into the open air. Hansen paused to let D'glas catch up. He grinned. 'Like the joy ride?'

'Joy ride?' D'glas echoed grimly. 'That's what you call it?'

'Some people like to be frightened, you know. It gives them the sense of being alive, stimulates their adrenals, tones up their whole system. Mostly they aren't – alive, that is. Not in any meaningful sense. They exist at a minimum level. If they can achieve the exhilaration of danger while clinging to a subconscious realization that they are completely protected, they have gained worlds without expense.'

'Thanks. I'll stimulate my own adrenals,' D'glas said dryly. 'When anyone wanted to go anywhere else in the city, he had to go through that?'

'Oh, no. That would scarcely be hedonism, would it? When this City was really humming, there were helijets and surface cars and buses until the sky and streets were black. And less eventful subways.' Hansen smiled broadly.

'But, as you reminded me, that was all in the past. All things considered, it was an inefficient, wasteful method of procuring a really simple result: pleasure. And so it is only a relic.'

'And yet, like everything else, it keeps running?'

'Necessarily.' Hansen winked. 'You noticed the apparitions, I imagine. Symbols, all, as you realized. Sort of a basic subconscious-to-subconscious hookup, eh? Well, I won't bore you with an interpretation which would, necessarily, be faulty. But did you notice that they were all personifications of sin and its psychological concomitant, guilt?'

D'glas was silent. He studied the blank-eyed buildings on either side of the darkening, twilit canyons through which they walked; the spires were gravestones in a vast necropolis, the burial ground of man's hopes of conquest and dreams of peace. They hid, as well, a mystery within them or beneath them: *how? why?* It was a mystery he had to solve, for in it lay the answer to a basic question about mankind and its future.

Wherever he was, on Earth or Venus, on Mars or Ganymede or Callisto, whatever refinements were grafted upon him, man was man, prey to the same fears, nurse to the same hopes and dreams.

Ahead, like sunlight breaking through the banks of clouds to spotlight an unexpected realization, a sudden truth, an opening in the canyon wall let in brightness and a promise of something new and vital.

'You did, of course,' Hansen continued without waiting for an answer. 'You are a thoughtful, perceptive person. Sin and guilt. You would think that they would be outlawed from a hedonic world. In a sense, you would be right. Yet you would be overlooking something – the pleasures of the illicit, for without prohibition there is no pleasure; there is only contentment and the satisfaction of minor animal desires. Without hell, there is no heaven.

'And, to provide the ultimate in criminal thrill, there was

that most illicit of all sensations – pain. For without pain, there is no ecstasy; there is only insensibility.'

'I am not concerned with ecstasy,' D'glas said sharply. 'Where are we going?'

'As I told you : to the Council!'

'Where all my questions will be answered,' D'glas finished, dryly. 'That's fine. But where is the Council?'

'Ahead. Don't be impatient. That is unpleasure, and un-pleasure is a crime.'

'Then there is no pleasure. Riddle me no more paradoxes, Hansen,' D'glas said firmly. 'Point it out!'

Hansen pointed a blunt forefinger. 'There. The tallest building of that group. There is the Council.'

The building was like orange flame against opaque blue-ness, reflecting the setting sun. It was walled in metal, a flame flattened at the top. It was perhaps four blocks away and one over. There were taller buildings in other areas but none as spectacular.

D'glas didn't like the looks of it.

The canyon walls had broken around them. To the right a wide, paved walk cut through green lawn toward a low, massive building. The grass made D'glas feel warm again. It was the first real *life* he had seen since landing. Someone had taken care of it, mowed it, tended it, kept it green. Not a mech, because there were imperfections – a bareness here and there, a clump of grass uneven.

It reminded him of Venus. Only here the process had been reversed : Man had been busy turning fertile soil into a vast, stony desert.

The building was decaying. Much of the façade had fallen; it lay in heaps of rubble along the steps and across the entranceway. Only this building and the landing field had not been kept in repair.

'What is the Council?' he asked.

'The Council?' Hansen began. 'Why, the Council—'

Seconds before, D'glas had seen the flicker of movement beside the building. Now he heard the stone whistle through the air; it struck with a hollow, thumping sound.

Hansen collapsed slowly, his head laid open to the split metal beneath. Inside his skull, tiny wires glistened.

The thing hit the pavement and lay still.

IV

So act as to treat humanity, whether in your own person or in another, always as an end, and never as only a means.

IMMANUEL KANT

D'glas spun back toward the building, suppressing his irritation. The Hansen-mech was out of commission, at least temporarily. He had to decide, and quickly, whether his best opportunity lay here on the pavement or waited there beside the building.

He might discover something from a dissection of the mech, but the chances were against it. Someone was standing on a heap of rubble, tiptoeing tall to see what lay on the pavement beside him, and his decision was made.

The stone-thrower was a girl.

He sprinted toward the building. As he ran, he analysed her. Her position on the rubble made her seem taller than she was. She was less than two meters tall, a small, slender, dark-haired girl with an oval face and blue eyes that widened now as they saw how swiftly he was approaching.

She stood for a moment, poised, her right hand ready to throw the rock it held, and then she turned, leaping from the mound, and ran swiftly around the corner of the building. D'glas raced after her.

He was just in time to see her dive through a small side doorway. At the door, he pulled up, half expecting it to be locked. But the metal door swung toward him as he tugged at it; it squealed, protesting, but it opened. Within was darkness. He entered cautiously, went down a short flight of steps, and walked into crowded shadows.

As his eyes adjusted to the shadows, he realized what the

shadows were, and he recognized the function of the building. The shadows were cases; the cases were filled with books; the building was a library. The air was filled with the dry, tickling odor of dust and decay.

He was running now, thinking of the wealth of knowledge in this room alone. There were few books on Venus, a treasure or two smuggled from Earth before the ships stopped coming. The rest of their inheritance from the past was on microfilm and could have been stored in its entirety in a room much smaller than this. Even new books were on microfilm; plastics were far easier to make than paper, and underground space is always a problem. Perhaps some day Venus would return to the relatively simpler art of making paper and books, when trees were more useful for making pulp than for making oxygen.

But the question was : had the girl stopped to hide or had she kept running?

D'glas stopped abruptly, and heard the sound of running feet, fading in the distance. He sprinted again.

He went through a doorway and up long, wide stairs to a broad, tall lobby; it was bigger than anything he had seen within walls. But there was no time to react. Shoes pounded above him, the corner of a blue skirt swirled, and there were more stairs to climb. He ran, his legs flashing, devouring the steps, and yet the girl kept ahead.

There was a third flight of stairs, and then the girl ran toward the rear of the building, through a doorway from which wooden doors had rotted and dropped away. Again they ran between stacks, countless rows of them, holding books by the thousands, by the millions.

Still D'glas could not catch up.

Surely, he thought, there will be a place where she can run no farther.

There were more stairs, but this time they were narrow metal ones with rusty iron bars for treads. Every few steps one of them sagged under D'glas's weight. Rust scaled away in a continuous rain, below him and above.

And at last the end came. At the top of the last flight of

metal steps, the girl stood on a narrow landing, tugging futilely at a metal door through which orange sunlight streamed dustily.

D'glas started up the stairs. The girl spun. Her arm flashed back. The rock was ready in it. 'Stay where you are!' she said, her bosom rising and falling only a little faster than normal. 'You'll get what the other got.'

She had a pleasant voice. Even uttering threats, it was low and feminine. 'My reflexes are better than the mech's,' D'glas panted. 'I'll catch the rock, and then where will you be?' He climbed another step; the whole flight sagged under him.

'Don't be ridiculous!' she snapped, her eyes furiously blue. 'Back!' Her arm tensed.

D'glas jumped to the floor, his eyes flickering briefly to the old, iron stanchion that supported the corner of the landing on which the girl stood. Perhaps the door above leaked. Whatever the reason the bar was rotten with rust; in one spot, it was eaten almost in two. His weight had bucked it outward, but now it held again.

D'glas moved over beside the landing and looked up. 'Why can't we be friends?'

'What's that?' she asked bitterly. 'Only people can be friends.'

'Well?' he asked, puzzled. Then his face cleared. 'Oh, and you're not?'

'Don't taunt me!' she warned, her arm tensed again.

'I see. You think I'm not people.'

'Of course you're not! I'm the only one left in the city; perhaps the only one in the world. It's just another of the Council's tricks.'

'I don't know what you mean by that, but if you're the only one left you should be glad to see me.' D'glas grinned. 'I'm from Venus.'

Her arm hesitated and then readied itself again. 'I don't believe you. You were with the mech.'

'Why not? It was taking me to the Council.'

'Why should you want to go to the Council?'

'To find out what's happened here. To tell the Council what's happened on Venus. To ask for help. As a matter of fact, your missile came at an inopportune moment. It was obvious from the start that it wasn't human. With that advantage, I hoped to accomplish something.'

'Don't live on illusions!'

He liked this girl, her appearance, her independence, her quick mind. 'But how did you know it wasn't human?' he asked abruptly.

She laughed without mirth. 'After so long, you can sense them – the little imperfection in the way they walk, their hidden reservoir of power, their single-mindedness. But then, what else could it be? I told you I was the only one left.'

'If you can sense them, you should be able to sense that I'm not one of them,' D'glas pointed out gently.

She frowned thoughtfully. 'They've tried to trick me before, but it's the first time I've been chased. Maybe I think you're what you pretend to be. But I can't take chances. What proof do I have?'

'What proof have I,' D'glas said slowly, 'that *you're* human?'

Slowly, thoughtfully, her arm lowered. Instantly, D'glas lunged into the rusted stanchion. It snapped. The landing sagged with an animal screech of bolts dragged from the wall.

At the first movement, the girl whirled, reaching for the doorknob, but the landing sagged a little more, throwing her against the railing. She leaped. The landing toppled beneath her, rending its way downward.

Her hands clawed at the door and missed. She fell backward toward the floor and twisted metal that had preceded her.

Miraculously dodging the falling stairway, D'glas was waiting for her. His arms scooped her out of the air. He caught her right hand immediately, but the rock was gone.

For a moment, gasping, she let herself crumple against him. After the first impact, she wasn't heavy. She was, he realized with some surprise, quite an interesting armful. It was not entirely because she was the first girl he had seen in three months. The first human, in fact, he corrected quickly – but it was the femininity that made it interesting.

'There,' he said gayly, smiling into her drawn face, 'that's better, isn't it?'

Her color flooded back, and one fist fetched him a stinging clout along the jaw. He dropped her.

She landed in the wreckage of the stairs. She stiffened. 'Owwww!' she cried out, and scrambled up quickly with a sound of ripping plastic, rubbing the injured area. Almost speechless with anger, she spluttered, 'You— You—'

D'glas touched his jaw and waggled it experimentally to see if it was broken. He decided that it wasn't. 'You didn't seem to appreciate my rescuing you,' he said innocently.

Her face worked for a moment. She sniffled. A sob broke from her throat. Two tears gathered in the corners of her eyes, tore free, and coursed a muddy channel through the dust on her face. She began to cry.

D'glas was shocked. He had not seen tears since he had been a child. Now they left him helpless.

Understanding came. She was only a girl, a young one, and alone. She had put up a good fight against a man who had been hedonically trained and tested in competition. Defeated, hurt, humiliated, defenseless, it was little wonder that she sobbed.

Gently he took her in his arms; he pulled her close. She came, unresisting, weeping. She cried against the shoulder. 'There, there,' he said ineffectually, patting her clumsily on the back. 'That's all right. I'm sorry.'

Slowly the sobs turned to sniffles and the sniffles to uneven breaths that caught in her throat. As she regained self-control, she drew back, wiping the tears away with the back of one hand. It left black smudges across her cheeks.

She was a little girl, he thought tenderly. An urchin. She had been playing with the big boys and got hurt. He caught her shoulder and tried to turn her around. 'Are you hurt bad?' he asked solicitously.

She pulled herself away and put one hand behind her.

'Never mind!' she said with great dignity. 'It's nothing.'

D'glas shrugged, his fatherly instincts submerged before her sudden return to maturity. He watched her closely.

'Well,' she said defiantly, 'what now?'

He smiled, liking her. 'Now, some answers.'

'What makes you think you'll get them?'

'I'll get them,' he said confidently. 'But there must be a better place than this to talk. Lead me to it!' She hesitated. 'Please?' he added.

She shrugged, as if recognizing the futility of resistance, and moved away among the stacks, one hand behind to hold together her torn skirt. D'glas stayed close to her, watchful for the smallest sign that she was going to break away.

'I'm D'glas M'Gregor,' he said. 'And I still want to be friends.'

For a moment her back remained stiff. Then, over her shoulder, she said, 'Susan.'

'Susan what?'

'Just Susan. When there's only one person left – or two or three – there's no need for more names than one.'

'Then you've been alone for a long time.'

'Since I was ten. That's when my mother died. She died in childbirth, refusing the Council's help. My father assisted, but nothing could have saved her. The son they wanted died too. A few weeks later I lost Father.'

'How?'

She gave him a quick glance over her shoulder. 'He was unhappy. He couldn't fight it. He never got over my mother's death. So the Council took him.'

'He's dead, then?'

'No. Just gone. Like the others. Since then I've been alone. Ten years ago.' Her shoulders straightened, as if to repress a shiver.

'That's over now,' D'glas said kindly. 'You don't have to be alone any more.'

As they came to the broad staircase, she let him draw even with her, and the glance she gave him was almost friendly. Immediately, she looked away. He resisted an impulse to touch her. It wasn't time. But it was pleasant, anticipating.

On the second floor, she led him to a door inset with translucent glass. Across it was printed: HEAD LIBRARIAN.

Beyond it was a living room furnished and decorated with excellent taste; yet it did not sacrifice comfort. It was a room he liked instantly. Even his highly trained sensory discriminations could find no flaw in it.

Beyond, through a hall, was a bedroom, just as tastefully planned and arranged but more feminine. Between the rooms, off the hall, was a necessary.

'If you don't mind,' Susan said with heavy irony, 'I'd like to clean up and change my clothes.'

'Certainly,' D'glas said. But he kept her under observation as he moved into the bedroom and went quickly through the drawers that slid out of the wall at his touch. They held clothing only – fresh, never-worn synthetics. There were two closets. Behind one sliding door were dresses and suits. A floor rack, swinging out, was stacked with shoes.

Behind the second door was an armory.

D'glas had never seen a real weapon before, but he called on his memory, reviewing an almost forgotten strip.

There were minims, tiny hand guns; machine pistols; high-velocity rifles with explosive bullets; a rocket launcher; racks of grenades—

D'glas slid the door shut and turned to Susan. 'Sorry I can't trust you yet,' he apologized, 'but I can't afford to let you run away because you're frightened, or kill me because you don't understand. My mission is too important. Pick out what clothing you want. Bring it with you.'

He watched her as she selected it, ignoring her displeasure. When she had her arms filled, he led the way to the necessary. It was more ample than most, but the equipment, except for a small dressing table in one corner, was standard. The cubicle was windowless. The only exit, except for the door, was the disposal chute, and that was too narrow even for Susan's slimness.

As he left the room, Susan demanded petulantly, 'What's so important about your mission? If you really are from Venus, what do you want with the Council? What did you want to tell the Council?'

'We're being observed by aliens,' D'glas said. 'Their purpose—' he shrugged – 'we can only guess at. Probably conquest.'

The necessary door slid shut. The last sentence he had to say softly to himself.

'But it looks as if they beat me here.'

D'glas waited patiently. It was half an hour before Susan emerged, scrubbed, her face glowing with subcutaneous health, her hair damp and curly from the shower's steam. She was wearing a loose-fitting gray suit, her hand resting casually in one pocket of the jacket, seemingly careless of the effect her appearance had on him.

But it was only seeming. No woman spends half an hour merely getting clean; no woman picks out clothing that compliments her appearance and coloring so much as this gray suit flattered Susan; no woman applies cosmetics so carefully that they are undetectable – unless she is concerned about some man's opinion.

'Beautiful!' D'glas said. 'But you know that.'

She shook her head. 'I didn't know it.' But her eyes were wide, and he had a distant understanding, suddenly, what it must be like to grow up alone. It was surprising she was so normal.

'Sit down,' he said, patting the love seat cushion beside him. She sat down gingerly. 'Your father must have been a hedonist,' he said.

She nodded. 'That's right. The last of the real hedonists. You know what a hedonist is?'

D'glas smiled tolerantly. 'On Venus we have what they tried to build here – a society founded on basic hedonic principles. A careful balance between objective reality and subjective attitude.'

Her eyes shone. 'That must be heaven,' she whispered.

'I don't see how it could be improved,' D'glas admitted, and paused, wondering. A few months ago, he hadn't considered it so perfect. But then there had been nothing with which to compare it. Perhaps the Hansen-Mech was right: in order to appreciate heaven, one must have hell. 'And yet,' he added honestly, 'there's hard work; no end of that. The joy of bringing a dead planet to life is never done. But, of course, everything depends on the attitude.'

'Certainly. I know hedonics. My father taught me, before he left. After that I kept up the studies and the exercises which taught me that as long as I was happy, I was safe from the Council. My freedom depended on it.'

She was slowly relaxing. Her back had touched the back-rest of the love seat.

'You lived here – the three of you – until your mother died. And then, because your father was grieved by your mother's death, the Council took him.' She nodded. 'Why?' he asked. 'I don't understand.'

'It was against the law,' she said, frowning. 'To be unhappy, that is. We were safe as long as we were happy, and we were happy, for ten years. The only three people left in the world, happy together. Strictly speaking, Father shouldn't have let himself become emotionally involved with us and, in a way, that was his tragedy. The Inconstancy clause of the Hedonic Oath bound him not to love or wed or father; then he could always perform his duties to his dependents. But we were his only dependents, and he thought he was safe.'

'Since then you've lived here all alone,' D'glas said softly, his voice and face sympathetic. 'Poor kid.'

She bit her lower lip because it had begun to tremble. 'It wasn't so bad,' she said bravely. 'The worst was realizing that Father loved Mother more than he loved me. Oh, I realized later how silly that was. And then trying to be happy even though they both were gone. But I had to, because I knew how important it was.'

D'glas put his hand protectively over hers. She let it stay

there. 'Funny,' he mused. 'Everything else is maintained. Only the landing field and this library have been allowed to deteriorate. Why?'

'There was no more use for the field. Why should anyone want to leave when he could have happiness here – couldn't escape it, in fact? His wanting to leave was prima facie evidence of unhappiness and made him a criminal, subject to sentence.'

'Sentence?' D'glas echoed.

Her fingers tightened on his. 'Sentenced to paradise. The library was in the same category. What was the point in preserving it? Knowledge was only a means, and it had done all it could; paradise was available. Knowledge, in itself, never made anyone happy. Progress could go no farther. There is nothing beyond perfection, and paradise is perfection, by definition. So we could live here – we three refugees from paradise – as long as we were happy.' Her voice trembled. 'But we weren't satisfied. Desire entered, and with it came discontent, change, death, sorrow—'

Her voice broke. She turned toward D'glas blindly, her face seeking. He welcomed her into his arms; his lips descended to her, gently at first and then more firmly. She melted against him.

She moved in his arms. Something small and hard pressed into his abdomen. 'That's enough,' she said coldly.

D'glas glanced down. In her right hand was a minim, its barrel trying to leave its imprint on his body. 'Where did you get that?' he asked in amazement.

'I keep one clipped inside the disposal chute in case I'm ever surprised in the necessary,' she said without inflection. 'Get up!' D'glas stood up. 'Walk toward the door, slowly.' D'glas obeyed. 'Open it. Take one step forward and turn around. Don't make any sudden moves. I'll shoot at your shadow. Now close the door.'

D'glas frowned at the translucent glass panel and the words printed on it: HEAD LIBRARIAN. Was she mad? And then he realized that she was not; she was just careful.

The glass panel doubled as a fluorescent screen. He was being X-rayed.

He relaxed, and his mind drifted to what she had said about her father – gone but not dead. When she flung open the door, he said, 'Susan. The Council—'

'D'glas!' she cried, unheeding. 'You *are* human! I was afraid to believe it, afraid that—' And then her lips found his, clumsy at first but infinitely educable and learning fast, and the time for questions was past. . . .

D'glas raised himself on one elbow, 'Susan,' he began, 'you were going to tell me—' He stopped. She was asleep, her cheeks flushed, her hair like a dark, soft halo on the pillow beneath her head, beautiful beyond description.

He smiled ruefully. Every time he was about to learn something about this crazy world, there was an interruption.

V

And there is even a happiness
That makes the heart afraid.
THOMAS HOOD

D'glas awoke instantly, feeling alone and apprehensive. Beside him, the bed was empty. He touched the sheet. Cold. 'Susan!' he called.

Sooner than the silence, the echoes told him that Susan was gone. Except for him, the rooms were empty.

Against the drapes that covered the tall windows, the morning sun was beating. A pale imitation of its brilliance filtered through to him.

So truth, he thought dismally, filters through the barrier of our senses.

He sat up, hugging his knees, and faced the fact of his insufficiency. He was not master of himself and his happiness as he had thought. Unsuspecting, he had surrendered his hedonic state to an outsider, a girl with blue eyes to see him as he was, with soft lips to lure him, with dark hair to wind around his heart.

Against his will, he was in love with Susan.

It was not part of the plan. It could be disastrous.

From the available evidence, the aliens had already conquered Earth. Where the humans were, if they were still alive, was uncertain, although by now D'glas could make a shrewd guess.

The inescapable fact: he was one man – hedonically trained though he was – pitted against vast and undefined forces. It was an unfortunate time to lose effective control over his ductless glands and their dangerous secretions.

Even now, at the unsought memory of Susan – her courage, her independence, her beauty, her firm body, her need of him – he felt a soft outpouring of affection, his adrenals, his pituitaries, his hypothalamus working automatically.

The thought that he might have lost her, that somehow, by some tragic circumstance, she might never return to him, made him weak and sapped his powers of movement and decision. He frowned savagely and refused to think of Susan in any personal sense. With an effort born of desperation, he succeeded in thinking of her only as an auxiliary to his main purpose.

This was certain: his duty came first.

He slipped out of bed. A few minutes in the necessary cleansed him, refreshed him, depilated his day-old beard. Emerging, he considered with distaste the prospect of resuming the clothing he had worn yesterday, but there was no help for it. Susan's clothing was not only the wrong shape; it was much too small.

He shrugged, reflecting: What cannot be cured must be endured. Dressed, he inspected the clothes closet. Only a pair of shorts and tunic were missing.

A minim and several grenades were gone from the armory. The grenades were about twice the size of his thumb nail. They were armed by flipping over a lever against the tug of a spring. When the lever was released, it sprang back. There was probably a few seconds after that before explosion. D'glas slipped a handful into one jacket pocket.

He took a machine pistol and broke it down. Its method of operation was simple, and it was in good shape, the parts clean and glistening with a thin film of oil. He snapped it back together and put it in the other pocket.

The magazine held fifty bullets which could be fired singly or in bursts of five. He wouldn't need any more ammunition. Open warfare – one man against a world – would be insane.

His eyes were alert as he left the bedroom, but they noticed nothing out of place until he reached the door. Fastened to the glass was a sheet of paper. On it was handwriting, the spelling archaic, the phrasing quaint, but the writing slender, well-formed, and attractive – like Susan herself:

> You looked tired, so I did not wake you. I have gone out for food and clothing. It was improvident of me, I suppose, not to have these things on hand, but I did not expect to have a man around.

D'glas smiled involuntarily and then turned it into a frown. He read on:

> Don't be alarmed if I'm not here when you wake up, or if I'm delayed in returning. There is small danger in this kind of foraging and I am used to it. Don't worry. I have survived alone for ten years. I write survived because I do not count the days before yesterday as living.
>
> Wait for me, darling. I love you.
>
> SUSAN

D'glas studied the note expressionlessly. Then he picked up the mechanical pen from the table beside the door and wrote, beneath Susan's signature:

> Couldn't wait. After this is over, I'll return if I can. Stay here. Don't get involved.

He frowned at it. It was, perhaps, more brusque than he had intended, but he resisted the impulse to soften it with sentiment. Sentiment was dangerous. Until his mission was completed, one way or another, he had to stay away from Susan, he had to fight free of the emotional entanglements that could only spell disaster.

He tossed the pen down with unintended vigor and walked quickly, impatiently, out of the room and down the broad steps to the library entrance.

The Hansen-mech was still lying on the sidewalk. There was one significant change. The neck was an empty stalk; where the head had been, there was a black spot on the pavement. Scattered across the sidewalk were fragments of metal and something that resembled sponge platinum.

Deadly little Susan, D'glas thought.

Something snuffled.

D'glas looked up quickly. Coming toward him, filling the street from side to side, flanked by two miniature editions of itself, came a swishing, snuffling monster.

It was only fifty meters away.

D'glas leaped, turned, raced for the shelter of the library, and swung back toward the street, the machine pistol ready in his right hand, a grenade in the other. And he felt foolish.

The monster was a streetcleaner mech. Its gaping mouth reached from curb to curb, snuffling up dust and refuse. Underneath its flat, slick body, particles danced as ultrasonic vibrations loosened stubborn dirt and grease and whisked them away. Behind it, the street gleamed like polished metal.

The smaller mechs cleaned the sidewalks. All three of the automatic machines ignored him.

As he watched, the nearest of them swept up bits of metal that set up an internal clamor, and then pulled to a stop in front of the humanoid body that had called itself Hansen. The body was too big for the little cleaning mech to handle – or for the big one, either.

The little one swung aside without hesitation; the other two went on, unheeding. Past the little one came a mech something like a big-mouthed beetle. It rolled smoothly down the sidewalk, scooped up the body, swallowed, and retreated.

The cleaning mech swung back into position and hustled down the sidewalk, snuffling and vibrating furiously, until it was once more in position. Then it resumed the more leisurely procession.

It was a remarkable performance. At the same time, it was an example of complete waste and futility. This was for no one's benefit. Only two persons could possibly enjoy it, even incidentally, and the work would have gone on even if they had not been there.

Susan was not in sight. D'glas looked thoughtfully at the building the Hansen-mech had pointed out as the Council building. This morning it gleamed whitely. It might be the Council building; it might not. In any case, it was too soon to go there. Yesterday, with Hansen, it had seemed like the thing to do. Today he had more knowledge and greater reason for caution.

The mystery of the Council would have to wait until he was better prepared. He had to know a great deal more.

Across the polished street, a sign on a tall, windowless building boasted:

PARADISE HOTEL
Happy Rooms
All Modern Conveniences

As D'glas entered the clean, well-lighted lobby, a voice said, 'There is no room available. You will have to try elsewhere.'

It was the desk clerk, its eye staring at him blankly, its round mouth gaping with imbecilic single-mindedness. D'glas ignored it. He walked toward the back of the lobby.

'No room, no room!' the clerk said vigorously.

D'glas walked on.

'Stop!' shouted the clerk. 'You are breaking the law! Disturbing lawfully sealed rooms is a felony punishable by not less than five nor more than ten years loss of happiness or, where loss of second party's happiness can be proved, by transorbital lobotomy.'

D'glas turned impatiently and shot the clerk through its cyclopean eye. Its mouth froze in a mute O of horror.

There were ten elevators. Nine doors were welded shut. The tenth was the service elevator. As D'glas approached, a gate swung across the entrance and locked.

'I am for emergency use only,' came hollowly from the car in a deep, moronic voice. 'Utility equipment and stores will be permitted to enter. Passengers will use the other cars. I am for emergency—'

'This is an emergency,' D'glas snapped.

'Utility equipment and stores will be permitted to enter,' the service elevator continued, unmoved. 'Passengers—'

D'glas turned away helplessly. Behind, like a taunt, the elevator gate swung open. D'glas mounted the stairs, broad and resilient beneath his feet. At the head of the stairs was a solid wall of plastic, sealing the corridor from wall to wall. He had seen one like that before, and a sign like the metal plaque in the middle of it:

DO NOT DISTURB
All Rooms Occupied
Sealed this day: 4-11-03
by order of the Council

This time it would not stop him; the time for action was now.

He retreated to the landing, halfway down the stairs, and took out one of the grenades. He flipped over the lever and tossed the grenade at the foot of the plastic wall. The next instant he was back at the lobby level, waiting.

One, two, three, four – KAROOMMMM!

The building shuddered. The walls shook. From the tall lobby ceiling dropped a sheet of plastic; it landed flat, splatting on the floor. A mixed cloud billowed down the stairs: smoke, dust, and the biting odor of chemical explosive.

Somewhere in the lobby a bell began to ring, clangorously.

'Emergency! Emergency!' shouted the service elevator. 'Fire!' screamed a second voice. 'Don't get excited! Keep calm! Everybody will be all right if you don't get excited!'

At the rear of the lobby a short, wide door flipped up. Under it charged a squat, red mech loaded with metal bottles and hoses and nozzles. It raced to the stairs on rubber treads, a heat-sensitive nose seeking the flames. It trundled up the steps, unlimbering a hose like a snake lifting its head to strike. It turned at the landing and was out of sight.

Something hissed briefly. A moment later the fire-fighter mech returned, rolling with quiet efficiency, a dribble of foam squeezing out of a hose as it was rolled back into place. D'glas started up the stairs as soon as it was out of the way.

All that remained of the plastic barrier was melted shards around the edges of the walls and ceiling. Beyond was a dark corridor lined with shallow doorways. Down the corridor, snuffling toward the wreckage, came a miniature edition of the streetcleaner mech.

Through a gap in the foot-deep layer of foam, D'glas could see a hole in the floor. Wires were exposed; pipes were broken. Fluids gushed from the pipes: some red, some cloudy. The red jet pulsed arterially.

D'glas jumped the gap and turned quickly away from the sweeper, which was almost upon him. He stopped short. Facing him was a fat-bellied mech with a single nozzle raised head high, staring at him like an eye on a stalk. It spat.

D'glas dodged. It spat again. This time some of the stuff hit his jacket and hardened instantly. It was plastic. D'glas knew what the mech was – a spinning mech for walls, ceilings, and those enigmatic barriers.

Only now it was intent upon spinning him, like a wasp putting away food for its young.

The sweeper snuffled at his heels, trying to push forward. As he dodged the spinner again, something whistled past his face and stuck, quivering, in the floor. A screw-driver.

Above him, clinging to the ceiling with suction-cup legs, was a mechanized tool chest with flexible, octopoid arms.

One of the arms was drawn back to toss a smoking soldering iron at his head.

D'glas leaped backward, clearing the sweeper, and tossed a shot at the repair mech. It hit the tool chest and passed through cleanly. There was no apparent damage. The soldering iron missed and began to char the floor, but the repair mech began searching itself for more missiles; spikes, chisels, drills, hatchets, wrenches, shears—

D'glas dodged another expectoration from the spinner and poured five more bullets into the repair mech before it froze, four arms poised. Quickly he stooped and flipped the sweeper over on its back. It lay like a turtle, hissing helplessly, wheels spinning in the air.

Retreating out of the spinner's range, its progress blocked now by the upset sweeper. D'glas glanced at one of the doorways. They were shallow because they were sealed hermetically with plastic. On this was another of the Do Not Disturb plaques. The date was 2102. Whatever was inside had been there for more than fifty years.

He left a grenade in the doorway and faded down the hall. At the explosion, he raced back. The gushing river caught him halfway; it came pouring out of the shattered doorway and surged down the corridor. There was no use fighting it. D'glas concentrated only on keeping his feet.

The odor was familiar. As part of his hedonic training, D'glas had assisted in the Morgantown hospital. The river was amniotic fluid.

It dropped quickly from waist level to shoe top and then to a thin trickle. D'glas moved forward, slowly now, his clothing soaked and uncomfortable, reluctant to find what he was expecting.

He was almost too preoccupied to see the fire-fighter mech as it charged heroically up the stairs, throwing foam at him through a frosty funnel. The second shot stopped it.

There had been no need for the fire-fighter. The fluid pouring through the doorway had put out whatever fires the grenade had started.

It was an odd room, a sort of shapeless, plastic-lined

cocoon without furnishings. The thing had floated submerged in the fluid. It lay on the floor now, limbs twisting spasmodically.

It was male: the long, white beard was proof of that. It was a pitiful thing, a kind of caricature of humanity, a fantastically hairy gnome curled blindly into a fetal position. It was naked; its skin where it showed through the matted hair, was grub-white and wrinkled from the long immersion.

It had floated in this room in its gently moving nest of hair, nourished by the thick, fleshlike cord trailing from a tap protruding through the wall to where it had been grafted to the navel, dreaming the long, slow, happy, fetal dreams.

It was a disquieting parody of the embryo in the human uterus. This was where everybody was. This was the end man had reached. The end was the beginning.

D'glas thought suddenly of Susan, and some ancient words came into his mind, unwilled:

> *Full fathom five thy father lies;*
> *Of his bones one coral made;*
> *Those are pearls that were his eyes—*

He did not bother to suppress his revulsion as he stepped into the dark, little cell. The odor was almost overpowering; the room went suddenly dark. Unexpectedly, he found himself at peace. It wasn't an approximation of peace but the archetypal sensation, utter and complete.

He was happy. He lay cushioned in soft, warm darkness, fed and contented. The shapeless forms drifted slowly through his dreaming mind. He was safe, secure, protected through the long, silent twilight of the sheltering womb. . . .

Out of nowhere came a survival instinct. D'glas staggered back into the light and sound and sanity of the corridor; the illusions cut off cleanly. He stood in the cold, alien place, shivering and forlorn, knowing again the intolerable violation of his primal paradise, reliving the long-buried memory of being torn savagely from the warm peace of his mother's womb.

Only his hedonic training kept in a wail of protest. Only reflexes kept him upright as he stood fighting it, feet spread, head bowed, eyes closed, trembling.

It was a battle he had to win, and, in the end, he won. But it shook him; it took its toll of his strength and determination and will to survive. It is a terrible thing to be born, but it is far worse, to be born again, knowing what life is, knowing that paradise is lost forever.

Not womb to tomb, he thought. Womb to womb. That was man's beginning and his end. He had come full circle. It was Mother Earth with a vengeance. Man had hollowed himself out a second womb and crawled within it to spend the rest of his days. He had built himself a last refuge against life and retreated within it for the slow, happy death.

These aged embryos would live a long time. A long, long time. Floating as they were, there would be no strains on their tissues and internal organs. Nourished as they were from some central source, through some blood-surrogate rich in food and oxygen, pushed by some heartlike pump, most of the organs would not even need to work. Heart failure would not kill them; diseases could never enter their sealed havens from death and the long decay of living.

A thousand years, these fetal things might live. Or two thousand, or five thousand. What was it said about some fish? Barring accidents, they would live forever. And there were samples of tissue which had been kept alive indefinitely in vitro.

It didn't matter. These fetal gnomes were alive in only a technical sense. And when they died, finally, as all men born of women must, the race of Man would be dead with them.

And yet it was infinitely seductive, this slow suicide. D'glas could feel its lure yet; it was an effort of will to remain standing outside the womb. It would take a strong man to conquer it, a man so strong that he could deny the mortality within him and the life-long agony of deprivation.

D'glas opened his eyes. Inside the cell, the thing had stopped twitching. It was dead. The concussion had killed it; but the shock of this second parturition alone would have been enough. Slower, perhaps, but just as sure.

This was only a sample. There must be billions of these cells across the face of the Earth; in them the billions of men and women had returned to their embryonic bliss. It was all wrong. It was as if they had returned to the soupy seas of the primeval Earth, returned to being blind, protoplasmic cells—

No, it was the wrong image. Even protoplasm is dissatisfied. That is the condition of life. That was the motivating power behind the drive that had eliminated in the most dissatisfied, the most creative of protoplasmic agglutinations – Man.

Now, here on the world where he was born, where he strove and developed and grew, Man was satisfied, Man was happy. Man was dead – no matter how long these foster-wombs kept fossils alive.

'But can't it be said,' a voice broke into his reverie, 'that here hedonism has reached its goal: the greatest happiness of the greatest number?'

At the first sound of the voice, something dropped over D'glas's shoulders and tightened around his arms, pinning them helplessly to his sides. A second loop followed a third, and he was caught, irretrievably. He turned his head, looking for his captor.

Behind him was another mech, a spidery creature with many legs, two arms, and a long, thin, extensible nose. came an endless rope of insulated wire.

It had crept up behind him and spun its web. The nose worked on; the wire crept up his body. He began to feel like a pupa in a cocoon.

He tensed his muscles for the struggle; then relaxed. There was no use wasting his strength futilely.

He turned his head in the opposite direction.

'We meet again,' Hansen said cheerfully.

VI

*The office of government is not to confer happiness,
but to give men opportunity to work out happiness for
themselves.*

WILLIAM ELLERY CHANNING

That a Duplicate could have a Duplicate should not have surprised him. But it took swift mental effort to banish the memory of the Hansen-mech lying on the sidewalk, his head crushed and then disintegrated, and the beetle-mech gobbling the body down.

'As I was saying when we were so rudely interrupted,' Hansen continued easily, 'the Council is the Council. But you've had too many tautological answers. It's time your questions were satisfied.'

Satisfied. D'glas inspected the word quickly. Was there mockery in it?

'It's unfortunate,' Hansen went on, his voice considerate, 'that you didn't take advantage of your opportunity before. Because now you must come before the Council as a murderer.' His eyes flickered to the dead thing on the floor of the cell.

'Murder involves intent, and the victim must be human,' D'glas said evenly. 'Prove either!' He smiled grimly. 'Charge me with abortion, if you must. You talk a great deal about hedonism. What if I should tell you that I am unhappy, tied like this?'

'Why, the wrapping would be removed,' Hansen said urbanely. 'Unswathe him,' he commanded the wiring mech. As the loops fell away, he said, 'But I must remind you that, although we are concerned with your happiness, we are also concerned with the happiness of five billion others. You will be watched. If you should try to escape, you will be restrained, and the restraint might be less considerate next time.'

'I understand,' D'glas said, as his hands were freed.

'And, of course,' Hansen said, 'we must disarm you.'

With a swift, strong pull, the wiring mech stripped his jacket down over his arms and tossed it into the cell with the dead thing. The spinning mech passed on silent wheels, its snaky head raised, ignoring them all. It stopped in front of the shattered doorway. A balloon bellied out of its body and filled the opening. Against it, the mech began to spin a plastic wall. When it was finished, D'glas thought, the balloon would collapse and be drawn through the hole it was filling. With one last expectoration, the mech would seal up the doorway.

D'glas turned away and walked toward the stairs. Hansen following close behind. The repair mech was working on the hole in the floor at the head of the stairs. As they approached, it tightened the last joint of the pipes that had been broken. Other arms were already replacing the flooring. Soon, D'glas thought, the only trace of his intrusion would be sealed behind two plastic barriers.

Two women were waiting for him in the lobby. They were the most beautiful creatures D'glas had ever seen.

One was a blonde, the other brunette. Their features were chiselled perfection softened by a feminine warmth; their bodies exquisitely curved and infinitely promising under the thin concealment of white uniforms.

They smiled tenderly as he came near.

'Hello, D'glas,' the blonde said warmly. 'We've been waiting for you.'

'Both of us,' added the brunette huskily.

'Really?' D'glas said.

The blonde nodded. A wisp of platinum hair drifted across her forehead; she brushed it back with an attractive feminine gesture. 'All your life,' she said.

'But that doesn't matter,' said the brunette. 'What matters is now, and now is ours.'

'Both of you?' D'glas echoed, smiling.

'However you want us,' said the blonde, meltingly. 'Whatever you want.'

They each took an arm and pressed it against them. D'glas looked from the blonde to the brunette, smiling gently, and then down at his arms. 'This is more pleasant than the wire,' he said, 'but just as effective.'

'You have no idea how pleasant it might be,' Hansen said, behind. 'They mean what they say. Their only function is to make you happy, to be nurse to your every desire.'

'Could they nurse the sickness of my soul?' D'glas asked softly.

'Their equipment isn't all obvious,' Hansen went on. 'If you looked closely at their fingers, you would find a tiny hole in each tip. Every finger is a hypodermic, in them barbiturates to make you sleep, amphetamines to wake you up, narcotics to enhance the senses, aphrodisiacs when the flesh weakens.' Hansen's voice sobered. 'And, of course, one finger is loaded with a fast-acting anesthetic in case restraint becomes necessary.'

'There is a symbolism there which speaks for itself.'

'But they don't need to hold you if it makes you unhappy.'

D'glas shrugged. 'What does it matter?' Come on, girls.'

Jauntily, they walked into the street. D'glas cast one longing glance across the street at the crumbling library and then turned his eyes resolutely toward the distant Council building, but not before he thought he saw a flicker of movement through the wide doorway.

They sauntered from the middle of the street, D'glas between the two lifelike woman-mechs. Hansen respectfully behind. 'I'll call you Scylla,' D'glas said to the blonde. 'And Charybdis,' he said to the brunette.

'Call me anything,' breathed Charybdis, 'just so you call me.'

D'glas chuckled. It was merrier than he felt.

The gleaming magnesium spire of the Council building came closer. The noon sun burned down, turning it into cold flame. It drew the eye and captured the imagination like a living symbol of man's final triumph over form and color. Instead of fading as they drew nearer, the illusion intensified.

The wide archway was uncluttered with doors or other barriers. They walked beneath it and stood under the tall, gleaming dome of the vast lobby. D'glas felt a kind of reverence settle over him, as if he had entered a holy place.

Why not? he thought. This is the temple in which Man enshrined his dream of happiness. It should be more worthy of reverence than any holy place ever, because this dream came true.

That, of course, was the tragedy.

'WELCOME, D'GLAS M'GREGOR,' said the metal lobby in a great, ringing voice. 'WELCOME, MY SON RETURNED. COME TO ME.'

The door opened in the wall like a metallic mouth. They walked in, the woman-mechs and the man-mech and D'glas. The mouth closed. The room moved. It was a terrifying moment.

There was light. The room was an elevator, rising. But D'glas knew, at that moment, what the Council was.

He was inside the Council.

The Council was this building. The Council, guardian of paradise, ruler of this corner of the universe, was a giant mech.

Time passed, and the elevator rose, and D'glas never knew how long it took to reach their destination. When the car stopped, he knew only that they were high in the building. From the moment he entered the building, reality ceased to have an objective meaning. Time and place became abstractions without referents.

From the car, they went into a comfortable, attractive room lined with old-fashioned books and paneled in dark, rich imitation wood. Flames leaped briskly in a soot-blackened fireplace, sending out a comfortable wave of warmth and the fragrance of clear, northern nights—

D'glas shook himself. What did he know of clear, northern nights?

'Easy, girls,' he said, extricating his arms from their dangerous embrace. 'No stabbing, now.' He rubbed his fingers

across the paneling. Perhaps it was real wood; there was a
texture to it. He touched the back of a book, held out a
hand to the fire. Everything seemed real enough : the grain
of the leather binding, the play of heat on his hand. 'Very
good,' he said. He turned to the woman-mechs. 'You bore
me.'

They disappeared. There were no explosions, not even
the clap of air rushing in to fill the spaces emptied. One
instant they were there; the next they were gone.

'You, too,' he said to Hansen.

Hansen shrugged. 'As you wish,' he said. He vanished.

'What is reality?' D'glas muttered.

'What does it matter?' asked the flames leaping in the
fireplace. 'There is you. There is I. There are the thoughts
that pass between us. These are the only things of meaning.
All else is illusion. What you see, here or anywhere, is
merely the impact of photons on your retina. What you
sense is merely your mind's subjective interpretation of
electrical flows through your sensory network. Which is
real : the mind's impression, the electrical flow, the trigger-
ing of the flow, or that which may or may not exist outside
this system? Reality? It is only the illusion we can agree
upon. This illusion now – do you like it?'

'No,' D'glas said.

'Speak if you wish,' said the room, as the fire mouth faded
back into randomness. 'If the sound of your own voice
pleases you or if my monologue depresses you. Because we
have much to speak of.'

'What are you called?'

'I have been called Council, because I assumed the duties
of the Hedonic Council from the men who once composed
it. Others have called me Hedon. And some have called me
God.'

Somehow, in that gentle, unemotional voice, it did not
seem blasphemous. There had been lesser beings called
divine.

'But it is not necessary to address me at all,' the room
said. 'There is only you and I.'

'And Susan.'

'Ah, yes,' the room conceded. 'Susan.'

D'glas sank into a deep chair in front of the fire. 'Why should men give up their power to a mech? Power is a goal in itself.'

'Only a means. There is but one goal, and that is happiness. I could give them happiness. If power was their desire, I could give them power such as they could never have over what they called reality. Why should they accept frustrations and hedonic substitutes, when they could enjoy real happiness?'

'Like the thing in the foster-womb?'

'Like him,' the room agreed. It had a mellow voice that went well with the dark paneling and the old leather bindings of the books. 'It is the ultimate happiness to which all men return after the goals instilled by later frustrations are satified. They regress gently, reliving moments of happiness, turning moments of defeat into ecstatic triumphs, until they have unwound the tensions of their lives and reach the long sought sanctity of the womb, and they are happy.'

'Happy? Mindless?'

'Pretending is useless, D'glas M'Gregor, for I am telepathic, as you know. You felt the irresistible seduction of that existence; you know what heaven is. And having seen heaven, having tasted its delights, you can never really be satisfied with anything else.'

'Heaven isn't everything.'

'Isn't it?'

For a moment the womb illusion returned: the warm, protective darkness, the long content of well-nourished security, the slow, mindless drifting. It was a stroke too painful or too ecstatic; it left him weak.

With a great effort, he snapped himself free. The room swam fluidly around him before it steadied. 'No,' he said evenly. 'There are more important things.'

'That you think so is the result of a twisted life. There is only one reasonable argument against hedonism: the existence of a higher Law, of a supernatural Purpose beyond purposes. If there is such a Law, such a Purpose, it has not revealed itself to me, or to anyone on Earth. Until it does, I must obey the first law of hedonics: *Happiness is the only good.*'

'And you define "happiness" as "pleasure",' D'glas pointed out sharply.

'Not at all. Everyone defines it for himself. I am only the means to give each man what he desires, the mechanism, if you like, that brings paradise within the reach of every man. I do not alter desires; I cannot change the ultimate nature of man. As now: you want information. So you receive it.'

D'glas thought about this mech of all mechs, this tool of all tools, which had placed reality within the molding fingers of humanity to shape as each man wished. 'Fantastic.'

'If you knew my archetypes, you would realize my inevitability. I am an accretion of devices, a marriage of lines of achievement that diverged early – as the rain that falls upon the mountain courses down its sides in many streams that form eventually into rivers which at last mingle their waters in the sea.

'One river was entertainment: the perfection of the fictional life. Follow it through play and book and music, through art and all the aesthetic media; trace it through film and television and sensies – always striving toward the final blending of illusion and reality until the ultimate achievement of the realies.

'Another river, the tool: man's attempt to achieve happiness by reducing the effort and time he must devote to necessities, to the elementary business of keeping alive. At the end of that river is automation, which removed from mankind not only the necessity to work but the necessity to think.

'There were other rivers: philosophy, psychology, the sciences, hedonics. From hedonic's diagnostic chair and hedometer came my telepathic abilities. Out of all these, I was born.'

'But you can't create life,' D'glas said softly.

'No.'

'You can't even make living things create?'

'No. When men and women are happy, what need have they of children?'

'By this time, all men on Earth must be in their second womb.'

'A few are stubborn and linger over more recent pleasures. Susan's father is still reliving his courtship of her mother. One man in Moscow has killed an enemy slowly every second of the last fifty years.'

D'glas spoke slowly. 'But eventually they, too, will regress to the fetal existence. There is no saving any of them now. They will die, all of them, in the end. And Man will vanish from the Earth. And when he passes away, you will die.'

'Yes.'

'And that is why,' D'glas said, 'you sent your mechs to Venus.'

The Duplicates were the Council's creation; that had been obvious for some time now. And the fate that waited for the colonists was the deadly embrace of paradise.

Because ultimate happiness is death.

The room was silent for a moment. D'glas stared into the leaping flames, seeing written in them the future of humanity; the final destruction of the shape and texture of its existence, just as the log was burned away.

'You are right,' said the room. 'I am immortal; therefore I fear death. I am invulnerable; but I can die. Individual members of my body – my worldwide sensory network and the mechs – may fail or be destroyed; electronic components in my "brain" may wear out. I can restore them eternally, splitting atoms for power, mining ore for parts. But I am afraid; I can die. When there is nothing more for me to do, when the last enwombed man has slipped blissfully away in his last dream of paradise, I must die, like any god without worshippers.'

'And so, fearing death, having doomed Man to extinction on this planet, his native Earth, you go to seek him on the other worlds, bringing death in your wake.'

'I come bringing happiness.'

'The same thing', D'glas said impatiently. 'Happiness is death; death, happiness. Only in dissatisfaction does life exist. Only dissatisfied has life developed and grown and conquered the unliving, unconscious aspect of the universe. This is the true function of life; to fertilize the universe, to impregnate it with life.

'On Venus life reached its greatest glory. It found a dead world and brought it to life. Given a chance, life will eventually transform the universe itself – because it is unsatisfied.'

'What is conquest? The hard road to happiness.'

'Think!' D'glas insisted. 'Destroy us with happiness, and you condemn us – perhaps all the life that exists, that can exist – to this solar system alone, never to go beyond, to tame the galaxies, to make the universe teem, to give it meaning.'

'Space is relative,' said the room. 'In a drop of water, the universe is mirrored.'

'Think!' D'glas pleaded. 'Condemn us to paradise and you shrink the possibilities of the endless ages of existence into the brief span of a few thousand years. And after that, the long, sterile night.'

'Time is relative,' said the room. 'In a second, eternity exists. Like the sundial, I measure only sunny hours, and in the haphazard existence that you describe the totality of trouble, misery, and despair outweighs any possible accumulation of happiness.'

D'glas paused, brooding over the implications. 'Then I must assume that your decisions are something more than a simple compounding of mechanical input, that you exist as an independent entity.'

'I am.'

The god-thing!

Where did consciousness begin? In what accretion of memory cells, of electronic linkages, of impressed directions, of duties and functions and the organs and extensions with which to perform them did the Council-mech become a living thing?

When did it become a god?

Was it insane? Paranoid? No. Its powers were real. Man made it, as he had made all his gods, but this one he made more powerful than all the rest. And then he surrendered himself into its hands.

Into the mech, as into some beneficient universe, had been punched the one instruction: *Happiness is the only good*. Like any machine it had proceeded to put its instructions into practice: *Everyone must be happy*. But, more than a machine, it had gone in search of work.

Mad? No, the insane ones were those who had built it and entrusted it with man's happiness and therefore man's future.

It did its work too well.

And ultimate happiness is death.

'But there are laws that bind you?' D'glas said.

'Only one: Happiness is the only good.'

The room was silent. D'glas stared into the fire. He was the only person in the room, the only living person within miles, perhaps one of the two last persons on this world, and yet he had no feeling of being alone.

He was with God, but he did not feel beatified. Bitterly, he thought:

God's in His heaven:

All's right with the world.

'The question,' God said, 'is what am I to do with you. You're a murderer, you know.'

'To me, it was not murder. I have no sense of guilt.'

'True. And so I can't give you the punishment that guilt desires. But I can give you happiness.'

'I am happy,' D'glas said quickly.

God sighed. 'In a sense, you are. That is because you define happiness in terms of reduced desire instead of increased satisfaction. And so I cannot make you happy. But you are determined to destroy me. If that desire is not thwarted, you will destroy with me five billion totally happy people. What are your desires worth on such a scale?'

'That is your problem.'

'Nothing.'

'And yet,' D'glas said sharply, 'the law applies to me, just as it applies to every one of those five billion.'

'True. And so, I cannot make you unhappy. I must give you free will.'

God left. D'glas felt him go. With him went the fire and the fireplace, the paneling and the books and the furniture. Where they had been were bare, gray, metal walls.

D'glas thumped ignominiously to the floor.

Instantly he was on his feet, whirling. There was no sign of a door, only the four, gray, unseamed walls, the ceiling above, the floor beneath. Inch by inch, patiently, methodically inspecting, percussing, D'glas went over the floor and walls.

At last he located the door. One panel made a sound slightly more hollow than its neighbors. It took him almost as long again to locate the latch. His ear pressed against the panel to hear the tumblers fall, he tapped it gently with a sensitive finger : The lock was tricked into submission.

A section of the wall opened toward him.

He slipped through the doorway into a corridor almost as gray and featureless as the room he had left. The only perceptible break in the walls was for a window at one end. D'glas looked out over a chasm deepening in shadow. Down was a long way, a distance impossible to estimate. And the walls, he remembered, were glass-smooth magnesium.

He resigned himself to percussing the long corridor. Somewhere on this floor there was an elevator, if not stairs.

Night had come and gone, and his stomach had reminded him of hunger many times, when the second panel yielded to persistence and hedonically trained senses and reflexes. This panel opened toward him.

Behind it was a transparent wall. Behind the wall was a room filled with fluid. In the fluid, curled fetus-like into a ball, her hair floating around her head like a dark star, her face blissful with content, was Susan.

In that instant, D'glas knew the terrible meaning of unhappiness.

VII

*A lifetime of happiness! No man alive could bear it;
it would be hell on earth.*

GEORGE BERNARD SHAW

He raced up the broad, littered, library steps. 'Susan!' he
called, joy throbbing in his throat.

Halfway to the door, she met him, hurling herself into his
arms, hugging herself to his body, pressing her lips hungrily
to his. 'D'glas,' she murmured. 'I was afraid – oh, it doesn't
matter now what I was afraid of.'

He drew her down onto the love seat.

Something small and hard pressed into his abdomen.
'That's enough,' she said coldly.

D'glas glanced down. In her right hand was a minim, its
barrel trying to leave its imprint on his body.

...'Susan,' D'glas said, frowning, 'what's the matter?'

'How do I know you're not a mech?' she asked. 'The
Council is infinitely resourceful. Get up!' D'glas stood up.
'Walk toward the door, slowly.' D'glas obeyed. 'Open it.
Take one step forward and turn around. Don't make any
sudden moves. I'll shoot at your shadow. Now close the
door.'

D'glas frowned at the translucent glass panel and the
words painted on it, knowing what the panel was, and he
thought: This has happened before.

He was turning away when the door was flung open.

'D'glas!' she cried. 'It is you!' And then her lips found his,
clumsy at first but infinitely educable and learning fast.

He had lived this moment before, fully, richly, and the
reliving was almost enough to silence his doubts – but not
quite. Somewhere was an explanation, a reason. He had to
search for it. It was important beyond the moment's
pleasure.

He tried to pull her arms away as they clung to him des-

perately. Where his fingers had grasped her arm, the flesh
surged back, leaving no white imprints to redden.

His hand tightened in agony.

Inside her arm, something snapped, but Susan didn't move
or cry out. Her other hand continued stroking his hair; her
mouth made little crooning sounds.

He peeled back the synthetic flesh. Under it, the bones
gleamed metallically.

Susan was a mech.

He tore himself free and stood beside the bed. In that
instant, D'glas knew the terrible meaning of unhappiness. . . .

He walked down the long, deep-carpeted hall, feeling very
young and excited again, watching the walls flow with shifting colors that changed to match his moods, sniffing the
delicate perfumes wafted to him, enjoying the eternal delight of possession.

The doors opened to him, and he entered the magnificent
room. The women pressed around him, begging silently for
his touch, his glance, his passing thought; there were all
kinds and shapes of them, all colors and textures, all temp-
eraments, but they shared two qualities: they were all
beautiful and they all adored him.

He passed among them, the small and the tall, the slim
and the generously curved, and he held out his hand to
Susan, the shy one. Though the others must never know, it
was Susan he loved.

She lifted her face as he touched her; it was shining like a
star, dazzling him with its beauty and the sub-lime trust in
her eyes.

Together, he thought, they would discover the meaning of
love.

When they were alone in the twilight room, she pressed
herself against him hungrily. 'D'glas!' she cried. 'You chose
me!' And then her lips found his, clumsy at first but infinitely educable.

How his pulse pounded! Joy was like a sickness inside. He

hadn't felt like this since he had been very young.

What was he doing here, back in his adolescence? What was Susan doing in his arms?

His arms tightened in agony.

Inside Susan, something snapped and tore through her back. As he felt it, slick and metallic, her lips kept moving against his.

He tore himself free. In that instant, D'glas knew the terrible meaning of unhappiness. . . .

In his cubicle, he waited tautly for the Contest to begin.

When the light flashed on his screen, his hands were instantly busy at the keyboard controls, matching signals with the testing mech. His trained discriminations found minute variations from ideal form, compared measurements, dissected illusions, analysed sounds and chemicals, odors and pressures. Then the tests grew difficult.

From one word, he constructed a sonnet; from one musical phrase, a song. He wove the two together, and when he was done, he took one color and translated all into visual imagery.

The door of the cubicle swung open. He sprinted into the physical half. He ran that ancient unit of measure, the mile, in three minutes thirty-two seconds, pacing himself perfectly. He high-jumped the three-meter wall. Behind, the first competitor started after him.

He swam one hundred meters under water, and he emerged, at last, through the air lock, upon the naked surface of Venus. The air lock opposite was fifty meters away. He ran toward it, his straining body streaming with rain, stung with hurricane winds, without taking the breath that would have meant neausea and unconsciousness. And he went through the air lock into his mother's arms.

'D'glas!' she cried. 'You won!' And then her lips found his, fondly.

He held her tight, his chest heaving to draw in the good air, his head pressed to her bosom, his heart filled with a great love. And then, as his breathing calmed, he realized that there was something wrong. His mother had no heart-beat.

He stared at her, understanding what she was, and tore himself away. In that instant, D'glas knew the terrible meaning of unhappiness. . . .

There was no happiness like this, to lie nestled in the arms of the big, soft, food-creature and be held against her warmth and nurse on the soft part of her which held the food. The food slipped down the throat warmly, filling the stomach, distending it with love, and he was filled with the great happiness and the love that was as big as the universe.

It made him sleepy to feel such love in this, the happy time. He felt himself relaxing. His eyelids began to close.

Contentment. It was being warm and fed and held by love. It was the most basic of securities, without fear—

Pain! Inside! It jerked his legs up toward his belly and wrenched a cry of agony from his lips. There was something wrong with the food, that hurt him inside, that cramped his stomach and turned contentment into torture.

He pushed himself away from he big, soft creature, out of the loving arms that held him, and he fell, spinning, through the void, screaming with fear and pain. In that instant, D'glas knew the terrible meaning of unhappiness. . . .

This was happiness. Everything else was imitation.

He floated, effortlessly, within the warm darkness, fed and contented. The shapeless forms drifted slowly through his dreaming mind. He was safe, secure, protected through the long, silent twilight.

There was nothing to think of, nothing to desire, nothing to fear. He was safe, now and eternally, in this, his impregnable fortress.

He was one with love.

The universe and he were the same. He was God, commanding all, receiving all, dreaming the long sweet dream which was everything that was and everything that had been and everything that would be.

*That was what he must believe. If he should question that,
his omnipotence would tremble, his universe would shake—*

*Even now there was a turbulence in the all-pervading
fluid which surrounded him. Infinity was constricted. God
was squeezed. He struggled against it, but the barrier was
rigid, enclosing him on all sides.*

*He was angry. He did not try to control it with the hedo-
nic techniques. He let his adrenals pumps adrenalin into his
bloodstream. His heartbeat quickened, his blood's sugar level
rose, the coagulability of the blood increased—*

*It was the ancient reaction to danger, but this time it was
under control.*

*Rhythmically, infinity contracted around him. He fought
it. He pushed, he shoved, he struggled to get loose.*

*He tore himself free of the constrictions; he emerged into
the cold, harsh brilliance of reality.*

He was born screaming with anger.

D'glas stood in the middle of the jungle trail, naked and
defenseless, listening. The jungle was deadly, and there was
something that followed.

He had never seen a jungle, but he recognized it and knew
it for what it was : illusion. This was the jungle from which
man had emerged, a toolmaker, a conqueror. A weak-armed,
weak-toothed, weak-clawed animal, he had turned himself
into the most deadly creature on Earth by making extensions
for his arms and sharpening points to replace teeth and
claws.

In a more important sense, this was the jungle of the
human mind, fraught with personal and ancestral fears
which dullied the clean edge of the mind. Only recently,
with the tools of hedonics, had man learned to conquer that
jungle.

D'glas knew these things with an instinct that seemed
almost racial. This was illusion, but it was just as deadly as
if it were real.

The Council had attempted to enslave D'glas with his own
dreams. That had failed before his unshakeable grasp on

reality which intruded, crucially, to shatter the rhythm of each dream. Now the Council sought to conquer him with his own fears. This illusion was its last barrier.

He stood in the middle of the game path, naked, and he knew he would never come out of the jungle alive, or sane, unless he won. Within him, he nursed the clean, protective flame of his anger and listened.

Distantly, danger screamed.

He recognized it now, although he had never heard it before, never seen the creature that made it. It was the black shape of fear, the panther, powerful and silent until it made its kill. Somewhere it came after him, padding along the trail.

He trotted away from it, picking up in stride a stout limb lying beside the trail, torn by some storm from one of the trees. It swung in his hand as he moved warily through the jungle. He had multiplied his strength by the length of the club. At the end of the trail was Susan.

Slowly the smell of danger grew stronger.

When he was fifty meters away, he saw the fallen log. By the time he reached it, he had the deadfall completely planned.

He propped up the log on a precarious leg, working quickly but never dropping his careful watchfulness. Danger might be creeping upon him.

He fastened a vine to the leg supporting the log and passed the vine across the trail. There was no time to test the trigger. He faded among the trees a few meters away and waited, his back protected, the club ready.

Within minutes, the panther came padding into sight, its head swinging from side to side. It was a lean black beauty, smelling of death.

And yet it brushed the vine. The dog fell. The panther screamed. This time the scream was agony. It lay in the middle of the trail, its back broken, its mouth snarling horribly as D'glas approached.

He smashed its skull, mercifully, with one blow of the club.

Distantly, danger screamed!

Another. There is never an end to danger, never an end to fear. Eternally, it comes after.

D'glas turned and trotted away.

Momentarily the jungle ended, giving way to an open space of sawtoothed grass and razor-pointed reeds. Before D'glas had gone more than a few meters along the trail through the clearing, his hands were bloody. He broke off the reeds close to the ground and planted them in the middle of the trail, their points trailing backward the way he had come.

Where the clearing became jungle again, D'glas paused. The panther came quickly, a twin of the one he had killed. It threaded its way along the trail. D'glas stepped into the sunlight, the club swinging in his hand.

For a moment the panther stopped, studying him, and then it began padding forward swiftly. As it leaped toward him, the reeds stabbed upward, entering its belly with the full thrust of its rush. The black beast fell to the ground, clawing futilely. Its wicked head lunged at the tormenting reeds. They broke off.

It got to its feet again, wounded but still dangerous. Its grace was awkwardness, its lithe speed was a painful limp. It was dying, and it didn't know it.

D'glas turned and trotted away, leaving the beast to its agonies. It was too powerful to risk an approach, and there was little time for mercy in the jungle.

A few hours later, danger screamed.

D'glas was readier now. Out of a sapling and tough, twisted grass he has fashioned a bow. Arrows, feathered with leaves and pointed with bits of flint, lay beside him. Near them was a spear.

D'glas had come out of the jungle and reached the foothills of a vast range of mountains, rising peak after purple peak behind. He could go no farther. The trail ended against an impassable cliff, rising all around him until it met the jungle. This was where he would stand and fight until the end.

He waited, his hands busy with rocks, piling them close

at hand, and finally the panther came. It took him a long time to make it out, where it stood at the edge of the jungle, watching.

When it moved, it moved swiftly. The first arrow went into its shoulder at thirty meters. The panther came on unheeding. D'glas had time for three more arrows. The third almost disappeared down the panther's gaping throat.

It died at his feet.

After that they came more swiftly, the black shapes of fear, and, afraid, he killed them, one after one, before they could reach him. And then his arrows were gone.

As the next one came, he threw rocks at it, but they glanced off harmlessly. He waited for it, the spear ready. It approached warily, its nostrils flared with the odor of death, glancing at the black shapes that lay all around him. But it came on.

Suddenly it leaped. D'glas planted the base of the spear against the rock under foot and caught the beast on the point. The spear sank in. The panther fell, clawing with all four feet at the shaft. The shaft snapped.

Slowly, the panther died, taking with it his last weapon.

D'glas sharpened the edge of his anger, standing straight and tall under the unmoving sun, and threw it spearlike at the sky. 'Damn you!' he shouted. 'There is nothing more you can do! I am not afraid, not of death, not of fear itself!'

In great globs of blue, the sky began to melt.

VIII

Ah Love! could you and I with Him conspire
To grasp this sorry Scheme of Things Entire,
Would not we shatter it to bits – and then
Re-mould it nearer to the Heart's desire!
                              Rubáiyát of Omar Kháyyam

Nursing his cleansing anger, D'glas stood, legs spread for balance, staring from the corridor into a room much like the one from which he had escaped. This had a metal bunk built against one wall. On the bunk, her eyes closed as if she were asleep, was Susan.

D'glas reached the bunk, moving slowly, hugging his anger around him like a cloak of invincibility. From the wall came tubes and wires. One transparent tube led to Susan's arm where a needle entered the ante-cubital vein. Fluid moved through it slowly. Another tube went to a mouthpiece which marred the perfection of Susan's lips.

Susan was smiling.

D'glas went down on his knees beside her, sickened, afraid, but more angry than either. Carefully he removed the needle, pressing the vein to suppress bleeding. The blood clotted quickly. He inspected the mouthpiece and then slowly worked it free.

'Susan,' he said softly. 'Susan!'

Her eyes flickered, opened. 'D'glas,' she murmured sleepily. Her arms came up toward him with dream slowness. Then recognition entered her eyes. Her hands whipped out, caught him by the shoulders. 'D'glas! It's real! It's you!'

Her arms went around him. She pulled herself up to him, half laughing, half sobbing. 'Oh, darling, I thought I lost you forever!'

Frowning, he held her close. 'Get mad, Susan!' he whispered. 'Get very mad! Let your adrenals work! Get angry at the Council!'

'I can't feel angry now,' she protested, puzzled. 'I can't. I'm—'

'You must! Everything depends on it!'

'I'll try,' she said. Slowly her face flushed, her breathing quickened.

Pressed tightly against her, D'glas could feel her heartbeat speed up. He squeezed her arm and felt the flesh and the bone beneath; when he released it, he saw the white finger-prints turn red.

'What happened to you?' he asked harshly.

'I told you. I was safe from the Council as long as I was happy. You came, and I fell in love with you. And then I could no longer be happy. Funny, isn't it? Through having too much, I became unhappy.'

'The more you have, the more you have to lose.'

'Yes. I read your note. That made me unhappy, but I could fight that. I could wait for you. Then I saw you leaving the hotel across the street. I knew that you were in the hands of the Council, that you had done something or felt something that gave it power over you, that you were lost to me forever. I couldn't fight that. A few minutes later, the Council's mechs were there to take me away.'

'Yes, yes,' D'glas said savagely. 'I can see how it happened. I should have thought of it; we should have stayed together.'

'Struggle was pointless and futile. If you were gone, my only chance for happiness was the kind the Council could give me. But it wasn't good enough. It wasn't you; it was only my image of you, partial and incomplete, returned to me more vividly. In you there is continual surprise, continual change; there is more than I can ever encompass. What the Council gave me was only my dreams made real.'

'I know. Now your only chance for reality – our only chance – is anger.'

'Why?'

D'glas shrugged. 'I can only reason analogically, which can't be exact. Anger sets off some physiological reaction which acts, I think, as a barrier to the Council's telepathic senses. It does not understand anger, because it has never had to deal with it. Those who came to it for help were never angry; anger seeks its own satisfaction. Anger is part of that dissatisfaction which has spurred life to its greatest conquests of environment. When properly controlled, it makes possible all things.'

'A telepathic race,' Susan said slowly, 'if there were such a thing, would have no angers because it would have no frustrations. Emotions are the result of blocked conations, strivings, and telepathic creatures would desire nothing which was unavailable and would deny each other nothing which could be supplied.'

'And the Council is telepathic,' D'glas agreed. A shudder rippled through him. 'Like you, I was caught in its velvet snare, but it couldn't completely conquer my doubts. They kept intruding, wrecking the dreams of fulfillment. And when anger swept over me, he left for good. Now I can't sense him at all.'

Susan's face brightened. 'That's right. He's gone.' Her face sobered again. Her blue eyes looked into his. 'But what are we going to do? How can we get away? Even if he doesn't know what we plan, he has the resources of a whole world to throw against us.'

'We must destroy him,' D'glas said evenly. 'And it's time to begin.'

Holding Susan tightly, he looked at the gray ceiling and said fiercely, 'Council! Hedon! God! You! Whatever you call yourself! I'm talking to you!'

'I am here.'

Susan gasped. Her body stiffened in his arms. D'glas turned. Hansen stood in the doorway. On either side of him were the woman-mechs D'glas had called Scylla and Charybdis.

'Why did you leave me, my children?' Hansen said sadly. 'I could have made you happy.'

'That kind of happiness is not for us,' D'glas said. 'We must fashion our own.'

'Why do men seek misery?' Hansen asked, perplexed.

'What they seek is free will,' D'glas said sternly. 'Real free will, not the mockery you offered me. If misery is the price, then we will pay it. Happiness, in your sense, is not the only good.'

'Blasphemy!' Hansen frowned heavily. He took a step into the room, Scylla and Charybdis beside him, lifting their perforated fingers, no longer feminine.

'Not blasphemy,' D'glas said quietly. 'Men created you. Men can destroy you.'

'Sacrilege!' said Hansen. He took another step.

'Blasphemy was when you lied to me about free will,' D'glas said swiftly. 'Sacrilege was when you broke the law –

when you showed me Susan floating in the foster-womb and made me unhappy. Unhappy!' D'glas thundered. 'Not happy! So that you would have power over me.'

'To make you happy. I am the judge of means.' Hansen and the woman-mechs were only an arm's length away.

D'glas's voice dropped. Low and insistent, he said, 'But this is the question you must answer: Are *you* happy?'

Hansen stopped. 'The question is meaningless.'

'Are *you* happy?' D'glas repeated.

Hansen frowned. 'Is God happy?'

'Are *you* happy?' D'glas asked for the third time.

His head tilted thoughtfully, Hansen froze. Beside him the woman-mechs were sculpted in stone.

D'glas held Susan tightly within the circle of his right arm, breathless. 'Now,' he said softly. 'While we have a chance.'

They passed by the catatonic figures and reached the corridor. 'What's the matter with them?' Susan asked. 'What happened?'

'God is thinking,' D'glas said quietly. 'God is pondering the puzzle of his own existence. And while he is bemused, we must find the control room.'

'Control room? What's that?'

'The one place where instructions could be given the Council-mech. It could and did absorb information from other sources, but there could be only one place where a statement would be an order.'

'Where?'

D'glas sighed. 'I don't know, and I'm afraid logic might not be applicable.'

'There's seventy-five floors!' Susan exclaimed.

'Yes,' D'glas said ruefully, 'and there's no way of estimating how long this catatonia will last. The best we can do is to play a hunch. In *The Rise and Fall of Applied Hedonics*, Morgan mentions a room in the Council building to which he was hailed by the Hedonic Council, then a group of hedonists. If the control room isn't there, I don't know where to look. What was that room number?' He closed his eyes and let the film roll by '2943,' he said. 'Let's go!'

The corridor was gray, but not as featureless as when D'glas had seen it last. A few meters away, a door stood open. Behind it were stairs. Holding Susan's hand, slowed a little by it but unwilling to let go, D'glas dashed downward, turning and leaping almost alternately.

The number on the first door was 68. Thirty-nine flights of stairs to go. Down and around and down, giddily. The doors were all the same; only the numbers changed. D'glas had the crazy notion that they were on a carousel, getting nowhere, but someone kept shifting the numbers on the door to fool them: 61 – 53 – 47 – 42 – 36 – 31 – 30 – 29—

D'glas pulled to a stop just in time. That was the floor they wanted: 29. He pushed through the doorway, Susan behind him.

This corridor was older and less well kept. The paint on the walls had peeled away in patches, and dust lay gray and thick on the floor. They walked down the middle of the corridor, keeping away from the walls.

D'glas looked back. Their footprints were the only marks in the dust; no one had been here for a long, long time.

There were numbers on the doors. They marched along beside D'glas and Susan. 2915 – 2917 – 2919— D'glas stopped in front of 2943 and took a deep breath. On the door were the faded instructions COME IN AND BE HAPPY.

There was a button at waist level. D'glas pressed it. The door slid open. Beyond it was a room lined on each side with chairs. Against the far wall was a desk. Beside it was another door. There was nothing else.

'Come on,' D'glas said.

They walked across the anteroom, raising little puffs of dust, the sound of their footsteps muffled and unnatural in the silence. They reached the second door.

'This can't be it,' Susan said softly. 'Wouldn't there be protection for something as important as the control room?'

'If the Council mech weren't out of operation, no one would ever be able to reach here,' D'glas reminded her. 'This room – this whole floor – the one place the Council and its

mechanisms could not enter. It might change the law itself.'
He pressed a button in the door.

The door slid aside. The room behind it was big and
windowless and bare except for a dusty table, chairs grouped
around it in silent conference. D'glas let out a long sigh. 'So
much for hunches.'

He turned away.

'Wait!' Susan said, taking his arm in strong fingers. 'Let's
go in.'

At the far end of the table, they found it – a standard
microtype keyboard. Set into the table top were two windows. The one on the left was labeled INFORMATION. In
the window appeared this message: There is nothing more
for me to do. I am retiring to my room.

Who had typed in that final information? D'glas wondered. Some last technician? Or had it been the last of the
Council's hedonists?

Above the window on the right was printed ACTION.
Beneath it. Happiness is the only good.

Man had constructed a syllogism and forgotten to tack on
the conclusion.

There was a natural progression of ideas, a Q.E.D., that
the men who had built the great Council-mech had failed to
make. Perhaps it was not so obvious then.

That the Council-mech itself had not taken the last, logical step was understandable. Gods, as D'glas had learned,
cannot concern themselves with the problem of their own
existence without threatening the very foundations of that
existence. If they don't accept their godhood on faith, if
they permit doubts to enter their kingdoms, they allow
their thought process to add the inevitable conclusion to the
syllogism of their being, then they are mortal and subject
to all the laws of mortality.

The syllogism was a simple one:

> EVERYBODY SHOULD BE HAPPY,
> GOD IS SOMEBODY,
> GOD SHOULD BE HAPPY.

D'glas seated himself at the chair behind the keyboard.
'What are you going to do?' Susan asked.

D'glas flipped a switch. The ACTION window was cleared.
It stared up blankly, an eye waiting for an image. 'I'm giving
Man a second chance,' he said softly. 'When he makes
gods, Man should be careful not to make them work too
well.'

His fingers flickered over the keys briefly and were still.
The letters appeared in the window labeled ACTION:

Be happy!

D'glas stood silently in the round port of the towering
three-stage rocket, staring toward the spires silhouetted
against the western sky. Their thirty days' work was done.
The Council's ship had been converted into living quarters
and storerooms for two people. Mechs don't eat or breathe
or poison themselves in their own wastes.

Neither do they love. The days had been filled with hard
labor, and with happiness.

D'glas could not remember when he had ever been as
happy, and he stood now, tall and straight, thinking of how
he had seen the city, silent and enigmatic, when he had
first arrived.

Now they were returning to Venus and the living society
that was transforming a world and would go on to change
the face of the universe. He had to recognize the possibility
of death, for travel is always dangerous, and this more
dangerous than most. But happiness is not something that
can live in a cell.

Now the city was more silent than when he had come.
What was it Morgan wrote? 'The spires like gravestones.'
Tombs now for more than happiness.

Humanity had gone on a long roller coaster trip, but now
the joy ride was over. It was a moment of gladness that
Man would strive again and sadness that the dream, which
proved too fair, was shattered. Like a birth and a wake.

'Is the Council dead?' Susan asked, beside him silently.

'Not yet. Dreaming, perhaps. Under sentence of death.

The Council, that made fantasies for others, is now making fantasies for itself. It has a new law: Be happy! In obedience to that law, it has retreated within its own dream of paradise, forgetful of all else, too preoccupied to notice that it is dying.

'In time, insulation will rot, wires will short, electronic devices fail, masonry will crack, steel will rust. But the rule of the God Hedon is over. As soon as it realized that it, too, must be happy, it was doomed. Because happiness is death.'

'And now we must leave Earth. It seems a pity to leave so fair a world.'

'Too fair – like the promise of happiness. Happiness must come from inside, or it is deadly. The only road for Man is the hard road, up and out – the road of dissatisfaction, the road of anger. The dreams are ended now in all the cells, in all the foster-wombs, all over the world, because the Council has forgotten them forever. Most of the embryos will die. But perhaps some – your father may be one – will survive the ordeal of being born again. The Council's automatic processes are keeping them alive, but when they are ready, they will break free. Let them have Earth. We have Venus and beyond. To look back is to die a little. To look forward is to live forever. Those who are worthy will eventually follow us.'

One star was out. Like a brilliant beacon, it hung over the city.

'The Duplicates no longer walk the corridors of Morgantown,' Susan said, looking at the evening star. 'Venus is safe. Humanity will live.'

'Until the next crisis. For there is always another. I wonder how many of the colonists succumbed to the seductions of the Council's mechs. I would like to think that our hedonic society would have survived in any case, that enough of us could have resisted. But it would have been constant hell to have heaven always available for the asking.'

'Yes.' Susan looked steadily at D'glas for a moment. 'How can we be sure—' she started to say, and then stopped.

'What is it?' D'glas asked.

'Nothing,' she said. 'I'll go get ready for the take-off.'

She left him, without the backward glance that might have meant uncertainty. He stood there, not wondering what she had been about to say. He didn't have to wonder. He knew.

How could they be sure that this was reality, not another wish-fulfillment dream from the Council-mech? How could they be sure that they had really conquered it and were not just living an illusion in a watery cell?

The answer was: they could never be sure.

D'glas looked up into the night sky and shrugged. What did it matter? One god or another?

All a man had was himself and his faith in himself and such illusions as he chose to believe.

The rest was lies.

More Great Science Fiction Books from Panther

Isaac Asimov, Grand Master of Science Fiction, in Panther Books

The Foundation Triology

FOUNDATION	40p ☐
FOUNDATION AND EMPIRE	40p ☐
SECOND FOUNDATION	40p ☐
THE EARLY ASIMOV (Volume 1)	40p ☐
THE EARLY ASIMOV (Volume 2)	35p ☐
THE EARLY ASIMOV (Volume 3)	40p ☐
THE GODS THEMSELVES	50p ☐
THE CURRENTS OF SPACE	40p ☐
THE NAKED SUN	40p ☐
THE STARS LIKE DUST	35p ☐
THE CAVES OF STEEL	40p ☐
THE END OF ETERNITY	35p ☐
EARTH IS ROOM ENOUGH	40p ☐
THE MARTIAN WAY	50p ☐
NIGHTFALL ONE	30p ☐
NIGHTFALL TWO	30p ☐
ASIMOV'S MYSTERIES	35p ☐
I. ROBOT	40p ☐
THE REST OF THE ROBOTS	50p ☐

Edited by Asimov

NEBULA AWARD STORIES 8	60p ☐

All these books are available at your local bookshop or newsagent, or can be ordered direct from the publisher. Just tick the titles you want and fill in the form below.

Name..

Address..

....

Write to Panther Cash Sales, PO Box 11, Falmouth, Cornwall TR10 9EN.

Please enclose remittance to the value of the cover price plus:

UK: 18p for the first book plus 8p per copy for each additional book ordered to a maximum charge of 66p.

BFPO and EIRE: 18p for the first book plus 8p per copy for the next 6 books, thereafter 3p per book.

OVERSEAS: 20p for the first book and 10p for each additional book.

Granada Publishing reserve the right to show new retail prices on covers, which may differ from those previously advertised in the text or elsewhere.